ACCLAIM FOR *HOME LEAVE*

"Sonnenberg writes about expatriate life with an easy authority...In the elegiac final third of HOME LEAVE, daughter Leah emerges as the book's emotional core...This sets up an interesting contrast between the psychologies of mom and daughter: one never wanting to be fully known, the other never expecting to be found familiar. It's a dynamic that whets the appetite for what's to come in American expat literature."

—Megan Hustad, *The New York Times Book Review*
("Editor's Choice")

"[A] striking debut."

—Bethanne Patrick, *Washingtonian*

"HOME LEAVE is a rich, lively novel. Original in conception and set in various continents, it describes migrations as a contemporary existential condition. More importantly, it shows how this condition effects change, loss, and growth in the migrants. It offers many insights that are true."

—Ha Jin, National Book Award winner for *Waiting*

"The lucidity of Sonnenberg's prose is notable for its stark honesty and sharply observed details...[An] ambitious debut."

—*Kirkus Reviews*

"A captivating *tour de force* that follows a nomadic family across generations and continents."

—filmmaker Wim Wenders

"Sonnenberg writes with clarity about the messiness of the expat Kriegstein family's lives...Sonnenberg captures beautifully what it's like to grow up as an American abroad, not as a tourist but not fully as a native either."

—*Cleaver Magazine*

"Brittani Sonnenberg, like the best storytellers, shows us what we carry and what we leave behind as we travel across time zones (from America to Germany to Singapore), as we sit in airports, alone with the aloneness, as we love, live, grieve, and then try to live once more. Authentic, beautiful, bravely-told, HOME LEAVE is alive with characters you want to protect and hold—characters you won't want to leave behind."

—Nami Mun, author of *Miles from Nowhere*

"[A] compelling debut... [HOME LEAVE] reveals a dialectical truth about families; they are places of joyous hope, and also crushing loneliness."

—*Los Angeles Review of Books*

"HOME LEAVE is a remarkable debut, notable for the insightful intimacy of its characterization and a restless formal invention which perfectly evokes the uncertainties of expatriate life."

—Peter Ho Davies, author of *The Welsh Girl*

"Sonnenberg writes like a house on fire. The opening chapter alone is worth the price of this book."

—ReadHerLikeanOpenBook.wordpress.com

"It's hard to believe that this astonishing novel is Brittani Sonnenberg's first—she writes about family with wisdom, humor, and native daring. Here is Persephone's journey, undertaken by an entire family, the Kriegsteins, who ricochet through time zones, moving from Berlin to Singapore to Wisconsin to Shanghai to Atlanta, together and alone. Sonnenberg's prose is so vital and so enchanting that you will read this book in the dilated state of a world-traveler, with all of your senses wide open. Her family members are so well-drawn and complex that you'll close this book certain they exist."

—Karen Russell, author of *Swamplandia!* And *Vampires in the Lemon Grove*

Home Leave

Home Leave

a novel

BRITTANI SONNENBERG

GRAND CENTRAL
PUBLISHING

NEW YORK   BOSTON

Scripture taken from the New King James Version. Copyright © 1982 by Thomas Nelson, Inc.

"1116 Arcadia Ave." was published in modified form in *Asymptote* (www.asymptotejournal.com) in 2012.

"Sonnets to Orpheus" by Rainer Maria Rilke, from *In Praise of Mortality*, English translation copyright © 2005 by Anita Barrows and Joanna Macy. Reprinted by permission of the translators.

Grand Central Publishing
Hachette Book Group
1290 Avenue of the Americas
New York, NY 10104

www.HachetteBookGroup.com

Printed in the United States of America

RRD-C

Originally published in hardcover by Hachette Book Group.
First trade edition: May 2015
10 9 8 7 6 5 4 3 2 1

Grand Central Publishing is a division of Hachette Book Group, Inc.
The Grand Central Publishing name and logo is a trademark of Hachette Book Group, Inc.

The Hachette Speakers Bureau provides a wide range of authors for speaking events. To find out more, go to www.hachettespeakersbureau.com or call (866) 376-6591.

The publisher is not responsible for websites (or their content) that are not owned by the publisher.

Library of Congress Cataloging-in-Publication Data

Sonnenberg, Brittani.
Home leave : a novel / Brittani Sonnenberg. — First edition.
pages cm
ISBN 978-1-4555-4834-7 (hardcover) — ISBN 978-1-4555-4835-4 (ebook)
I. Title.
PS3619.O54H66 2014
813'.6—dc23
2013024371

ISBN 978-1-4555-4833-0 (pbk.)

For Karen and Steve Sonnenberg

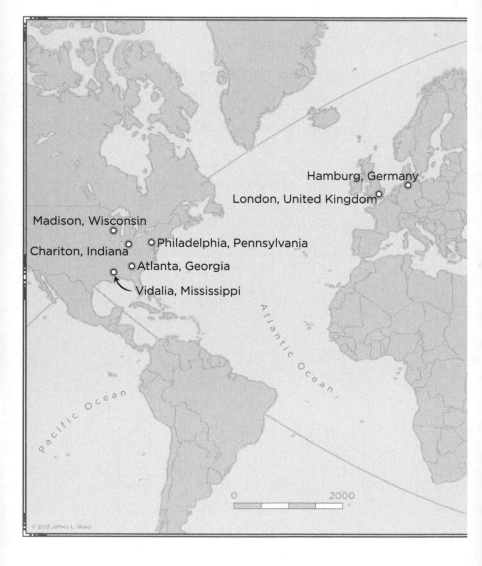

Hamburg, Germany

London, United Kingdom

Madison, Wisconsin

Chariton, Indiana

Philadelphia, Pennsylvania

Atlanta, Georgia

Vidalia, Mississippi

Atlantic Ocean

Pacific Ocean

0   2000

© 2013 Jeffrey L. Ward

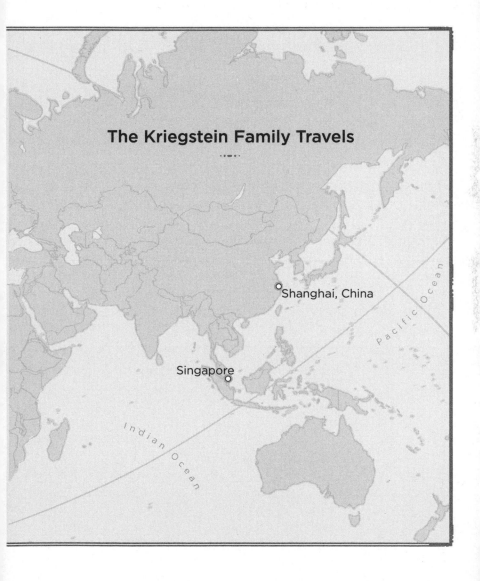

The Kriegstein Family Travels

Shanghai, China

Singapore

Pacific Ocean

Indian Ocean

The purpose of home leave is to ensure that employees who live abroad for an extended period undergo reorientation and re-exposure in the United States on a regular basis.

—*US State Department*

Be ahead of all parting, as if it had already happened,
like winter, which even now is passing.
For beneath the winter is a winter so endless
that to survive it at all is a triumph of the heart.
—*Rainer Maria Rilke, from* Sonnets to Orpheus
(translated by Anita Barrows and Joanna Macy)

Home Leave

Part One

1116 Arcadia Ave.

Vidalia, Mississippi

E lise Ebert rang the doorbell to greet her mama and me on a hot October afternoon in 1977, sweaty as July. She'd been gone five long years. The sight of her face, waiting on the doorstep, cool as all get-out, made me shiver. Or perhaps it was the shrill yell of the doorbell—everyone in Vidalia usually just knocked, or walked right in after a courtesy tap on the window. Whoever heard of ringing the bell at your own home? But I was so thrilled to see Elise that I didn't dwell on her odd behavior, or on the fact that my insides felt like they had ten years earlier, during Vidalia's only recorded earthquake. Most of my friends, the older ones, can recall similar incidents of shakiness or decay and the depression that followed, knowing they were now officially over the hill. I couldn't read the warning sign for my joy. My best friend down the block—1118 Arcadia Ave.—who I just call Caro, has always said I am an optimist to a fault.

All I thought was: Elise is back. That's one thing they never tell you when you're newly built: your youngest inhabitants will walk out on you one day, in search of new dwellings. I had heard that people die, of course; I saw the Ebert children grow and Charles and Ada age, even as my paint chipped and my linoleum cracked. But I was naive enough to believe I would shelter the six of them for as long as they were walking this earth. Not so.

At first, Elise's unexpected homecoming had me feeling brand-new, the way I used to after a fierce vacuuming by Bessie Stipes, whom Ada always hired to clean before parties. Bessie viewed dust as a theological problem, the devil made manifest (and considered her beliefs confirmed when they started selling Dirt Devils at Kmart in the mideighties). Seeing Elise that day sucked all my sadness out, set my surfaces shining. Yet Ada never caught on that Bessie Stipes stole, and it would only dawn on me thirty years later, as Ada was limping out of my side door for the last time, that it was Elise's return on that blistering autumn afternoon that spurred her mama's eventual exodus and my emptying out.

By then, the rest of the Ebert clan had left me of their own free will, except for Charles, who dropped dead in a bowling alley at sixty, collapsing before he could see if he'd made a final strike (he hadn't). Without Elise there to drive Ada to the nursing home, Ada would have stayed put: none of the other kids had the gumption or the guilt keeping them from sleep, insisting that they do right by their mama.

The guilt: It's funny, isn't it? That Elise would have felt one lick of guilt after all that passed between her and Ada? Makes you think Elise might have stuck Ada in the old folks' home to get even. For Elise's sake, I nearly wish this were true. But her face betrayed no satisfaction that day, hauling her mama in the car. They both wore the same expression: long-suffering, dulled, duty-calls, southern female martyrdom.

⁂

You'll have to forgive my appearance. It rained hard last night and that's never good for those in my state. Back when I was young, a night rain would make me look brand-new in the morning sun, such that Charles, heading to work, would sometimes stop the car in the driveway, get out, and take me in: his sparkling abode, his prizewinning azaleas, his family sleeping inside. With a small, tight smile, which was all Charles ever showed of his happiness (as if joy were dollars he ought to be saving), he'd get back in the car and drive to his dental practice, head high. Those were the only times I ever felt close to Charles, and I did my best to look imposing and expensive in his regard. It's tough for us: a girl can run to the powder room and slap on some lipstick, a little rouge. We can only wait until our owners summon the will to work on a Saturday and paint our exterior or weed the flowerbeds. For as long as Charles was alive, he kept me looking good; I'll give him that much. He was the kind of man who preferred home maintenance and gardening on the weekends to lying in the hammock.

The years have taken their toll. In 1960, when I was first built, my ranch-style layout was pleasing to the eye, as were my warm red brick and my modern carport. I was a fortress against all kinds of things. Weather, naturally, and the snakes that slithered up and down the ravine to my right. I kept out small, maddening creatures like mosquitoes, as you can observe in the protective features of my side screened-porch addition, which I acquired in the late seventies, a year or so after Elise's return. That's when I thought I was getting a second wind. But no, it turned out to be a last gasp before a slow decline, like the American economy today. Recovery, my foot. If I squint I can still read the headlines of the newspapers they slap onto the driveways of the other houses around me every morning at seven a.m. One hasn't stung my concrete for years.

❧

I haven't mentioned the real incentive for my construction, the biggest keeping-things-out motivation of all: white flight. Though that's an indelicate term, and one I prefer not to use. After all, were it not for the panicked glances and raised pulses of the good upper middle class of Vidalia, Mississippi, followed by the determined talk and long-suffering sighs after integration was decreed—when *you know who* started moving onto Main Street—I wouldn't be here today.

Look who's *not* coming to dinner was the general line of thought among the self-appointed upstanding citizens of the town, so they relocated their dining tables and fine china and children up to the top of Vidalia's single hill, evacuating downtown like Atlantans heading out before Sherman.

They abandoned languorous, jasmine-scented southern porches that could have graced the cover of *Veranda* for a more modern look: me. Not to be self-deprecating—an unappealing trait, to my mind— but I am the first to admit that the houses they sold for near nothing were of a higher class than my squat brick design.

Most of Main Street is falling apart now, given the poverty— although my former owners and their friends were always quicker to blame it on the ignorance of the new occupants, who "just didn't know how to take good care of things." Well, since my own decline began when my white-as-rice owner Ada, God rest her soul, was still living here, I think I can say with authority that it can happen whenever inhabitants, white or black, feel a sadness that works like lethargy on the mind, a Deep South "leave it be" overwhelming the Yankee can-do spirit. Such tiredness spreads through the soul quicker than kudzu over a yard car.

How do you think I wound up steeped in mildew, pine needles

clogging my gutters, and Parmesan cheese from 1995 sitting in my refrigerator when it was 2002 outside? All because Ada, the family matriarch, was in her own none-too-graceful decline, in direct opposition to the Miss Manners books she had adhered to closer than the Bible from the time that she was a young bride. Elise, after her initial return, would drop by every now and then, or the boys, and insist on repairs, but Ada would just let it slide. My point being, it's not a race thing, like they try to get you to believe. Those run-down houses now owned by black Vidalians look that way because the only things keeping the economy alive around here are a state prison, a Piggly Wiggly, a Dirt Cheap, and a dollar store.

I wasn't always so open-minded. But I find that, as death approaches, clarity does too. It's fearsome and breathtaking. I know it happened with Ada, because I heard her mumbling and caught revelations that damn near made my bricks crumble. She wouldn't brush her hair or pick up the mail (a personal indignity to me), but that's because the girl was *busy*. Seeing and feeling things she couldn't keep down anymore, no matter how loud she turned up the TV or how many glasses of Sauvignon Blanc she treated herself to, despite the doctor's orders. Elise hated to hear the booze in Ada's voice on the phone. "Mama, you sound loopy," she'd say.

But Ada was allowing herself to see things for the first time, and it scared the hell out of her. I tried to make the cushions plump and the windows let in only the softest of dusk light, but there was no denying that Ada was in the valley of the shadow before Elise carted her off to White Gables. I saw the brochures and it looked like hell. Not a gable in sight. My Ada.

⚘

It's a funny thing, moving up on a hill to protect yourself. All of Ada's kids resisted it, pointing out that not even Dodge, the stronger of the two boys, could pedal his bike up. Ivy, the baby, would just walk two steps from the foot of the hill and cry until someone carried her. But what I mean to say is, why go to all that trouble to escape when your biggest trouble's right there with you? Might as well have a big old cardboard box that reads TROUBLE in all caps, red marker, to remind yourself. Sure it might feel better for the first few weeks, thanks to the smell of fresh paint and the doors that don't squeak, but by the second month it's as present as any piece of furniture.

I was fooled too. What with being newly built, and them my first inhabitants, my family, as I thought, I fell in love right away. *Honeymoon phase,* my neighbor-houses hissed (aside from Caro, who just took pity), but I didn't believe them. Not until I heard sobbing in the middle of the night and a silence at the dinner table miles thicker than the casserole Ada was cutting into.

Of course, all houses have their own trouble, Caro let me know. (Caro is a few years older than me, like all the others on the street, but she looks a hell of a lot better than I do now.) Caro and I always confided in each other when things got bad. The hardest thing for a home, much harder than not having control over your appearance, is you can't stop any of what happens inside you. You're just a witness to it all. How many times have I wished that I could have shrugged one of my bookcases onto Paps, Ada's weak, evil-through-his-weakness father, who took his granddaughter into his shadows and made Elise afraid of my nights.

Can you imagine the torment? Being built to shelter, and then keeping the rain off the devil himself? I don't mean the old man alone. I just mean the poison that grew and grew, more toxic than asbestos. At the worst times, I wished flooding upon myself, or fire, so I wouldn't have to see anymore, and, in my own way, sanction it. It was in my corners that he would trap her. It was in my unlit study at dusk, when the TV was on loud in my living room, so Elise's brothers just heard Wile E. Coyote instead of her crying, which she was trying to stifle after Paps had moseyed off, as sickly satisfied as he'd ever be.

All I could do was try to let in soothing breezes on a child who couldn't sleep, or make a certain armchair spot feel uncomfortably drafty for a dozing old man, never sure whether or not those efforts made an actual difference.

∻

From what I know of humans, their hope for God lies in their desperation for a loving witness. As a loving witness, I was always desperate for my yearnings to have physical expression. For example: Elise, as a little girl, had a favorite spot to play with her dolls, behind the curtains in her parents' bedroom, as though she were sitting under a giantess's skirt. And in those moments (although Caro insists this is pure superstition, what she disparagingly refers to as my *esoterics*), I would filter the sun falling on Elise, make it soft and gentle, like bathwater, warm but not too hot. I would keep the curtains folded loose around her frame so no one would walk in and spy her there. I can't prove that I have these powers, of course. Humans only have one word for that sort of thing: "haunted." They assume that a door slam or a stray wind on a still day signals ghosts of old souls. They never stop to think that it's the houses themselves talking back, desperate to show their affection.

During her years under my roof, Elise hoped someone heard her prayers; I hoped my responses made sound, or at least manifested themselves as light, presence. Not that I saw myself as godly. Caro says that this is our gift, to be silent, unmoving (but not unmoved) witnesses. I balk at such a helpless notion of love.

Or hate. It's an awful moment, to suddenly realize there are humans you hate, in addition to the ones you love. Some houses start hating right along with their hateful inhabitants, because it hurts less to be on their side. But then you take on an abandoned look, even when everyone's home.

I remember Elise tried running away one time, when her grandparents came to visit. I watched her neatly folding her clothes into a sleepaway suitcase, and even taking along a spelling book, for some reason. But then, when she was at the front door, her mama called them to dinner and it was fried chicken, Elise's favorite, and she got hungry and lost her nerve. She threw it all up later that night.

How mysterious desire is to a house. Of course we can ache, but that burning towards someone else—for revenge, or love, or greed, or shame. The closest I guess I've come to that is when things in me have suddenly broken—a beam, a tile, a fuse. Or my muscadine grapes swelling and thudding to the ground each summer, untasted now, except by the ants.

But the air around such an act changes, and I can sense that. Both good and bad. With Paps it was like a winter storm, with hail coming, spelling permanent damage. With Charles and Ada's occasional lovemaking, or Grayson and his girlfriend necking with Grayson's bedroom door half-open (Ada's rules), the air was a warm summer storm.

I probably sound melodramatic. Caro always jokes that I talk more like an antebellum plantation than a modern ranch. But those intuitions are in our frames just like humans have DNA, I tell her. You can't escape being southern architecture just because you were built after the Civil War and don't have big old columns. You also have a back door, I remind her, where the colored help would come in and out.

Ada, Ada. Dead now, rest her bones. I was always the closest to her, in a way that houses aren't close to their mistresses anymore, as Caro tells it. (She's on her sixth renovation, and looking young as ever. She gets grouchy when I call it plastic surgery, but that's all it really is—not that I'm jealous.) I loved Ada because she confided in me. Washing dishes, baking cakes, even whispering into the night after Charles had fallen asleep. In her last years, Ada spoke nonstop, not always making sense, trying out new confessions, revoking them the next day. Yet it was Ada who betrayed me, and betrayed her own family.

You see, at fourteen, Elise had finally gathered her courage. Paps and Gran had driven back to Arkansas that morning, and Elise had come home from youth group with fire in her eyes. I watched her sitting at her desk, hunched over a Bible, going over Psalm 10, verses 12 to 15, with a yellow highlighter.

Arise, O Lord!
O God, lift up Your hand!
Do not forget the humble.
Why do the wicked renounce God?
He has said in his heart,
"You will not require an account."
But You have seen, for You observe trouble and grief,
To repay it by Your hand.
The helpless commits himself to You;
You are the helper of the fatherless.
Break the arm of the wicked and the evil man.
Seek out his wickedness until You find none.

Then she prepared herself to deliver the revelation. Not with the usual half-nervous, half-delighted glances at the mirror that generally characterized her preparations (for she was a great beauty, from the age of ten). I don't believe she even looked at the mirror once. Just changed into her pajamas, read the psalm out loud (slaying me, of course, on the fourteenth verse: "But You have seen, for You observe trouble and grief"), and marched into the kitchen, like she was going off to war.

Ada didn't see it coming. She and Elise often had little night chats, about boys at school or what had happened that day. So she just cut Elise a piece of chess pie, then one for herself.

When Elise pushed back the pie and told Ada in a cold, flat voice what had been going on with Paps, I watched Ada closely, delirious. Finally. Finally. We would be a normal home again. I waited for my beloved to sit down in shock, to reach for Elise, to gasp, to cry. Anything. I wanted anything but what happened: Ada's eyes getting small and hard, and her back stretching just as straight as Elise's. And then in that same cold, dead, even tone, which they'd never used with each other before, I heard Ada say it: "You shouldn't tell such tales, Elise."

She said it again. And to my surprise, Elise, who would cry at the end of every other *Lassie* episode, or when Ada played Bach on the piano, stayed completely still. If anything, her face froze in a terrible small smile, not unlike Charles's pursed grimace, after a long pause in which it looked cracked open, like a face peeled from a skull, or a house after it's burned. No tears, no sound. Just that look of raw wreckage, then frozen tundra.

I hated Ada for that. It wasn't until years later, when Ada began to mumble her own ugly memories of Paps's deeds at my walls, that I could even begin to think of forgiving her, and even then I still couldn't, not all the way. Ada couldn't see what was happening to her daughter because she had willed herself into blindness when she was little. Still, she had a choice that night. She had what I would have given anything for: the ability to intervene. For a second, she glimpsed that chance. Then a little child's terror stole over her, and her face closed up. Ada, who'd taught Peter's denial of Christ in Ivy's Sunday school class just three weeks earlier.

⚬

There's one human quality that I've never come close to grasping. How they manage to wring beauty from their pain, or even throttle it until joy comes out. It's perverse. But I've seen it a million times. The sadder things got here around that time, the tighter the family's harmony grew when they sang Baptist hymns, especially Ada, Elise, and Ivy, like they were reaching out for each other, desperate, protecting each other with their voices, unable to do it any other way.

Or the laughter. I'm telling you, on the very worst days, when Charles was treating Ada worse than a stranger or a servant, when Paps was up to no good, and Ivy was drawing into herself like an overgrown forest, and Elise had turned her back on her mama and reinvented herself as a religious nut, those were the times when high giggles escaped at the dinner table, and Dodge's uncanny imitation of Mr. Hardy mowing the lawn made Elise wet her pants. I never could fathom it. The sudden shining, the addictive cascade of laughter— easing everyone and tiring them out with joy until the clouds drew in again, just as dark and just as close.

⚬

Later on in her life, Ada took to watching *Law & Order*. At first I was skeptical, but then I got hooked too; who wouldn't? She'd watch four, five episodes a day, and dream about them too, her face taking on the dismay and horror in sleep that it had in front of the screen. It was even more extreme when they'd have marathons a few times a year. She'd barely turn off the TV then, just microwave some Lean Cuisine and watch them catch the crook.

At first I was ashamed that that was the only noise inside of me, after so many years of piano practicing and butter sizzling and whispered prayers, but then I grew to like it, started feeling like those detectives and the funny folks on *Frasier* were my real inhabitants, just as Ada must have felt like they were her friends, or family, even. But I knew it was lazy, too. I saw how Ada breathed a sigh of relief as soon as the show got started and her mind could switch to their troubles, not hers. Is it cruel to say I begrudged her that happiness? Perhaps. But in the end I felt like she had her own crime stories to work out, so why waste time watching other ones get solved?

Of course it's not as simple as that. I know: I'm no prefabricated house you plunk down on a lot, dumb as its own faux timber. It was just that Ada would get so close to it sometimes, the truth I mean, or some kind of solution, ugly as it was. I'd see it in her eyes, hear it in her quickening breath. She might be looking up from washing her face in the bathroom, or entering the living room from the hallway, and there it would be: a stark realization of former events, of what they signified and how they might have played out differently. It was as though all her failures were seated on the couch, chatting with each other, pouring sweet tea and eating cheese straws, like the ladies in bridge club used to every fourth Wednesday. Ada's face would take on a kind of rapture. Then it would close with shame and she would back out of the room or march to that TV and flip it on, until all the failures shrugged at each other and took their leave, hugging each other at the door, trying to hug Ada, who just turned a cold shoulder and turned up the volume.

⚘

In the last few years before Elise moved Ada out (and, in so doing, sentenced me to my own slow death, like a spinster aunt whose final prospect has just taken the last train out of town), Ada and I would religiously watch the six o'clock news. Monstrous, most of what they'd show on there. But I recall one clip that caught my attention, a report on a new educational effort called "No Child Left Behind." I don't presume to grasp politics, but I loved the name of that program, and all the children they would show hard at work in those schools, frowning over their math books, the walls trying to whisper the formulas to them, they loved them that much.

And that's what I always thought about Ada, until the very last day: How could y'all leave this child behind? They all did, one by one. Elise was as good as gone after Ada called her a liar. Ivy departed the day she picked up a guitar, even if she lived at home until she was twenty-five. The boys went off to college. Charles died of a sudden heart attack while bowling, as I said, at the age of sixty. Typical of him, to bow out like that, so painlessly. I realize I'm being unfair.

After her initial five-year boycott, Elise was the only one who called regularly. She had every right to hate Ada, and in some ways, I think she did. There was a chronic tightness in her voice, an accusation that wouldn't lift, which joined the guilt echoing in Ada. Not that Ada would admit to that perpetual trial, worse than *Judge Judy*. Often, Ada treated Elise with a seasoned criminal's wariness and contempt. In her last years, Ada wanted peace, and the sight of Elise just stirred too much up.

For a while, after Charles's death, though the kids were worried about her living alone, Ada bloomed, as though she had a new lover. But I knew better: it was the pure delight of not having to explain herself anymore. Charles was a faithful husband, didn't drink, and came home each night at seven. But he was fanatic about saving money. The one time Ada asked him if they might go out for supper, he wouldn't speak to her through the whole dinner, which just made her dreamed-of steak taste like sand. After his passing, she deposited flowers on his grave weekly and went shopping. She bought lots of clothes, some in leopard print. She left me for weeks at a time and returned smelling like suntan lotion and margaritas.

That's when I felt sure things would get solved. I don't even know how I thought it would happen, exactly, maybe something like they have on televangelist shows, the witnessing, "come to Jesus" part of the service, where people fall on their knees before the rest of the congregation and sob. I pictured it taking place at Christmastime, after the grandchildren had gone to bed and the grown children had loosened themselves with a little wine.

I wasn't sure who would go first, but I tried to catalyze the chemical reaction, tried to make the lighting appear both reassuring and urgent, kept the room at a temperature where they wouldn't get too sleepy, tried to take on the colors and mood I'd had for each of their Christmases as small children, so that their memories would stir and they'd begin to speak.

Instead, they avoided one another's eyes and played with the toys that had been opened by their own children earlier that day, went to the kitchen and made coffee, or turned on the ball game. And what would they have said to one another, anyways? I never knew what happened to the people who confessed their sins or shames on-screen, if they went and had a burger after the service, or sex, or found a VCR and watched the tape of their moment of fame and honesty, over and over. What I'm trying to say is maybe it wouldn't have done any good, or maybe it wouldn't have lasted.

But they each dreamed about the unsaid that night. I spied with all my eyes, and sure enough, there was Elise in a river, trying to drown her mother and resuscitate her at the same time; Ivy, swinging at snakes in the ravine; Dodge, dreaming about long-dead dogs; Grayson, dreaming about his father yelling at him on the football field; and Ada, dreaming about sitting on her father's lap, her legs concrete so she couldn't move.

⤜

My Ada. My Elise. Elise couldn't get far enough away from Vidalia, or, let's face it: me. My smells, my rooms, my locks. Charles had decreed that she would go to a Baptist college in Mississippi. Blue Mountain College was near Tupelo, just an hour up the Natchez Trace Parkway, but you would have thought the girl was in the North Pole for all we saw of her. Charles shouldn't have worried about Elise losing God once she left Vidalia. Soon as she hightailed it out of town, the only father she paid attention to was the Lord.

At first she made excuses about not coming back for Thanksgiving (exams) or Christmas (traveling with her contemporary Christian band, Jericho!), until finally she stopped calling and just sent nondescript postcards on campus stationery. *Doing fine, much love to everyone at home. —Elise.* Infuriated, Charles stopped paying her tuition, but Elise's summer job as a counselor at Camp of the Rising Son, a modest scholarship, and waitressing during the semester helped make ends meet. The only person Elise would see was Ivy. They met for milk shakes in a town halfway between Vidalia and Tupelo, and Ivy would come back from those secret meetings loaded with prayer pamphlets from Elise, which she threw straight in the trash. If Jesus was Elise's salvation, pleasure was Ivy's. Both were gorgeous singers, and their harmony gave you goose bumps. When she was fifteen, Ivy ditched church choir and took her heavenly soprano and flaming red hair to nearby honky-tonks, where her older biker boyfriend kept her supplied with RC Cola and rum and fended off burly admirers, often on the same nights that Elise was singing Christian pop in bell-bottoms in church basements across the country.

⁊

Ada always wondered what prompted Elise's return to Vidalia, but it was no mystery to me. Paps had been buried for a full year. Elise had skipped the funeral (which Ivy had attended high as a kite). When I saw Elise, I was shocked by her change. In order to stand being back home, she'd had to seal something off deep down. She was back in Vidalia, but she might as well have been in Tibet. It killed Ada, but she was too scared to say anything: didn't want to drive Elise away again. But Elise left anyways, married a Yankee, Chris Kriegstein, then went even farther away: Atlanta, London, then Germany, of all places. Gave Ada a hell of a time trying to figure out the calling codes and time zones.

For a while Elise and Chris were back in Atlanta, and then we were getting Christmas cards from China and Singapore. Ada told everyone in town that Chris and Elise were doing Baptist missionary work in Asia, a distinct lie: by that time Elise was a stark agnostic.

She had two little girls—the younger one, Sophie, looked just like her mama: same beautiful blond curls. Having those children inside me, when they would visit during the summer, nearly made up for their mother's departure, and I guess Ada felt the same way. Then, one year, during their annual visit, it was just Elise and Leah, her older daughter. Chris was working in Singapore, I gathered, but Sophie was absent, and Elise was walking around with a look of doom, worse than she'd had in the Paps years. That summer was the first one since she was fourteen that Elise let Ada hug her properly, but Elise's eyes held an eerie unfocus, as though there was a word on the tip of her tongue that she was trying to remember, and if she could just recall the word everything would go back to normal.

⚘

The day Ada left me began warm and clear. It was May, not too hot yet, my favorite kind of weather. I had known she was leaving for weeks, months, even—the brochures, the boxes—but hadn't quite believed it until she stepped outside of my walls for the last time. Sure, there had been times when I wanted her gone, times when her confessions had crawled up my walls like termites. I tried to summon all my old resentments in response to her gaze, so her walking out would hurt less.

And then the surprise—as the car rolled off, as the tangerine sunset hit my naked walls: the lightness. I always thought I'd want to be a house that was occupied, even if it meant being haunted by homeless people or teenagers looking for somewhere to have sex or get high. Instead I felt a huge burden shrug off of me, and it felt good when the mold started growing and the rain began moisturizing my interior. That's something Caro can't understand; she urges me to stop slouching, reminds me that the For Sale sign out front won't ever go away if I don't make more of an effort.

Some houses have generations that pass under their roofs. Some see several family cycles. I only had my one, and there's something beautiful in that, too. Ada. How I envy the simple path her body took: out of breath, then underground. I felt it when she died, even though she was all those miles away. It mimicked the feeling I used to get when the power went out.

Given my strong brick and my storm glass, I'm not going to fall apart anytime soon. But I find I am entering a state I thought only possible for humans: I have begun dreaming. I drift most of the time; I see deep summer thunderstorms in winter and then it's Charles at the dinner table and the chicken and dumplings not being ready yet. I only stir, briefly, at Caro's insistent chatter, and then I doze off again. I will wake one day, I suppose, to my eventual disassemblage, or, Sleeping Beauty–like, to the kiss of new heartache repairing me, moving the unspeakable back inside.

Wittenberg Village

Chariton, Indiana

A high school kid calls up, asking is Chris Kriegstein still in town, or nearby. They're doing a "Chariton High Athletes: Where Are They Now?" feature in the school paper, *Tiger Tracks*, and he needs to know how can he get in touch.

"Aren't you on summer vacation?" I ask.

"Summer school," he says, and sounds so down about it that I give him Chris's cell phone and office numbers and email address, even though Chris and Elise have repeatedly asked me to keep them private. I warn him that Chris is pretty hard to track down; half the time he's in Saudi Arabia or China or God knows where. The kid mumbles his thanks and hangs up, just as I'm about to ask him about our team's chances for regionals this fall.

"Frank," I yell from the kitchen, putting down the phone, "where's Chris this week, you know?"

"Dubai until Thursday," yells Frank. He always knows. He gets these updates on our email from Chris's secretary, and he reads them as close as the weather and the obits. You want to know who died of what and how Tuesday's gonna be and which time zone his son is in, you just ask Frank.

I join him on the patio outside, carrying two frosty Diet Cokes; he's watching across the street, where the county fair is in full swing. "Best seats in town," Frank likes to say when anyone calls, asking us how it is to be living at Wittenberg Village. If they're friends of ours, still living in their own houses, they sound smug. If they're our kids, they sound guilty. Tomorrow will be three weeks since we left the farm.

It must look strange to anyone who pulls into the parking lot: all of us out here on our tiny porches, staring out across the highway like we're at a drive-in movie. Most of us in bathrobes, though Frank and I are still wearing the clothes of the living, as I like to say. Frank doesn't like it when I make jokes like that, and I think his forced cheer about moving out here is bullshit. But the anger that used to rise up in me at him has lulled now; before, when we were young and he'd say something to rile me, it would be like a rattlesnake in the room, something I had to either kill or escape from. Now it's just like an old fly buzzing around in August that you tolerate because you're too hot and lazy to get out of your chair.

All of northeast Indiana has had a terrible drought this summer, and the fields fringing the fair are a tawny brown. Frank frets about it, even though we sold off our corn- and bean fields shortly before we moved here.

"Only chance is winter wheat," he says to me now. We sit in quiet after that, sipping our Cokes.

My stomach rumbles and pretty soon his does too. We're both hungry, but we're putting off going to the cafeteria for lunch; meals are the most depressing times of the day. Vegetables for vegetables, I call it, another joke Frank doesn't appreciate.

When his grumbles for a second time I say, "Why don't I just heat up some Campbell's? We have a stove."

"The meals are already paid for, Joy," Frank says, with a dead determination in his voice.

"You got a point," I tell him, because you can only contradict your husband so many times in one day without starting to feel like you're on your own, and Frank and I need each other now, badly.

⚬⟋⚬

Three days later, the kid calls again, sounding whiny and desperate. It turns out the article's due tomorrow and if he doesn't get a quote from Chris he'll fail the assignment and have to repeat tenth grade.

"Well, there's no use asking me to make up a quote about him," I say sternly, going into recess monitor mode. I performed that duty for twenty years at the elementary school, and I never liked it, making kids play nice. He's silent on the other end of the line. I start feeling bad for him again.

"I can tell you about Chris," I say. "What do you need to know? You got the records of his best season?"

"Yeah, I got that," the kid says, grumpy. "It's posted on the plaque outside the cafeteria." As if I should know.

"You want a picture?" I ask.

"Can you scan it?" the kids says.

"Can I what?"

"What do they want?" Frank hollers from the patio.

"Something about Chris playing ball at Chariton," I yell back, covering the receiver. The kid starts explaining scanning to me, and then Frank's in the kitchen, waving a newspaper clipping in my face. It's the one he always carries in his wallet about Chris's senior basketball season. I've got the kid yammering about resolution something in one ear and Frank shouting about regional high scorer in the other until I yell, "I get it!" and they both shut up.

I hear the kid rustling some papers and then he says, very softly, "Could you at least tell me what he's doing now, please?" And I hand the phone over to Frank because the truth is I don't really know what my son is doing.

Frank takes the phone and barks "Frank Kriegstein" into it, as though he were speaking to the president of the United States. "Who wants to know?" he says next, suspicious, and then calms down when he hears it's just the school paper. "He's the CEO of a company called Logan," Frank says proudly. "What do they make? Instrumentation. Well, if you don't know what that means, get a dictionary."

I realize, for the first time, that Frank doesn't understand what Chris does, either, which gives me no small satisfaction.

"Send us a clipping when it comes out, will you?" Frank is asking, more pleadingly. And then, stiffly: "We're at Wittenberg Village. No, it's not a nursing home; it's assisted living. Across from the fairgrounds. We'd like a couple copies."

He hangs up, looking pleased with himself, which is how he's always looked when Chris was getting credit for something. From the time Chris was in middle school, I worried the boy's success would take him away from us, and I was right. First the basketball, which took him down south, to the University of Georgia. Then Elise, who kept him down there. Now work, which has him hopping countries like James Bond, and worries me sick.

"It will be a fine article," Frank says.

"He could have at least had the decency to write the boy back," I say.

"He's in Dubai," Frank says, all touchy, as though I were accusing Frank himself of being absent.

"Even so," I say, trying to picture Dubai. I can only summon Jerusalem, where we went on a church trip in '83, where I ate the best food of my life.

⁂

A week later, we get the article, not from the kid, but from my fifty-five-year-old unmarried daughter, Beth, who works as a part-time librarian in the high school and who missed her train, as far as I'm concerned, when she broke off her engagement with Sam Lehmann, the high school geometry teacher, in 1975.

Beth brings it by with some potato salad and ham sandwiches, and we take the newspaper out to the patio, putting down pickle jars to keep it from flying off in the wind. It's shorter than I expected.

CHARITON'S TOP SHOOTER MOVES TO THE MIDDLE EAST
By Jim Laurence

Chris Kriegstein, who scored more points in his senior year than anyone in Chariton has since (even though the baskets were closer together in the old gym), is now living in Saudi Arabia, says his mom, Mrs. Joy Kriegstein. She says he's very difficult to get in touch with. His dad, Mr. Frank Kriegstein, says that Chris is making instruments there, although he didn't say which kind. Chris played the trumpet in sophomore year. I guess, given Chris's famous three-pointer (which is actually a two-pointer in the new gym), you could say Chris was always good at long distance!

Below is a fuzzy black-and-white picture of Chris in the air. *Indiana's Best Jump Shot* is the caption. It's a beautiful photo, one so familiar

I can summon it when I close my eyes. I've always been astonished that my own child could look so graceful, like someone from another world.

After reading the article, Beth snorts and spits out Mountain Dew, she's laughing so hard. "I always underestimated that Jim Laurence," she says.

Frank is so upset he can't speak. As usual, he waits until Beth leaves to explode.

"Saudi Arabia! What did you tell the kid?" he fumes at me. I haven't seen Frank so mad since the church bulletin accidentally wrote his name as "Fran" under the list of ushers.

"Instruments!" he continues. "It sounds like he's making bombs, like he's bin Laden's personal assistant."

"Bin Laden's dead," I point out.

"Don't believe everything you hear," Frank says testily. "And what's that bunk about a smaller gym? What's the kid's last name? Who's his father?"

"Laurence," I say.

"Sounds Catholic," Frank says, and I say, "Oh, come on, Frank."

He stews all afternoon, doesn't even get cheered up when we sit on the porch and watch the swings swirl and the roller coasters pitch.

"Chris can't see that," Frank says suddenly, later, lying in bed, long after I think he has fallen asleep.

"He won't," I say. "And besides, he wouldn't care."

"He deserves better," Frank says, sounding kind of choked up.

"For chrissakes, Frank, it's a dumb article, not his tombstone."

Then I can hear Frank crying. "Tombstone" was not the right choice of words. I used to wish all the time my husband would be more sensitive. The one time I tried to bring flowers from the fields into the farmhouse, shortly after we'd married, he yelled at me for bringing wild carrot under his roof, as if the limp white blooms were going to turn into vines and choke him in the middle of the night. To be fair, they did wreak havoc on the soybeans.

"In some places it's called Queen Anne's lace," I'd shouted back once he'd slammed the door, and cried into the strawberry jam I was making.

Things like that. But about five years ago, Frank started tearing up a couple times a day. Just a thin streak leaking from his eyes, soundless. It took me a while to catch on to what it really was. At first, I worried he had an eye infection, but he got so gruff and defensive when I asked that I put two and two together. He would cry at the most obvious, embarrassing stuff on TV: sappy airline commercials where families get reunited, or after the Hoosiers lost a ball game.

The crying at night is a new development, since we moved here. I'm worried about him. I'd like to bring it up with Beth, but it's hard to get a second alone with her and I don't want to embarrass Frank. So I just pretend I don't hear him. Our first night at the Village, when I put an arm on his shoulder in the dark and asked him about it, he jerked away. The next morning he wouldn't look at me, like nights in bed years earlier when he'd been a little rough. I'd always liked those nights, and I'd like his new, crying self, if he'd just let me share it a little with him. Sixty-one years of marriage: What's there to be private about?

⁂

The next morning, after breakfast, Frank begins writing a letter to the editor. I've never seen him work on something so hard, not even when he had to give a county commissioner campaign speech. Meaning I have to sit alone, outside, on the best day of the fair. It's the last day, when the kids are awarded 4-H prizes, just like ours were, just like we were. I call to Frank when the kids start spilling out, clutching blue and red ribbons, and he glances up but stays inside, pecking at those keys. So I reminisce by myself, remembering Beth and her turkeys, Chris and his calves, the awful day when Chris's calf died the day of the fair, how I always suspected Beth of poisoning it with stuff we kept in the barn for rats, but I never said a thing. I picture the little pond we built for the kids to swim in, in the summer, in front of the barn; the neat rows of tomatoes I tended; my favorite spot to sit on the porch, where it was always shady.

But thinking back on the farm is a mistake, something I promised myself I wouldn't do when we moved out here. The first meal we ate at the Village, when we were just visiting the place with Beth, all the talk was farm talk. How the crops were doing, corn prices, pesticides. To hear it, you'd think that all the men were taking a lunch break from field work, and that as soon as they emptied their plates they would be back up on their combines, the women in the kitchen, keeping an eye on a mean thundercloud, hedging bets on how long there was before we needed to grab the laundry from the line. That kind of nostalgia depressed me, and I decided to inject some hard truth into the conversation.

"We sold ours off to Nesbit," I said, referring to the farm conglomerate that had bought our land a month earlier. "They'd been bugging us for years. I almost miss talking to James Yancey on the phone each week, telling him no."

The others laughed ruefully, and Frank scowled at me. It was an unspoken rule that James Yancey's name not be said aloud in polite conversation, and my misdemeanor was swiftly punished with silence and the sad scraping of forks, the way I had once punished kids who said "goddamn" on the playground by sticking them on the time-out bench. Most of the Village residents had sold to James Yancey too, long before Frank and I had. The few lucky enough to have passed their farms down to sons or sons-in-law now beamed silently at me down the table: I'd done them the favor of broadcasting their good fortune.

At the end of lunch, Beth strode into the cafeteria clutching several folders, having finished her meeting with the director. "You guys ready?" she asked, hovering over Frank and me. "Wow, Mom, that brisket looks delicious."

"It's not bad," I replied, employing the phrase that everyone at the table, and everyone in Chariton, has relied on for years to complain without risking offense, a statement that summarizes our beliefs more neatly than the Nicene Creed. We didn't expect anything in the first place, it implies, so how could we be disappointed?

⌘

Once the prizes are given out, they pack up the whole county fair in a mere twelve hours, and it is just another empty lot across the way. That isn't bad to stare at either, even though all our neighbors go back inside.

The following evening, Frank asks me to read the letter he's written to the newspaper editor. I've never really read his writing before, aside from what he's signed on Christmas cards, plus his letters to me during the war, when he was in the Pacific.

> *To Whom It May Concern:*
> *I was troubled to find several errors in a recent article of your venerable publication, concerning Chariton High alum Chris Kriegstein. I have included the correct information below. I was*

saddened to see the sinking of the newspaper's standards. I remem-
ber when you could turn to Tiger Tracks *for solid information, not*
made-up crap.

"I don't think you can write 'crap' in a letter to the editor," I object,
putting it down.

"Well, that's what it is," Frank says.

"What about hogwash?"

"Nothing with farm animals in it."

"Trash?"

"Read the sentence to me out loud."

"All right," Frank says, nodding appreciatively as I read. "Trash. I
like it."

I continue.

Here are the facts: not only was my son Chariton High's top scorer
in basketball, he was also the only student to make varsity, in three
sports, from his freshman year onwards. He took his team to the re-
gional finals his senior year, a game against Vernon, a school four
times as big as Chariton, where he scored 45 points.

He is not living in Saudi Arabia making instruments; he lives in
Madison, Wisconsin, with his wife, Elise, where he is the CEO of
Logan Mechanics. He is a very successful businessman and has lived
in the following countries: the USA, Germany, England, China,
and Singapore. He and Elise were blessed with two daughters, Leah
and Sophie. Sophie died in 1996 and is buried at the Lutheran
churchyard in town.

"That's nice you wrote about Sophie," I say. "But shouldn't you
mention Beth, too?"

"What about her?"

"I don't know, that she's his sister?"

"Everyone knows that already," he says, and so I leave it be.

⚸

The next week they run Frank's letter (he refers to it as his "editorial"), and Beth brings us five copies. The editor has taken out "made-up trash" and put in "misinformation."

"Censorship," Frank says, darkly.

We take it with us to dinner and hand out the other four copies to the vegetables who can still read. You would have thought that Frank had won the Nobel Prize. Lina Bauer, who was known for letting boys touch her chest back in middle school, goes on and on about Frank's "talent" and asks him to write her a poem from the voice of her late husband, which sounds fishy to me. John Hartmann, who has a funny shrunken left hand from a threshing accident, suggests that Frank start a regular column in the school paper.

"But Frank's not in high school," I protest. "It's a high school paper." The whole table stares at me, shocked, like I'm some kind of Judas.

"That's the point, Joy," Frank says, quietly, dangerously. "To give the teenagers another perspective on things."

The high school journalism teacher says no, of course, just like I thought he would, but that doesn't stop Frank. He was up two days after his knee surgery last year, and back when our farm was dairy, he milked the cows every day at four in the morning, even when it was pouring, even when he had a raging fever.

Frank decides to start a weekly paper at Wittenberg Village.

It lasts for three weeks, until the staff shuts it down for the anonymous editorial criticizing the lasagna and a scandalous column by

31

Lina about the "Ten Most Irritating Habits of Residents" at Wittenberg Village. She comes out of the director's office crying. "They called me unchristian," she tells us at dinner that night.

I am relieved when the whole thing blows over, but Frank takes it hard. He starts watching a lot of TV, and his eyes leak at the littlest thing. I feel bad for not encouraging him more with his journalism. Frank's always needed something to do. I haven't minded, whenever I had a spare minute, just sitting on the porch at our old house, watching the corn, or the clouds, or petting our dog, Jenny, now long gone. It always got me in trouble as a girl, my habit of just staring at something, "dreaming," as my mother said, "idle." But on weekends, Frank wasn't happy unless he was fixing something. If anything, he got busier when he retired. A lot of the old farmers were like that, up until a couple years ago: they still had breakfast at five a.m. together at PeeWees, down on Miller Street.

I mention some of this to Beth when she comes over to check on us and Frank is out playing cards with some of the guys in the fellowship hall.

"Oh, give it a rest, Mom," she says.

"But I'm just worried—"

"You always have to make them look so good," she says.

"What? Who?" I ask.

"Your men," she says. "Chris, Dad. Why don't you just back off? Let Dad fend for himself. And screw Chris."

"Beth!"

"Forget it," she grumbles, and starts gathering her things. "I'm making a trip to Walmart this afternoon. You guys need anything?"

"Sit down," I say. "What do you mean 'make them look good'?"

"So Chris made some baskets in high school and makes a lot of money now," she says. "Who cares?"

"You know how important it is for your father," I say.

"But why do you get caught up in it?" she asks, her voice tight, like I haven't heard since she was a teenager. "You just encourage it."

"Is this about the newspaper article?" I ask.

"Jesus, that's what you think? No, Mom," she says. "Never mind."

"Do you want an article too?"

She stops and stares at me. "Do you really think I'm that pathetic?"

I don't know what to say to that. I don't think she's pathetic, but sometimes Beth traps you into saying things you don't mean. I learned a long time ago to be silent with her when it got to thin ice. She sighs and comes over and gives me a cold hug. "I don't need an article," she says. "Unlike Dad and Chris, and you, apparently, I'm not obsessed with my high school years."

After she leaves, I write one anyways.

CHARITON ALUM EXCELS IN SHELVING

Beth Kriegstein, who received Honorable Mention for her turkey, Feathers, in 1965, at the Chariton County Fair, and who had 100% attendance in 11th grade, has gone on to become Chariton High's star librarian.

What else is there to say? That she almost wore my wedding dress? That I know she goes to the Mexican bar for salsa nights, because of what Gladys Maynard told me? I suddenly understand poor Jim Laurence's predicament. I want to spice things up, to give Beth a husband and a volleyball medal and a great career. But that isn't Beth, or it isn't who Beth has become. I start over.

BETH PUTS THINGS WHERE THEY BELONG

Even when she was a little girl, Beth Kriegstein had a real talent for organization. I don't just mean she was tidy. She had a certainty that everything had a place. She would drive her dad crazy keeping stray kittens or storing all her magazines in the barn, never throwing anything away. About a year ago, she noticed that her dad and me weren't doing so hot. I was dizzy and Dad was having trouble getting around. That's how we wound up here, at Wittenberg Village. The way she used to know the second it was time to move her calf to a bigger stall, she knew it was time for us to leave the farm. I'm not saying she forced us here. She watched us close and she knew it was time. To be honest, I don't like it here all that much. The food doesn't look the same as it did on the brochure, and it's creepy to me when I hear folks cry out at night. But I trust Beth to know what's best and where we belong.

I hadn't meant to make it so much about myself. But when I try to rewrite it I just come up blank, so I keep it as it is. The next day, when Frank is at physical therapy, I go to the director's office and ask if I can make some photocopies, something I learned how to do when I used to help the church out with secretarial work. I make enough for every vegetable. Then I call up Jim Laurence and tell him I have extra-credit work ready for him; he just needs to pick it up. He starts blabbing about scanning again until I tell him to shut up and drive over here.

I meet him out front, so Frank won't see. Jim is taller than I thought he would be, with dyed black hair. He sounded so weak on the phone I'd pictured a short, fragile kid with freckles and glasses. I ask if he plays ball, and he says he is more into video games. I hand over my article. Tell your teacher you interviewed me, I say.

"Who's this?" he asks, skimming it.

"Chris's sister," I say. "Your librarian."

"I don't go to the library," he says.

"Well, you make sure she gets a copy when it comes out." I make him promise.

⚭

The article isn't the big hit I imagine when I hand out the photocopies at the cafeteria that evening. People glance at it, then spill gravy all over it. Frank doesn't like it one bit.

"You didn't even mention her 4-H prize," he says. "And you make me sound like a jerk."

My media privileges are revoked for one month. "I thought she was photocopying songs for the choir," the secretary explains to the director in the meeting I have to go to the next morning.

Even Beth hates it when it appears in *Tiger Tracks* a week later. "That's what you think of me, Mom? Someone whose greatest talent is being obsessive-compulsive?"

I don't ask her what that means.

Some would describe it as a disaster. But I feel oddly satisfied. I know that we can't live on our own anymore. I know the farm is gone, that Chris has his own life, that his taking over the farm was never a possibility. As soon as I saw the whole crowd roar and rise to their feet as Chris sunk a shot from the half-court line, even the opposing team, I knew that he would leave Chariton soon enough. I know that assisted living is what's done with old folks nowadays, even though I waited hand and foot on Frank's mother when she was ill and bedridden.

Ever since we moved here, I've wanted to turn over the dining room tables, or let all the stupid canaries out of their cages in the lobby, or bite the nurse who comes to take my blood pressure. I'm too mad to cry like Frank.

In school, I never did a thing wrong. I didn't pass notes, I never skipped class, and I didn't drink beer at polka dances. But ever since I got in trouble with the article about Beth, I know what a thrill the bad kids must have had. I walk around the halls, and the residents regard me the way I used to look at the delinquents in high school. I think of Jim Laurence, I adopt his slouch, his sighs, his uncaring.

The only time I drop my new pose is out on the patio. I look at that empty lot, the maples that just turned red at its back border. It says, *Be nothing,* and slack-jawed, staring at it, I am.

Part Two

Sei allem Abschied voran
(Be Ahead of All Parting)

Hamburg, Germany, 1981

C hris rides his bike to work each weekday. Elise sleeps in, rises around ten, and tries to finish her German homework before class at three. The apartment is always cold. Sometimes she takes three baths a day. This gives her a chance to examine her belly's growth. She spies on her nakedness with a curiosity that she would not have permitted herself back in Mississippi. This morning, a rare sunny winter day in Hamburg, she lowers herself into the steaming water. She craves the bath as much as breakfast. Shadows from the windowpanes—a fragile cross—play across her stomach and swollen breasts.

Last summer, when they'd traveled to Munich for a weekend, she'd spied naked sunbathers sprawled across blankets in the English Garden. She had felt repulsed and enticed. She could barely tear her eyes from the bodies, the way she had once stared at an older cousin dressing. Donna, in her early teens, had sensed Elise's gaze and had turned her back to finish buttoning her blouse, prompting a flood of shame in Elise, one of her earliest memories (aside from the ones that Ada had insisted she forget).

⚬

The first time Elise visited Chris in Germany, the year he was study-ing abroad in Stuttgart and she was teaching in Atlanta, they'd at-tended a birthday party with some of his local basketball team bud-dies. The party had climaxed in naked swimming at Lake Bissingen, just outside the city. Sitting on a blanket by the shore, Elise had en-dured a drunken conversation with Sandra, the only other American in Chris's study abroad program, which was surprisingly dominated by Koreans. The amount of Riesling that Elise, who rarely drank, had imbibed, plus the low-lit surroundings, hadn't disguised the fact that Sandra was stark naked, which struck Elise as irritatingly exhibition-ist. Elise had identified Sandra as an ally earlier in the night, given her compatriot status, but her nakedness now made her more foreign than any of the German women around them, who had generally put on clothes or towels once they'd come out of the water. Elise was shivering in a sopping-wet evening gown from one of Atlanta's nicest boutiques. It had cost more than she could really afford on her teach-ing salary, but she'd justified the purchase by imagining where she would wear it: a sophisticated, candlelit restaurant in Stuttgart, which had turned out to be a laughable overestimation of the night's trajec-tory. The silk was certainly ruined.

As Sandra embarked on an extended anecdote about the drugs she'd done during a road trip across America, in between semesters at Berkeley, Elise scanned the crowd for Chris. She didn't want him coming up and talking to them—the last thing she needed was a memory of him trying to make out Sandra's naked breasts in the moonlight—but he was at a safe distance, roughhousing in the water with friends. As Sandra continued her monologue, warming now to the theme of LSD episodes with her poetry professor, Elise reflected silently on her own years at Blue Mountain College, a Baptist all-women's school. There had been streaking—it was 1974, after all—

but that had been limited to girls running across campus in shorts, paper bags over their heads to hide their identities from the dean. Elise had never joined in, but she did get kicked out of the talent show for singing "All You Need Is Love" in front of a map of Vietnam, which had brought a swift end to her phase of political activism. She contemplated telling Sandra about the road trips she'd taken with her band, Jericho!, with Elise as lead singer, but didn't want to admit to her that it had been a Christian singing group, and she didn't feel sober enough to lie convincingly about psychotropic drugs she'd never taken.

During her Blue Mountain days, Elise would have seen Sandra as an "unsaved," her naked body a cry for help. Elise would have felt her pulse rise, her eyes begin to warm with an empathetic glow, and she would have taken Sandra's hand, walked with her to somewhere the two of them could sit alone, put a blanket around the woman's narrow shoulders, and murmured to her about Christ's unconditional love, His plan for Sandra, and Elise's own journey. Next to singing, witnessing was one of Elise's great talents. The other members of Jericho! had always teased her, claimed she could never last a Sunday service without responding to the preacher's call to come forward and testify. But tonight Elise was drunk, and she didn't feel the Holy Spirit; she felt tired and cold. As Sandra droned on, Elise held her cup out to a young man passing through the crowd with a bottle, and the secretive smile he gave her, as he filled her cup and toasted her with his own, felt as good as Communion ever had. After taking a long sip and looking around, marveling at her presence at such a party, Elise let out a wild, private giggle that made Sandra shut up and turn to her suspiciously. Elise suddenly felt a throbbing missing for Ivy, and threw her arms around Sandra's bare frame, rubbing the woman's bony, goose-bumped back before abruptly walking away.

Driving home that night, Chris was wildly enthusiastic about the party and about Germany. Elise, already consumed by guilt for her drinking, wasn't so sure. The next day, sitting by the same lake, with a picnic basket filled with cheese, bread, and a bottle of Prosecco, Chris had proposed. Elise had a flash of the party the night before, a terror that saying yes now would mean a life of debauchery and drunkenness and scant-to-no clothing. Then she looked at Chris, in his buttoned-up shirt, and the gently lapping lake, so innocent in noon light, and the kind diamond resting in red velvet, and acquiesced.

⸎

Elise's child will arrive in three months, according to her gynecologist, Frau Liebmann. *Drei Monate.* Elise knows these are the last three months she will have to herself and that she should be relishing them somehow, according to the advice of women's magazines, but instead she craves the baby's arrival like the promised visit of a best friend. In Hamburg she knows only a few people; it is nothing like London, where she and Chris lived prior to moving here. And the people in German classes don't count.

Unfairly, the water is already cold. With her big toe, Elise turns the hot water faucet, then sinks lower and lower as steam rises from the surface, the way fog would sift over Wolf Lake, near Vidalia. She closes her eyes, slides deeper, although she must compromise for the melting mercy of bathwater covering her torso and stomach by sticking her knees out of the water in two Vs.

Why had she agreed to this move, away from what she loved in London, where she and Chris had lived for the first two years of their marriage? Away from British dinner parties filled with wine and dripping wax and pork roasts and the tiniest, exhilarating hint of misbehavior—much more subtle, and thus more dangerous, more delicious, than German nakedness. Away from Elise's best friend, Mina; away from stubborn, fragrant sprigs of lavender and the dry, mischievous English humor that had shocked Elise at first and then been as warm and comforting as this bath. Away from the enormous old churches, the echoing whispers within them, the terrible bravery of what the pastor at All Souls had said from the pulpit, asking questions about God, belief, and goodness, unlike the Baptist ministers of her youth, who had only talked about the quickest way to get to heaven. "I don't think there is a heaven," that sad, elderly, wonderful British reverend had admitted one Sunday, as though the congregation were his oldest school friend, sitting next to him at the pub. Then he had read a dismal poem by Philip Larkin, "Church Going," and sat down heavily, as the choir burst into flames of Bach.

Of course she had said yes to the move. It was going to be good for Chris's career; he'd been miserable at the London office, and Elise could find ESL teaching work easily enough. The idea of discovering another country had excited Elise. She had imagined massive German castles on the Rhine and a plate piled high with mashed potatoes, for some reason. Both images had seemed simultaneously reassuring and thrilling. And she and Chris would be there together, with the baby on the way. But in her dreams of Germany she had excluded the fact that Chris would spend all day at work. And she hadn't seen mashed potatoes once since their arrival.

⚘

Moving to Hamburg also meant leaving Mississippi again: putting another country, another culture, between the delta and herself.

Elise's southern accent is barely detectable now, though it floods back when she makes long-distance calls to her family. Five thousand miles from Vidalia, Elise misses the five of them more than ever, a longing that gently tugs at her each day and inevitably evaporates the second she calls home. With her mother a sharpness creeps into Elise's voice, a dismissal that Ada, ever since Elise left, seems only too happy to accept. Her mother's timidity never fails to fill Elise with fury. It is admitting guilt without saying sorry.

With Ivy, who is now nineteen, still living at home, Elise feels herself going preachy, doing a secular kind of witnessing, asking about college plans, expressing skepticism over an album that Ivy is thinking of recording with her high school friends. From her brothers, Elise knows that Ivy has been mixing with the wrong crowd: her boyfriend got picked up by the cops for drunk driving last month. But on the phone Ivy is breezy and evasive, and Elise doesn't have the energy to demand a confession and exact punishment: Ivy has their father for that.

After these calls, Elise hangs up the phone blinking away tears. Chris assumes she is homesick, gives her a tight hug, but it's not that, she mutters to him, pulling away, going to run a bath: it's that home makes her sick. An hour later, flushed, dazed from the hot water, Elise steps from the tub feeling baptized and reborn, shed of home's cloying insinuations: *How could you leave? You shouldn't tell such tales, Elise.*

⚬

When Elise is not in the bathtub, and when Chris is at work, she finds herself rackingly lonely, a condition she can compare only to a monstrous two weeks at overnight camp in Alabama when she was twelve, where her nickname was Snot because of how much she cried at night. These days she desperately looks forward to German class and then hates it when she is there because the words don't come out right.

Plus there is the fact that the teacher, a handsome man in his midtwenties, perhaps even a bit younger than Elise, who is twenty-six, won't look at her. Men like him—a little shy, a closeted romantic— have been falling in love with her since she was ten, and it greatly unnerves her that this one stares at the unremarkable midthirties French student instead, who admittedly has much better German pronunciation. Elise supposes it is because of her pregnancy. It makes her feel grotesque and resentful of the baby, then ashamed. In the middle of class, while the rest of the students are declining verbs, Elise longs to be back home in Mississippi, singing a solo in First Baptist with everyone staring in wide-eyed admiration. After each German class, she rushes back to the apartment and runs a bath.

⁂

The doorbell rings. Probably a delivery service, Elise thinks; they'll try at someone else's. But it shrills again, insistently, petulantly, like a newborn woken from sleep, and she lifts herself from the now luke-warm water and wraps a towel around her dripping body.

"Coming," she yells. How do you say that in German? *"Kommen!"* Something like that. Then she remembers the bell is downstairs, outside.

She puts her nightgown back on and runs a washcloth over the foggy mirror, glances swiftly at her image. She is sweating. Her hair is plastered to her forehead in small curls. Minus a world of pain, she looks as she will in three months, pushing her baby out.

She lifts the receiver. "Hello?"

"*Hallo,* Frau Kriegstein?"

"*Ja,*" she responds, her voice, as always, an octave higher in German. She tries to place the elderly female voice.

A flood of incomprehensible German follows. Elise buzzes in whoever it is, and turns to her bedroom to retrieve clothes. Shivering, her hair still wet, she returns to the door and opens it halfway. A small boy with white-blond hair, five or six years old, stands there. When she opens the door fully, he holds a letter out to her, on which *Liesel Kriegstein* is written in a lovely, flowing dark script. But this little boy is not the older woman who just spoke into the intercom below. Elise tries to frame her confusion into a German question but can only think of "*Warum?*" Why? Meanwhile, the boy has entered her apartment, politely removed his boots, and joined her in the foyer.

He lifts the letter up to her and says something in German she cannot understand. She shakes her head, shrugs, makes all the miming movements foreigners use to show they cannot follow. She sees with alarm that his lower lip is beginning to tremble, and she takes the letter from him to prevent the storm approaching on his brow. But the tears begin, with the embarrassment of a child who is too old to be crying.

"Tea?" she asks desperately. "*Heiße Schockolade?*"

He simply stands and shudders. Appalled, she leaves him there and runs down the stairs in her socks to the street. There is no one there. It looks emptier, in fact, than it ever has before. There is only a man walking a small dog in the distance, and the sound of traffic from another intersection. Back inside, a wail fills the stairwell, growing louder as she walks back up. She finds the boy hugging his knees in her front hallway, crying like a kid lost in Macy's.

Not knowing what else to do, she hauls him upright and leads him gently by the hand, as she used to her little brothers and baby sister, into the living room, and brings him to the sofa. He clambers up like a sleepwalker, still sniffling. She takes him to her and rocks him awkwardly against her balloon-shaped belly. He continues crying, but softer, until it is just a wave every now and then of renewed misery. Then, eyes closed, he lies against her baby, and she smooths his hair.

The letter is still in her hand. Careful not to disturb the boy, she opens the envelope and removes the letter, one page of onion-skin-thin, old-fashioned stationery that the pen fairly bleeds through.

Liebe Liesel, it begins. And then German sentences that she cannot make out, aside from easy words like "we" and "you" and "weather." There has obviously been a huge mistake; the boy must be reunited with whomever left him here as soon as possible. She glances down at him. His eyes are shut with the concentration of fake sleep. He is waiting, she sees, for her reaction.

"I'm not Liesel Kriegstein," she says to him. He does not look up. "I'm Elise Kriegstein. There's been a mistake." What is the word for that? "*Fehler.*" Usually she is proud to reveal her German last name, acquired from Chris's ancestors, gratified by the nod of approval from the gynecologist's receptionist. But now the farce has been revealed; Elise is not German, not Liesel, and she cannot help this boy.

He won't budge. Carefully, she shakes him and gently urges him into a seated position. He opens his eyes. They are the bright blue of the cold February sky outside. He turns away from her with tear-streaked cheeks, digging moodily in his pockets for something: a white handkerchief. Somehow this strikes Elise as laughable; it is something an old man would carry. He blows his nose, and this makes her giggle out loud.

Then he says, still looking away, in a crystal voice, "*Ich liebe dich.*"

Why would he say that? It is the most intimate thing she has ever been told in German; somehow it strikes her as one of the most stirring things she has ever heard, even words from Chris before sleep do not plummet down her well like the words of this little boy. She feels suddenly afraid and looks down at him severely, as though he were much older. "*Nein,*" she says. "I'm not Liesel. We need to get you home."

Home. The boy leads the way. They leave Elise's apartment, stopping at the bakery, at the boy's tugging insistence, to get a few cookies. He orders and she pays. The baker, whom Elise sees every few days, gives her a quizzical look but does not inquire what she is doing with this boy. Thank goodness for German reserve. In Vidalia she would have been given the third degree, and she isn't even sure how she could have answered the question in English.

As they exit the shop, Elise is suddenly lighthearted, as though she were playing an enormous prank on Hamburg and her life in Germany. She will miss German class but she doesn't care; on the contrary, she feels eminently relieved. The day has taken on a snow-day feel, like the one or two times flakes would fall in Vidalia each year, and Ada would make the children hot chocolate with whipped cream and cinnamon on top.

With the boy marching ahead, Elise no longer feels like a foreigner. She sees the street before her in a new light, as Liesel might see it. Who is this Liesel? The boy's estranged mother? An aunt? Should I be going to the police? Elise wonders. But what would I say when I got there? Would they speak English? Elise's initial imaginings of Germany had also excluded the fact that everyone would be speaking German.

Rationally, of course, she had known this would be the case. Months before the move, she had listened to language tapes on her drive to the school in London where she taught third grade. But the emotional reality of living in another language didn't sink in until they arrived at the airport and the words buzzed all around her, like summers in Vidalia when the cicadas came.

Chris speaks some German from his days as an exchange student in Stuttgart. He also comes from a farming town in northeast Indiana, where each of his ancestors can be traced back to farms around Hanover. Chris and Elise took a train to Hanover in the early fall, the trees as yellow as dandelions, their first excursion from Hamburg. Elise had found it depressing that the Hanover farmland looked so similar to Indiana, that Chris's great-great-greats had traveled so far from home to face the same landscape. What kind of escape was that? Then again, the same regrets and insecurities haunt Elise now as those that haunted her in Vidalia, Atlanta, and London. Her moves have never resulted in the new personality she always hoped would come as a reward for the upheaval.

Elise doesn't notice when the boy turns a corner, until he shouts, "Liesel!" and waves furiously. She breaks out into a cautious run, holding her belly. She could begin the *I'm not Liesel* line of argument again, but she doesn't want him to have a breakdown here and draw attention. So she follows his surprisingly quick gait for another fifteen minutes through small streets filled with bright balconies and large trees stretching their naked limbs to the sun.

Then he stops at a small gate and they enter a series of private gardens, where city dwellers own small plots of land. She has noticed these *Gartenkolonien* scattered in pockets throughout the city, with their carefully tended rows and doll-like sheds, but she has never been inside. Now, in winter, the plots are all dead, the gates locked, apples rotting in brown grass. For the first time since leaving her apartment she feels uneasy and wonders if the boy has led her astray, or is simply lost himself. "Excuse me," she calls out to him, coming to a stop.

"*Entschuldigung?*" but he keeps going. As she catches up to him she can hear he is absorbed in humming a childish tune, the sort of thing you sing in grade-school choir. She can almost recognize it. He slips a hand confidingly in hers, and she falls silent.

Then they hear voices. The boy quickens his step and grips her hand tighter. At the end of the path, on their right, is an open gate. Inside the garden, on a picnic table, are an enormous cake and a steaming thermos. Four people, so bundled as to make their age and sex anyone's guess, huddle around the table, picking haphazardly with mismatched forks at the cake and passing around the thermos. No one has their own silverware or plate or cup. The air of disorder is decidedly un-German, Elise thinks, and for a second she feels a strong sense of camaraderie with the wayward winter picnickers.

"Oma," the boy calls out, and one of the bundles turns around and opens her arms. The boy lets go of Elise's hand, and she watches with anguish as he falls into the old woman's embrace. "Come back," she wants to call, knowing she has no right to him. As soon as he leaves her side, the familiar lonely ache begins again, and Elise thinks of her bathtub and tries to picture the walk back home, how to get back in the hot scented water as soon as possible. The group regards her with silent curiosity, and the boy points to her and announces, simply, "Liesel."

"*Auf Liesel!*" one of the men shouts, lifting the thermos to her, and they all drink from the thermos, crying "*Auf Liesel!*" before they drink.

"*Nein,*" Elise protests. "*Elise. Ich bin Elise.*" And then "*Tut mir leid,*" at the man's look of offense and the boy's scowl.

"*Natürlich bist du nicht Liesel,*" says another man at the picnic table, offhandedly, picking at the cake. "*Liesel ist tot.*"

Elise understands what the man is saying, even as the words fill her with an undefined dread. Liesel is dead. Elise feels nauseous and dizzy. She needs to sit but there is no place at the table for her. *"Komm,"* the boy's grandmother says, and gestures for Elise to sit beside her. Elise freezes, recognizing the voice. It is the woman who spoke into the intercom, back at Elise's apartment. The woman gestures again, patting the seat beside her. Weary of trying to make sense of it all—Germany, German, the old woman's voice—Elise acquiesces, childlike, and finds herself sitting on the rough wooden bench between the boy and his grandmother, leaning her head on the old woman's shoulder. The grandmother offers Elise the thermos. Elise realizes she is shivering, despite her heavy jacket and boots. Elise accepts the thermos, then discovers from its ripe, rich perfume that it is mulled wine, the smell of the Christmas markets that popped up all over Hamburg in mid-November. She gives the thermos back to the grandmother, pointing at her stomach by way of explanation.

"Kein Problem," the grandmother insists. *"Gut für das Kind."*

Inscrutably, Elise obeys her, for a small sip, and a rich, sour, cinnamony taste flies down her throat, hot and safe, like the Russian tea, made of Tang, cloves, cinnamon, and sugar, that she'd drunk at Christmas back home. Shyly, Elise takes a closer look at the other women around her. They remind her of a ruddier version of the women her mother plays bridge with. Last week, her father told her over the phone that, despite Elise's request in a recent letter, he and Ada wouldn't be coming to Germany for the baby's birth; it would be a waste of money. Chris had fumed at the news when Elise told him; it hadn't occurred to Elise to argue with her father, just as she'd stayed tongue-tied when he'd told her she had to stay in Mississippi for college. She wishes she hadn't asked, hadn't scrawled the letter in a moment of weakness when Chris was on a business trip, hadn't given her father the power to say no. It is her punishment, she knows, for the five years that she stayed away from Vidalia, for living abroad now. Elise closes her eyes.

Suddenly, the table erupts in raucous laughter, except for the grandmother, who is shaking her head, looking mildly offended. One of the men is wiping tears of mirth from his eyes. Elise feels herself entering invisibility. Usually, it is an exclusion she deeply resents; if she were at a dinner party with Chris right now, she would be tugging on his sleeve, demanding a translation, faking laughter once he'd told the joke in English, but right now she feels her ignorance is a privilege, an excuse to opt out of the present company. The sip of mulled wine has warmed and calmed her, not unlike a bath. She eases herself off the bench. The grandmother gives her hand a squeeze; the boy gives her a questioning look but does not protest. The others take no notice as she wanders away from the picnic table, deeper into the garden.

Elise meanders along the tall hedge of evergreen that separates the garden from adjacent properties. At the far right corner is a small gap in the branches, a gate leading into the next garden. Elise tests the latch. Unlocked. She glances back at the table. The grandmother and the boy are playing a handclap game. The others, from their increasingly impassioned gesticulations, seem to have entered some kind of argument. No one is watching her. She pushes down the latch and walks boldly through, as though the property were her own.

⚬

On the other side of the gate, Elise encounters not another garden, but a large greenhouse. Emboldened by the afternoon's growing shadows and their gift of anonymity, Elise heads towards the tall glass structure. She tries the door handle and finds it is also unlocked. After a moment's hesitation, she enters.

Inside, it is spring. Colors crowd Elise's winter-starved vision: lemon-hued forsythia, tulips the color of Dreamsicles. The air is humid; Elise can almost hear an exhaling. Or is it her own long sigh? She steps slowly down the aisles, bending her head over the blooms, pausing to fill her lungs with scent. At the end of the hall is another door that Elise continues through, this time without a second thought.

The next room is a good ten degrees warmer, and Elise shrugs off her coat, lays it on an empty plastic chair. The plants here, arranged on shelves in neat rows, are suited for warmer climes. She spots her father's favorites: gardenia, jasmine, lilies. All the flowers he tends with such care, the one luxury he allows himself: rare bulbs, heirloom seeds ordered from distant states. Usually the thought would make Elise scowl, roll her eyes at the irony of it: a father better suited for plants than children. But right now, in this warm, perfumed air, she feels a swelling gratitude to him, for working so hard on beauty. His garden (for it was always referred to as his, never the family's) often won first prize in the annual Tri-County Gardening Society contest. And he would bring cut flowers for Mama in the spring, Elise thinks, surprised by such an easy, happy memory of tulips on the kitchen table.

"*Ist da jemand?*"

Elise jumps at the voice, which comes from the other side of the room, behind a dark, waxy bush.

"*Hallo?*" Elise stammers back.

A woman, whom Elise guesses to be in her late forties, emerges from behind a row of shelves, her hands in gardening gloves, her face streaked with dirt, her graying hair tied back in an unkempt ponytail. She is sporting blue coveralls with innumerable pockets: the ubiquitous uniform of handymen and laborers throughout Germany. Elise has never seen such clothes on a woman before.

"*Was machen Sie hier?*" the woman demands.

Where to begin? Elise takes a deep breath. "*Ich bin—es war—* Liesel.*"

"Liesel?" the woman says suspiciously. "Liesel Kriegstein?"

"Do you speak English?" Elise asks, giving up.

"Yes." The woman's tone is arrogant, testy. "What are you making here? This is not a public garden."

Racking her brain for an answer, Elise realizes that language is not the issue. How can she begin to explain to the woman what remains a mystery to herself?

"I came from a party over there," Elise says, pointing in the general direction of the first garden.

"Yes, for Frau Kriegstein, I know. They invited me also. I do not go. It is a strange habit, *nicht?* To have a birthday party for the dead. A tradition, where they come from, but for me, it is strange. I do not like it."

Elise nods, trying to look sympathetic, cataloging the new information. "It is Liesel Kriegstein's birthday?"

"*Was* her birthday. She died six months ago. But to continue to celebrate, after death, is not good. *Besonders* not good for her little boy. Time to move on, *nicht?* I am taking care of Frau Kriegstein's flowers for many years. All of the gardeners from this *Kolonie* come here to my—how do you say—warmhouse, to give me their flowers for the winter. I keep them alive through the cold months, give them back in the spring. Every year, until now, Frau Kriegstein too. Now, her mother, the old woman, has the garden."

In her telling of Liesel's garden, the woman's tone has changed, grown wistful, and her face has softened into sadness. She turns to Elise with a hungry look. "Do you want to see Frau Kriegstein's plants?" It is an order.

Elise follows the woman to the room's middle aisle, where about twenty potted plants—rhododendron, azaleas, begonias—bloom beautifully, on a shelf marked *Kriegstein*. "It was terrible to watch Frau Kriegstein being sick. *Krebs*. She always had the best garden, always a nice, polite customer. She came to the garden even when she was very weak. Last winter, she would visit me here, check on her flowers. But to make such a birthday party now, it is *Unsinn*."

Looking around the room, at the quiet order of the plants, everything in its place, Elise can understand why the woman would feel terrified by the chaos of the tipsy festivities happening in the garden nearby. She remembers the same look in her father's eyes, regarding the wild chatter of his offspring at the dinner table, the obvious relief on his face when they excused themselves, one by one, to do homework or watch TV.

The woman looks at Elise sharply. "You were a friend of Frau Kriegstein? I never knew she was speaking English."

Caught again. Elise tries her best to shrug helplessly and smile. She lifts the letter from her pocket. "It was a mistake," she says. "My name is Elise Kriegstein. The little boy—Frau Kriegstein's son?—came to my house with this."

The woman swiftly takes the envelope from her. As she unfolds the letter, shaking her head, Elise regrets having showed it to her.

"What does it say?" Elise asks, her voice unconsciously dropping to a whisper, as the woman reads silently.

"It is from Liesel's mother," the woman announces, and then, unnecessarily: "To Liesel. The stupid old woman, she thinks you have some way of connection to her daughter, because of the names. She saw your last name on your building's directory."

"But why? How?"

The woman shrugs. "She is strange. She is—how do you say it—

suspicious? No: superstitious. Believing in spirits, connections. Ever since Frau Kriegstein dies, she is getting crazier, the way old people do—my aunt was the same. Talking to the plants, talking to her dead daughter, telling the little boy ghost stories. He believes her, of course. Such people should be in an *Altenheim*, not out on the street, giving letters to strangers. But she is not from around here," she finishes, and shrugs, as though that explains everything.

The woman returns to the letter. "Ah, wait—this is beautiful. *Großartig*. Listen," she commands, as though Elise were her student. "Liesel's mother quotes here a poem by Rilke: '*Sei allem Abschied voran, als wäre er hinter Dir, wie der Winter, der eben geht—*'"

Elise is unwilling to admit that not a word of this makes sense to her, but the woman is already translating, in her pedantic tone. "It means something like 'Be in front of all separating, as if it is already behind you.'" She pauses, searching for the English words. "Like the winter, which is leaving."

Elise nods politely and the woman continues reading. "*Denn unter Wintern ist einer so endlos Winter, daß überwinternd, dein Herz überhaupt übersteht.*" She frowns, struggling with the translation: "For under winter—is a winter so long lasting—that..." She sighs and gives up. "I don't know. Too complicated. Something with winter and *überstehen*...surviving."

"A good poem for a greenhouse," Elise interrupts, feeling witty.

"Where are you from?" the woman asks abruptly.

"America," Elise says.

"Ha! Hollywood!" the woman shrills.

As Elise is trying to find a subtle way out of the conversation, the woman removes scissors from her pocket and heads to a trellis smothered in honeysuckle vine, which Elise has not seen until now. The woman clips a short piece of the vine, with six pale, buttery blossoms, and hands it to Elise. "From your *Heimat, oder?*" she asks, smiling unnervingly. "I can smell it on you."

"Thank you," Elise says, frightened now, but clutching the honeysuckle (a shade lighter than the one that grows in Vidalia, in the Eberts' backyard, close to the ravine) as though it were her plane ticket home. She holds out her other hand. "Can I have the letter to Liesel, please, so I can give it back to them?"

"Oh no," the woman says, nonchalantly. "I keep it."

"But—"

"It is none of your business!" the woman cries, in a sudden rage, waving the letter. "Like you said, you are a mistake!" She calms herself and looks away. "I am sorry. But I loved her too, you understand? In your country, you are quick to love, *oder?* It is easier to talk about love in English than in German."

For a moment, in the wake of this awkward outburst, both women are silent, and then Elise clears her throat, preparing to go. But the woman speaks first, in a low tone, almost to herself. "Frau Kriegstein, before she falls sick, has the same hair like you. *Locken.*" And suddenly, as quick as a garden snake, the woman's hand is reaching out towards Elise's face, fingering one of her curls. Despite the heat of the greenhouse, the woman's dirty gardening glove, which glances Elise's cheek, is cold, and Elise shivers before startling to movement, drawing back violently. Unperturbed, the woman smiles, a bullying grin that Elise remembers from the older girls in high school, taunting her in the cafeteria. Her cheeks hot, Elise snatches the envelope from the woman's grasp. The second it leaves her fingers, the woman cries out but does not protest further. They stare at each other for a second, and then the woman lets out a bitter cackle.

"You Americans. Always having to win, always hungry for the happy ending. The liberators."

"The letter was delivered to me," Elise says evenly.

"*Ein Fehler.* It does not belong to you. But that has not stopped you before."

Elise is both bored and irritated by this thinly veiled political critique, and moves towards her coat. "I should get going."

"Of course!" the woman begins moving to another aisle, where she picks up a spade and, with a manic energy, starts digging around the roots of a rhododendron bush. "Get going, get going! I am also busy! I have fifty gardens to keep alive! What do you have to do, *Hausfrau?*" she spits. "Who do you have to keep alive?"

Elise, holding her stomach protectively, as though to protect the unborn from such venom, hurries away, as repulsed now by the gaudy blossoms as she was enchanted when she first entered the greenhouse. She considers tossing away the honeysuckle at the gate to the other garden but thrusts it in her pocket instead, next to Liesel's letter.

⁂

Back in the first garden, the picnickers are gone, and only the boy, the grandmother, and a few cake crumbs remain. The boy is asleep in the old woman's lap. The grandmother gathers Elise in one look and then shakes the boy, who moans. "*Los,*" she says. The boy opens his eyes and looks at Elise, full of longing. Elise opens her arms to him and he burrows into her, nestles against her neck.

"*Es ist kalt,*" the grandmother states, as pragmatic as ever, and begins marching off, jerking her head, indicating that the two follow her.

The sky is pinkish. Elise feels more tired than she can ever remember feeling. She wants to lay her head down on the picnic table, but the grandmother looks back at her and shakes her head no. Elise recalls what the woman in the greenhouse said about the grandmother's dementia. She was wrong, Elise thinks. I trust this old woman more than I trust myself. Elise feels for the letter in her pocket. I will translate the letter, Elise thinks. I'll spend the next week at home with the dictionary, skipping German class, poring over the looping letters. I will read it aloud to Liesel. It is an unhinged idea, Elise knows, but to live so far from home, in Germany, is just as unhinged. That's what being foreign is: being lonely enough to follow a small boy through a city, unbalanced enough to believe you can help a dead woman receive her mother's letter. Ironic, Elise thinks, that the visions she craved so badly back in Vidalia as a child, thinking if she prayed hard enough, she could glimpse what others sometimes claimed they witnessed—a holy light, the voice of Christ—never came. It is only now, in Hamburg, where she feels herself so lost, that the uncanny unfurls, godlessly, in spring's saturated colors, throbbing with secular love.

The grandmother and the boy lead Elise back down the series of gardens slowly, as though she is a recovering invalid. They walk back through the darkened streets, gone dim and busy with the work crowd and dinner preparations, turning corners until they are back at Elise and Chris's apartment. Elise can see the lights on in their apartment; Chris must be home.

"*Tschüß, meine Liebe,*" the grandmother says (or does she say "Liesel"?), and pinches Elise's cheek. The boy looks up forlornly at Elise and grudgingly accepts a hug; he is angry that she is leaving. Elise is also afraid to go, until the grandmother gives her a tough little shove and turns away with the boy. Elise considers following them, but the baby does not want to and kicks roughly. It is Elise's first intuition of her child's stubborn will, opposed to hers. It shocks her into movement. Elise walks to the door, rings the bell, and slowly climbs the stairs to her glowing foreign home.

Good Luck

Bombay, India; and Philadelphia, Pennsylvania, 1982

Chris likes to travel. Likes every last detail of it, from tenderly laying his ironed oxford shirts in his suitcase; to the sudden tilt backwards when the plane lifts—which body memory greets with anticipatory joy, from a jerky Chariton county fair roller coaster, August 1969—to the quiet melancholy of opening the hotel room door; to Chris's pounding heart, greeting a conference room full of foreign customers the next day, hoping the words come out right.

What he likes best of all, though he would never admit this, is exiting the airport's baggage claim in a foreign city and seeing his name on a handwritten sign—typically black marker, all caps—held high by the chauffeur. A curt nod from Chris, and the driver assumes his heavy luggage, leads him to lush leather seats. Chris relaxes, savoring the city humming silently by, the feeling of easy power, even if it leaks away as soon as he exits the car. That first glimpse of his own name seems to confirm everything, the same way seeing his mother's handwriting on his T-shirt tags at 4-H camp, in her cramped cursive, gave Chris a safe assurance of return. Those signs the drivers hold now remind him he is heading somewhere big, somewhere inevitable.

There is a certain kind of luck that Chris has learned, over the years, to hone. An instinct in his gut, the kind you can't overthink, because it might dissolve. Chris played basketball from middle school all the way up through college, and that's where he first learned about the luck and how to milk it. When you walk onto a court with that light certainty in your insides, your hands shaky with eagerness to palm the leather, the one thing you cannot, you must not, do is meet the eyes of this luck. The trick is not to question it and not to believe too strongly in it. It's like a shy dog or a pretty girl: let them know you're interested, and you can forget it. Instead, focus on grabbing rebounds and making sharp passes, get back quick on defense, and soon enough the luck will wind its way into your jump shot. Then you hold your follow-through, hear the swish, feel how scoring makes your calves go weightless. Luck paid Chris's tuition at the University of Georgia, gave him an engineering degree and a bad knee.

Chris realizes he's had a lot of luck so far. Getting out of Chariton, Indiana, for one. Not waking up at four a.m. every day like his father, not breaking his back trying to coax fertility out of the stubborn, cold ground, or rain out of sullen skies. Meeting Elise—stroke of luck number two—on the night of November 17, 1977, at a party after a basketball game. Elise was primly sipping 7UP, while everyone around her did keg stands and took generous bong hits. Chris, still elated from the night's victory against their rivals, Georgia Tech, floating on a three-beer buzz, had sauntered up to Elise and struck up a conversation, all casual confidence. He was shocked by her delta drawl; she'd looked so alone and vulnerable, leaning against the wall, that Chris had assumed she was a foreign exchange student or at least a fellow midwesterner. Her sweetly sassy attitude (it turned out she was a Georgia Tech fan and lived in Atlanta; she'd been dragged along to this party by a girlfriend) combined with her unabashed beauty (he'd noticed plenty of other guys checking her out, taking gulps of whatever they were drinking, trying to summon courage for the kill) and the irresistible innocence she exuded, sucking her straw like a ten-year-old, culminated in what Chris's coach would have called a "triple threat," against which Chris, who had just played one of the best defensive games of his life (four blocks, five steals, fifteen rebounds), was utterly helpless.

To Chris's astonishment, their talk that night led to a date a week later, which led to more dates, in Atlanta and Athens, which led to writing letters every day when Chris left to study abroad in Stuttgart, which led to Elise visiting Chris, Chris proposing, and everything that has unfolded since: marriage, a tiny row house in London, a chilly apartment in Hamburg, a baby girl, a small brick house in Philadelphia. Chris is still unsure why Elise chose to be with him, aside from his aforementioned luck. Elise doesn't know the only girlfriends Chris had before, back in Indiana, were Tanya White, with buckteeth, and June Schiller, whose only distinguishing feature was her body's uncanny square shape.

Aside from Elise, the only other woman Chris has slept with—another fact he has kept to himself—was the only one who might have vied for Elise's beauty: Twyla Lincoln, the little sister of his teammate Ben. After Chris and Twyla's one-night stand, which began with a party on the edge of campus that got kind of wild and ended in Chris's dorm room, Twyla never spoke to Chris again. Chris wasn't sure if it was because he wasn't cool enough or because he was white. Perhaps they were one and the same. Until Twyla, he hadn't been aware that racism could work the other way, too. And though he'd felt disappointed and hurt when he saw her with Dontelle, another teammate, at the next party, he'd also felt a little relieved: his parents had never forgiven his younger sister, Beth, for attending school dances with John Young in high school, and he was just Catholic.

Chris counts his career now as his third major slice of luck. The fact that he flies first-class and he's under thirty-five. The trust his boss puts in him, how quickly Chris has risen in the ranks at Logan since he started six years ago. Of course, Chris knows it can go downhill just as quickly as it got good. That's what happened at UGA: the team improved but Chris got worse, or maybe just stayed the same, until he was benching games as a senior that he would have played twenty-six minutes of as a freshman. And that was before the knee injury.

But at least things with Elise feel steady, Chris tells himself, especially now, with their little girl, Leah. Chris loves the glint of his wedding ring; it calms him when he's far away and gives him a noble, if not primal, feeling of protectiveness, as if traveling to meet customers in India were akin to hauling a boar back to the cave for his family's sustenance. When he pictures Elise, he sees her rocking Leah in silvery moonlight, even though Leah, at fourteen months, is nearly too big to be rocked like that. Even back in Hamburg, when Leah was a newborn, Chris rarely saw Elise holding Leah at night, since they always went to her in shifts. He slept like a stone during Elise's turns to comfort the crying. On his own shifts, too tall for the rocking chair, Chris's sprawling, near-seven-foot body had felt feminine holding the baby, humming off-key. After the initial agony of waking, once Leah had drifted off to sleep, Chris had enjoyed those unearthly moments with his baby daughter. Sometimes, he had wished he could stay home with Leah the next day and send Elise to the office in his stead, urges he always dismissed with embarrassment in the morning light.

These days, Chris wishes that Elise would display a little more gratitude for his breadwinning, or at least make some show of missing him when he has to travel for work. More like his mother, who heaves tragic, disapproving sighs over the phone whenever Chris announces an international trip, and who was horror-struck when he went south for college. Instead, Elise cheerfully waves good-bye, doesn't even offer to pack his suitcase. It's a recent development: in Hamburg she wept whenever he had to take overnight trips to the London office. But that was probably just pregnancy hormones, and it's good that she's independent, he chides himself, as the plane bounces onto the tarmac in Bombay; he's lucky it's not the other way around.

⚘

It's true: Elise loves it when Chris travels. She knows this is a strange reaction; the other mothers in Leah's playgroup always give Elise pitying looks when she says Chris is out of town. But Elise feels something in herself shake loose when he departs. She is relieved to be back in America; the loneliness that was a constant whisper to their ten months in Hamburg reasserts itself less frequently now and seems to strike when Chris is in town, rather than when he's gone.

Part of it has to do with accountability: when Chris is around, Elise feels observed. Before, this struck her as one of the most beautiful things about marriage, this daily witnessing. Now it feels intrusive. Elise's repatriation was accompanied by a new sense of recklessness. In Germany, she had been so careful: cautious not to offend, not to mispronounce, not to leave a bad impression. Here the stakes are much lower: in Wynnside, a small suburb of Philadelphia, Elise feels deliciously anonymous.

Elise tried to explain this new feeling to Chris, hoping he would relate. It came up over a discussion about finding a babysitter for Leah. Elise was going to need some hours each day away from Leah, which Chris didn't understand. She hadn't craved this in Hamburg, he pointed out. But now she did, she responded. Why? She tried to describe the new feeling, the new urges, the new apathy towards mothering that reminded her of the clarinet when she was twelve. For three years Elise had devoted herself to the instrument, and then one day she simply couldn't summon the desire to practice. She never missed it afterwards, either.

Elise omitted mentioning this final comparison to Chris, sensing it would not go over well. In truth, this inclination towards both overachievement and abandonment frightens her: you can't just drop a child the way you drop band class. She still loves Leah deeply, of course. But she just can't give from the same place that she used to.

Do you miss teaching? Chris asked. Elise nearly said yes out of wanting this to be the case. But she doesn't miss teaching, at least not yet. She believes it will all come back: her relentless sense of obligation and responsibility, her tireless caretaking, her real *self*, in other words. But for now the absence of all these duties feels wonderful—when Chris is gone, that is. When he is there, the new, irresponsible impulses feel embarrassing, like growing breasts at eleven: a private development made public. Then Elise feels ashamed by her new habits: Since when is she someone who leaves a fourteen-month-old with a sitter to have lunch, alone, at an expensive restaurant downtown? But her craving for these clandestine indulgences—she only glancingly mentions them to Chris—overwhelms her hesitation.

Elise discovered masturbation when she was fourteen. She shared a room with Ivy, who was seven. It was the year she tried to tell her mother about Paps. It was the year Elise masked herself with religion the way other girls in her grade masked themselves with makeup, the year Elise burned all her Beatles records at the summer revival. But even as she was desperately trying to give her soul to Jesus, Elise discovered that when she pressed down hard on one part, sucked her muscles in, and put a finger inside, elation happened, which Paps's wandering grip had never wrought. Glorious. When Ivy was asleep, Elise would explore. When Ivy was awake, Elise's impatience made her feel rackingly guilty. Something similar feels like it is happening with Chris now. The only place that Elise feels natural with him lately is in the bedroom. She is wilder, hungrier. He is both excited and baffled by it, she can tell. Yet she cannot bring this ease or abandon to breakfast the next morning—she sits as stiffly through cereal as though their sex the night before were a one-night stand.

Elise has begun traveling, too, when Chris travels. Since her father suddenly passed away, she has some money and a private account. Given Charles Ebert's extreme thriftiness, it is not a small sum, yet it feels sinful to spend it on beach cottages on the New Jersey shore, or a night in New York City. This sinfulness is one of Elise's greatest pleasures. Sometimes she brings Leah along; more often she leaves her with the babysitter, Becky. So far, Chris hasn't caught on: Elise has trained Becky to say, if Chris calls, that Elise is out shopping or with a girlfriend. If he calls at night, Becky is not to pick up the phone. Elise knows it's a game of Russian roulette, that her dalliance is bound to be discovered. What a pitiful thrill, she occasionally thinks. I'm not even having an affair. But she loves the feeling of hurtling misbehavior, of irrational rebellion, even if she can't quite pin down what or whom she's rebelling against. And so, when Chris announces a business trip, Elise's first response is a slow-spreading smile, imagining where she will wind up, picturing starched sand dunes in midmorning light.

⚬

For the past two days, and for an indulgent two more, Elise is staying in a small bed-and-breakfast in the Poconos. She wakes to a fresh pine breeze and saunters over to the main house for breakfast. The only other guests are a fidgety old couple celebrating their golden anniversary, according to Elise's eavesdropping. Over French toast, Elise slowly reads the *New York Times*, thoughtfully left on each table by their perfectly invisible hosts.

After all those months surrounded by German, Elise is still thrilled by the English language surrounding her, even though they've been back in the States for more than a year. Since repatriating, she has taken to reading in an entirely new fashion. Growing up in Mississippi, brains were the equivalent of crooked teeth, and about the time Elise got braces she also picked up a laugh that put people at ease, reassured them they never had to feel intimidated in her presence. There were smart girls in her class, but their fates at school dances were a clear enough warning, and the last time Elise was back in Vidalia, she'd run into Macy Lane Cargill, who'd won every spelling bee, working in the local library. So that was where intelligence got you below the Mason-Dixon Line: shelving cookbooks and shushing teenagers.

But here in the Northeast it is different. The women read, have fierce opinions about politics, and cancel their husbands out at the polls. Elise has to admit she likes the lifestyle section of the paper better than the front page, but she has begun to feel an unprecedented hunger for the news. Part of it, perhaps, is simply being back in *her* country, reading about *her* president, feeling permission to feel invested again.

It is a relief, too, to be away from the German criticism of everything American: the pettiness of Hollywood, the rampant consumerism, Reaganomics, the Iran-Contra affair—even the American habit of smiling, as Elise had learned over one particularly painful dinner with Chris's boss and his wife, back in Hamburg.

"Let me ask you something," Frau Müller had said, as the men had begun talking business. "Why are Americans always smiling, when there's nothing to smile about? Like right now. Why are you smiling? I've never seen you any other way. Are you honestly so happy, all the time?"

Elise had grinned more widely and laughed her most nonchalant laugh, shrugged, and changed the subject, a reaction that only confirmed Frau Müller's assumptions, she realized afterwards, with consternation. As dessert came, Elise considered the accusation. Did she really smile all the time? Of course she wasn't always happy. What an insulting suggestion. But how did you go about mounting a rebuttal? She glanced at Chris. He was beaming at his boss, nodding his head at an unfolding anecdote, and his expression suddenly struck Elise as idiotic.

Feigning a headache, Elise had left the dinner early and gone home. Lying in bed, a hand on her stomach—she was three months along with Leah at that point—Elise had sworn to herself that she wouldn't force her child to be cheerful. What had Ada always said? "I want to see that frown turned upside down. Before I count to five. One. Two. That's better." After that dinner with the Müllers, Elise had tried to be cognizant of when she was smiling, and why. Ultimately, it was an exhausting, punishing exercise, and she was glad to drop it when they returned to the States, where she could smile as much and as stupidly as everyone else.

Not that those smiles, including her own, don't drive her crazy some days, since moving back. And that isn't the only allergy Elise has developed to her home country. After their first move overseas, to London, Elise had become increasingly critical of the US. The outlandish food portions at restaurants. The death penalty. Oprah. But in Hamburg, when she would discuss such matters with Germans, even when she was on their side, Elise had often intuited a tiny, perverse relish in their critique, which had never failed to incense her and had inevitably resulted in her vehement defense of America by the end of the conversation, on a topic as silly as whether the first Thanksgiving was as mythical as the Creation in Genesis. Elise had decided the German dislike of America had something to do with the Marshall Plan and the postwar Allied occupation—resenting the person you owe something to, the one who is calling the shots. Elise had felt that way with Chris after she stopped working, before she received her father's inheritance four months ago.

It is still a man's money, but it wasn't bestowed conditionally, as a reward for toeing the line, the way Charles Ebert had always given his daughter money before. This time, Elise had earned it through her daddy's helpless death. She can spend it any way she wants and he can't do a damn thing. Elise is puzzled by the savage nature of her reaction. While he was alive, her fights with her father had been largely silent, characterized by symbolically aggressive acts (Elise not coming home for Christmas her freshman year; Charles withdrawing tuition the following semester), like pushing chess pieces across a board, each player tensed for the other's next move. Elise misses having an opponent. She spends Charles's inheritance with a kind of focused revenge, studiously frivolous (Charles had despised nothing more than frivolity), vaguely craving a stern reprimand, which never comes. Although the minute the notion of revenge comes to her mind, Elise dismisses it. She is just having a good time, after a long period of not having a good time. That is the least she deserves, the least they owe her after all those childhood years hiding in hot, humid shadows.

What is Ivy doing with her money? Elise wonders. The irony being that, of all the siblings, Ivy now needs cash the least. Her band,

Choked by Kudzu, which Elise dismissed for so many years, deciding it was an excuse for Ivy to stick around Vidalia with her high school buddies, get high, and "write music," has had considerable regional success. Elise watched Ivy perform the last time she was in Vidalia, and Ivy is rapturous in front of a crowd, her red hair long now, her voice alternately crooning and harsh, belting out the band's mix of bluegrass, roots, and rock. Offstage, Elise isn't sure how Ivy is doing. It's hard to catch her sister sober; that's for sure. Then again, Elise thinks, maybe she's just looking for ways to deny Ivy's success now, the way she dismissed the band's potential before. After all, Ivy is still young, in her early twenties, having a blast. You're just jealous, Elise scolds herself.

While this theory is hardly flattering, painting Elise as the uptight, petty older sister, Elise settles on it because it reassures her that she doesn't have to go back down South to check on Ivy, doesn't have to go into guardian-angel mode. A role that's never worked anyways, Elise thinks, a tight, bitter smile flickering across her face, remembering Paps's visits, how Elise would make sure to skip choir and rush home from school to check on her sister, only to find the two of them innocently perched on the sofa, Paps reading *A Hundred and One Dalmations*, Ivy gnawing on a Snickers bar. In response to Elise's hesitant inquiries over the years, Ivy has always insisted that Paps never laid a hand on her. But Elise has her doubts.

Such thoughts make it difficult to concentrate on the paper. Elise puts it down and turns her attention to the French toast and the breakfast room. Thankfully, the antiques here are tasteful and restrained, the dining room shelves lined with crystal wineglasses, not crowded with potpourri sacks and mildewing teddy bears, like the old plantation homes-turned-inns in Mississippi. That's another thing that Elise likes about the North: the interiors don't suffocate.

The crotchety couple across from Elise is rising now, arguing about their morning schedule. The man wants a walk; the woman is pushing for the private zoo in town. Elise shudders: she saw a billboard for the zoo on the drive through town yesterday. The sign featured a photograph of cougars that looked like alcoholics and tired, gray flamingos. Elise revels in the only debate about her day being an inner one: Hike in the state park or read in the sun?

There are always men who approach her on these "field trips," as she calls her excursions. That is another forbidden pleasure to them. Older men, younger men, usually unsure of themselves, clearing their throats as they walk over, their hands anxiously balling and unballing a napkin. She consistently sends them away after a beguiling chat, relishing their starved glances from across the room. It is unclear why her recklessness always stops here, why she never kisses anyone or accepts a drink. Perhaps Chris, after all, is accepting such invitations across the world, even as she is turning them down. The thought rather thrills her. But following through with it seems boring somehow to Elise; she is after something slightly wilder, a fling being too predictable. Sex does not seem dangerous. Being alone does, so that's what she chooses.

She will go on a hike with a book in her backpack, she decides, scraping her chair from the table. She grabs an apple from the fruit bowl and returns to her room feeling giddy, the way she imagines the bad kids at Vidalia High—her mother called them the "dead-end crowd," until Ivy was one of them—must have felt playing hooky.

⁂

Chris's presentation the following day does not go well. Not my fault, he insists to himself, but he still feels guilty. He often rates himself—

after presentations, board meetings, sex—and this time he got a four out of ten. The Indian clients wouldn't let him finish. They began barging in with questions halfway through and then argued among themselves. He stood at the front of the room feeling like a helpless substitute teacher, trying to bring them back to the subject at hand: how his company's product could dramatically reduce pollutants during crude-oil extraction. Nobody was listening. When the hour and a half was up, they were still arguing, and he slipped out with his briefcase and the slides.

Now he is trying to psych himself up for dinner with his Indian joint-venture partner, although he has a strong urge to order room service and watch ESPN. You've got this, no problem, he tells the mirror as he shaves. But does he? The doorbell rings. A lovely hotel worker—gleaming black hair, turquoise and gold sari—stands there with a bouquet of orchids. From Eastern Energy Incorporated, she says, inclining her head. Chris smiles and accepts the flowers, enjoying her appreciative gaze at his physique, his American friendliness. He'd hoped the bouquet was from Elise. But she isn't really the flower-sending type. He glances at the clock. He is late.

Dinner actually helps. The wine, and then the gin and tonics, and the smooth, even tones of the tan-hued bar soothe Chris the way luxury is meant to soothe. He lets himself be flattered by the CEO, he flatters back, the game as familiar, by now, as flirting. He is reminded of how much better he is one-on-one than with groups. Eight out of ten, he tells himself, brushing his teeth. Maybe even an 8.5.

The next day, Chris wakes up early, thanks to jet lag. The clock blinks five a.m. He flips through the channels to kill time before the breakfast buffet in the hotel restaurant opens at seven. After breakfast, with five hours to go until his meeting, he decides to walk around Bombay a bit. He is soon sweating, so he meanders to the dusty shade of a park and watches the morning slide by. One of the best things about his travel schedule is the constant momentum. Like his first basketball season as a freshman, Chris finds, work demands leave him exhausted. But such a ruthless schedule keeps him on his toes, and he relishes the challenge. Right now, for instance, as he sits here, watching India, his mind is also on the factory tour he will take at three, and which questions he should ask. Sure, you could call him distracted, but that's how he works best: multitasking. Chris spends the next ten minutes brainstorming questions he might be asked on Logan's profit margins. But it's impossible to concentrate in the heat. He gives up, feeling suddenly jet-lagged, listless, and a little lonely.

His mind wanders to the States: to Elise, Leah, his parents. What is his father doing now? This is one of Chris's favorite mental games to play, and it always cheers him up. Eight a.m. in India: six p.m. in Chariton. Mom and Dad must be sitting down to dinner, Chris thinks, the same kind of thing they always eat this time of year, sloppy joes on white buns, corn on the cob, and Jell-O salad. His sister might drive over and join them. Then prime-time news and bed. While I, Chris thinks, am securing the future of business in India for my firm. Exploring Bombay, one of the world's largest cities. Representing my country overseas. Chris loves playing this game of comparative realities because he always wins.

Chris's pride at the miles he's put between himself and his hometown is an ease Elise does not share; something he has often tried to impress upon her, with no luck: there's no need to feel guilty for getting out when they did. They both escaped their small towns, both dodged the pointed finger of their respective fates: Chris, as the eldest, the only son, narrowly eluded farming; and Elise, just as mercifully, skirted becoming a preacher's wife, handing out lemonade at prayer meetings, or God knows what she would have done down there. But whereas Elise frets about having "abandoned" her family, Chris sees their absences in the family pews of First Baptist and Pilgrim Lutheran, respectively, as cause for celebration. We're American, Chris tells Elise, we do whatever the hell we want, and we do it better than the last generation.

What Chris does not tell Elise, what he himself could not put into words, is that every day he shows up to work at Logan he is nonetheless obeying his father's commands, a stern inner voice with a slightly nasal midwestern accent: Work your tail off. Don't take a thing for granted. Forget the easy way out. Don't blame others for your mistakes. Even though his current white-collar tasks are a far cry from his teenage chores (hoisting hay bales into trailers, cleaning cow stalls), Chris is following in his father's footsteps, and he knows that he has made Frank Kriegstein proud. (It is only thirty years later, when the farm is finally sold, and his father's voice, over the phone, is heavy with grief, that Chris will come to understand Elise's dull guilt, and the once stern, authoritative voice in his head will grow petulant, accusing, cracked with sorrow.)

"Do you mind?" A middle-aged Indian gentleman with glasses and a newspaper indicates the space next to Chris. Chris does, but there's no way to politely refuse, so he simply nods. He considers standing up and continuing his walk, but his new sense of satisfaction feels somehow tied to the bench, and he is loath to leave it.

The man unfolds the paper. He reads as though he is listening to a friend relate a story of deep misfortune, shaking his head ruefully, clicking his tongue, sighing deeply. This man, Chris thinks, is probably a member of India's rising middle class. His clothes suggest he has a good job; the English paper he's reading is proof of his cosmopolitanism. If I can speak with him, Chris thinks, growing excited, I can get some man-on-the-street insights into the joint venture, see it from a different angle, come up with a good question for the factory tour. But how to initiate such an exchange? Chris is skilled when the script is predetermined, the roles clear, less so with improvised conversations with strangers. That's Elise's terrain: after church, at the playground, on the airplane.

Chris clears his throat. "So," he begins after a pause. The man is still reading. "I'm new here. Any suggestions on what I should see in town?"

"Wouldn't know." The man folds his paper crisply and turns to Chris. "I'm not from here either. I'm on a business trip from Singapore. Bloody Bombay," he grumbles, looking around the park. "It gets filthier every time I visit."

"What's your line of work?"

"Biotechnology," the man says. "We just discovered how to extract an enzyme from papaya."

Chris stifles a yawn. Ever the diplomat, however, he masks his boredom with flattery: "That sounds important."

The man shrugs. "It pays well. But I'm counting down the days until my plane lands in Changi. Have you spent time in Singapore?"

Chris nods, about to reply, but the man is no longer interested. "Singapore's the only country in Asia that's really got it together. China's booming, but it will explode in everyone's faces. Japan is like an old retiree who still shows up to work in a tie. And India..." He shakes his head as a beggar approaches them. "Too bloody populated."

"I'm from America," Chris offers, though the man hasn't asked.

"America is a continent, my friend," the man observes snippily. "Do you mean the United States?"

"Exactly," Chris says, and falls silent.

"I admire Reagan very much," the man says. "It was the media's fault that the business with Nicaragua got out of control. In Singapore this would never happen. What Lee Kuan Yew sees fit to do, we trust as the right outcome. None of this obsession with hush-hush security."

Chris doubts everyone in Singapore feels this way but is cowed by the man's aggressive confidence.

"It's your Christian guilt. That's the problem. We Indians have Hinduism. Much more forgiving. Much more modern."

"I thought you said you weren't Indian."

The man glares at Chris. "Well, do I look Malay to you? Of course I'm Indian. Just not Indian Indian."

The man opens his paper again. Chris rises, irritated that he has gained no more insight about the Indian middle class than when he began. "Well, have a good day," he tells the man.

"Are you on business here?" the man asks him, oddly invested now that Chris is departing.

"Yes."

"One piece of advice. Don't be the American nice guy. It always fails. I've seen it a million times. They'll eat you alive."

Chris has an urge to respond with something equally cutting and condescending, but all he can think of is "Shut up," so he simply nods and says, "I'll keep that in mind," in a tone that he hopes is sarcastic.

"Very good, very good," the man says absently, and returns to the paper, dismissing Chris before Chris has a chance to leave first.

But at the factory, Chris takes the man's advice. He is cruelly scrutinizing of sloppy mistakes he observes, complains about the behavior of the Indian colleagues yesterday, and leaves halfway through dinner, simply saying he is tired. His new sharp, uncompromising self is thrilling. Emboldened, Chris dials home, only to get the answering machine. Again. "Hey there. Give me a call," Chris says, and hangs up, not even saying, "I love you," as he always does on overseas trips. The man on the bench was an asshole, Chris thinks, but he might have been on to something. Chris has been too nice, too lenient, too accepting. That was always his problem in basketball, too: passing too much. "Get a little more selfish, Chris," his high school coach would say. "Why the hell did you give up the ball?" his college coach would yell, and bench him. Raised on a strict diet of Lutheran modesty, Chris had always piously assumed this behavior would reward him in the end. But that was bullshit. That night he dreams of robbing banks and kicking things until they crumple.

∎

Annoyingly, Big Pocono State Park, which Elise has driven an hour to reach, is crowded and noisy. It is Saturday, after all. Kids everywhere. Elise feels a tug of missing for Leah, which surprises and pleases her, and she impulsively calls home from a pay phone near the parking lot. Becky puts Leah on, but the second Elise hears "Mama?" she has an urge to hang up. She tries to keep her voice kind and interested when Becky gets back on the phone and describes their day at the playground. "I'm out of coins, Becky—better run," Elise lies, and hangs up after one minute.

Elise had only planned to do the loop trail, but the phone call has rattled her, and so she follows a sign to a higher summit, a farther two miles up. There are fewer people here. Elise moves quickly, trying to leave thoughts behind. She is glad she has brought along a large bottle of water by the time she reaches the top. She is alone, and she stretches out over the rocks. With the sun's warmth and all the exercise, she begins drowsing, flitting in and out of dreams. In the first one, she is back in Hamburg, trying to return a dress in a department store, trying to remember the German word for "receipt," then in Vidalia, in Charles Ebert's study, the lights off, struggling to concentrate on the patterns of light from the shutters, her nails digging into her palms, breath close to her face, sniffing near her right thigh. She scrambles, terrified, into a sitting position, stifling a scream. But it is just a dog.

Elise laughs shakily. "Hey there," she says. It looks like a mutt but has a Lab's friendly-dumb disposition. He pants at her, smiling. He has a collar that Elise examines. "Robo Cop." That is unquestionably the worst name she's ever heard for a dog. As though he agrees, the dog lies down mournfully next to her and closes his eyes.

"Robo?" Elise hears through the woods. "Robo!"

The dog doesn't stir. They are on an enclave jutting out from the mountain. *He's here!* Elise knows she should call out, but she doesn't. Robo Cop's owners don't try very hard to find him. There came a few more halfhearted "Robos" and then there is just the sound of sparrows chattering, Robo's panting, and the faint whine of cars from the road far below. This is not good thinking on her part, Elise knows. Lately, she's been shedding responsibilities, connections, as though they are clothes and she is bent on skinny-dipping. She couldn't even talk to her own child on the phone an hour ago. So why not reunite Ro (she can't bring herself to call him Robo) with his owners? Why end up disappointing and abandoning another creature?

He is beautiful. Marmalade tiger stripes over dark brown fur that glints gold when the sun hits it. He looks to be around three or four. Back in Vidalia, Elise loved the two Dalmatians her neighbors owned. She's always wanted a dog with Chris, but they've moved around too much. Honestly, Elise wanted a dog more than a baby. She kept this to herself. Maybe she shouldn't have. One of Elise's favorite lines from the Bible is at the beginning of the Christmas story: "Mary kept all these things, and pondered them in her heart." It doesn't read, "Mary called Joseph and asked what he thought of Immaculate Conception." Elise loves the hallowed privacy of that verse, but it does have its pitfalls.

"You thirsty?" Ro looks up at her expectantly. She pours what is left of the bottle near his mouth, and he laps and catches about one-third of it.

"Okay, buddy," Elise says. "Let's head back down." Ro rises enthusiastically, turning in circles a few times joyfully before continuing on the trail ahead of her. On the way down, he darts in and out of the woods but always comes trotting back. At the foot of the trail, near the parking lot, his owners are waiting.

"Robo," an overweight woman in her fifties cries. The dog trots over to her, tail wagging. So much for thinking he needs a new family, thinks Elise, feeling strangely betrayed by the dog's goodwill.

"We thought we lost him for sure," the man says. "Robo. What were you thinking?" He takes out a leash and snaps it on the dog, who turns to Elise, as if in apology.

"Beautiful dog," says Elise, and then, struggling to keep her voice kind, "I'm so glad I found you guys. I didn't know what to do with him."

"Thank you," the woman says, but with a tone of suspicion.

The man is less perceptive. "Yeah, we owe you. Ever since our daughter left for college, Robo here is pretty much our baby."

"What kind of dog is he?"

"Mutt," the man says. "He just showed up at our house one day, two years ago, starving."

So I could have kept him, Elise thinks. Shit. She feels like a sucker. Ro whines. I've got to get out of here, Elise thinks, or I'll kidnap that dog.

"You guys have a good day," she says, heading to the car. On the drive back to the bed-and-breakfast, Elise considers her needs, what they might be. Is it a dog? Would a canine companion rein her in? Sometimes she fears that if someone, or something, doesn't curb her new inclinations soon, she'll head off the rails: wind up as a bartender in Vegas or one of those permanent backpackers she and Chris always made fun of in European airports: dreadlocks, wrinkled, sundrenched skin, empty eyes.

∖∘

Eight thousand miles apart from each other, en route to the Bombay airport, and walking through a small mountain town after lunch, Chris and Elise are deeply shaken by similar sights, though neither will ever think to mention it to the other: they each encounter a corpse. Chris sees a Hindu funeral: mourners, marigolds, the dead body being carried through the street. He glimpses the scene through his car window, shudders, and goes back to his yellow legal pad, where he is scrawling notes for an upcoming meeting with his boss, apprising him of the Bombay trip. On Main Street, after a chicken salad sandwich at a local café, walking down the street, Elise sees a woman lying on the sidewalk whose torso and lower body are covered in a sheet. There is a trickle of blood somewhere on her face. Later, Elise will not be able to recall where the blood was—at the corner of the mouth? On the forehead? Medics surround the woman, and beyond them, a scattered crowd of gawkers, half tourist, half local.

For some reason, Elise is certain that it is a suicide. The choice to kill herself radiates from the woman like the choice to marry coming from a bride. Elise does not cross the street to avoid the woman, but she does not look at the body as she passes the scene, either. No one in the horrified crowd is crying, only whispering. Elise walks back to her car in a trance. After seeing the dead woman, she thinks, I should want to go home, hold Leah tight, call Chris. But I don't.

She pulls off the road at a sign for a lake, and wanders to the shore. Clouds have gathered and it is chilly, too late for swimming. Again, she curses herself for giving Ro back. She settles into the sand. Her own mother's duties were clear. Across the lake, a dog barks. Elise does not know how to be a mother without putting on a straitjacket. A door slams. The darkness deepens. How to be so giving, every goddamn day. Mary kept all these things, and pondered them in her heart. Who am I to cut myself loose? What have I done to deserve that? Across the lake, light flickers on inside a house. Dinnertime.

Chris, sitting in 2A of a Northwest flight, removes a James Patterson novel from his briefcase and sips his gin and tonic. His tough-guy act has already faded; he felt it seeping away this morning, and by the time he got to the airport he was spent and nice again; he tipped the driver too much and didn't cut anyone in line at the ticket counter, didn't even protest when others cut him. He is lucky, he knows. There is no reason to demand anything from the world beyond that. It could scare the grace away. He pictures Elise and Leah, at the dinner table, Elise spooning mashed peas into Leah's mouth.

Elise lies on the beach until the stars come out and she is shivering.

Leah wails in her crib. Even after Becky comes in to sing her to sleep, Leah is inconsolable: her bear has fallen below the bed.

⚘

He gets home before she does. The house is silent. He calls out both their names as the taxi drives away, knowing by the empty garage that they're not there. But where are they? Why can't she ever leave a note? He feels insecure; he wanted to hug both of them, to swirl Leah around, to hear her giggle. He wanted Elise to milk out all the stories about India from him, so that he could understand his trip better, feel her quiet sympathy. But instead it will be Chinese takeout and college basketball games. It's the Sweet Sixteen, so it could be worse.

Elise eases in around ten. She looks caught. "You're here!" she says to Chris. "I thought you were getting in tomorrow."

"Where's Leah?" Chris asks.

"Babysitter's," Elise says offhandedly.

"But if you're here—"

"Shhh," Elise says. "You've had a long trip." And she brings him up to bed.

Her hunger makes him shy and despondent. She's met someone. He's sure. But his body reacts, almost against his will, and he finds himself drawn to this new, unfaithful Elise, even as he is gasping, she is gasping, and after he comes he doesn't feel angry, just small and in need of protection.

She, too. They curl together like the stuffed animals that Leah arranges in her bed each night.

"Did you have a good trip?" Elise finally asks.

"Yes." It's hard for Chris to keep his voice from sounding bitter.

"I did too," Elise says.

A pause, as Chris's mind races. "What do you mean, you did too?"

Elise's laugh is high, nervous, the way she used to laugh when she was speaking German. "I've been meaning to tell you. I've been going on trips as well, when you go away. I don't know why. Just for the hell of it."

"By yourself?"

"Yes. Not with Leah." She hesitates and then adds: "But not with anyone else, either."

Silence again, and then her voice, horribly kind: "Is that what you were worried about?"

He doesn't reply. He wishes the light were on. Isn't it easier for her to lie in the dark?

"I need it right now. I don't know why." She sounds almost angry.

"Why?" he asks, stupidly.

But she responds. "It has to do with being back here, in the States—"

"I thought you wanted to come back!"

"I do! These trips, short travels—it's a good thing. I think it's a good thing."

"What about Leah?"

"She stays with Becky."

"Great," Chris says, his voice flat, furious.

They lie in the dark, each pricked by the stony silence of the other, throats tight with resentment and a creeping fear. Chris has the feeling he used to get in games his sophomore year at UGA, their worst season. Inevitably, a moment would arrive in the third or fourth quarter when it was clear their team was going to lose, that they would never make up the ten-point difference. Watching the clock wind down, the shots fall short.

"I don't know, lately I just feel like traveling. Exploring. Like you," Elise says, "with your business trips."

"Like me? What do you think I do when I travel? Hang out? Go to the beach? I'm working my ass off, Elise. For us. I don't know what the hell you're doing, but it's definitely not for us, and it's certainly not for Leah."

Too far. Elise turns her back to him, draws the covers over her like chain mail.

"Elise—"

"Look, you obviously don't understand. So there's no point staying up talking about it. I'm tired. Good night."

She's right. He doesn't get it. He feels very, very tired and helpless, like when his calf died right before the county fair. His mother told him about it in the morning. Lucky was gone before Chris could see him one last time. That was the worst thing about it.

"Hold me?" he asks. He hates the strangled tone in his voice, hates himself for asking anything of her now. Wimp, he hears in his head: from his father, from his coach, from that Singaporean Indian jerk on the park bench in Bombay.

But the request softens Elise. She turns to him and spoons his back, her small breasts pressed flat against his skin, both of their bodies still moist.

"Good night," she says again after a while, more gently.

"Good night."

He can't sleep, of course. Typical jet lag—you enter the point of pure weariness and stay there, as if it were a cruising altitude. His thoughts are in several time zones, feverish. He keeps seeing the Indian hotel attendant with the flowers, bringing him good news. He pictures Elise on her "trips" with a shadowy stranger, and he tosses in bed, trying to erase the stranger from his thoughts, wanting to trust Elise, telling himself that he is lucky to be married to someone so independent. But by the time he falls asleep, at six a.m., as the neighbors' sprinklers go on and dogs are being taken out for early walks, luck seems like its reverse, and he desperately wants something dire to happen, to bring them back together.

❧

Two weeks later, sitting down at breakfast, Elise tries to coax Leah to eat her Cheerios. Chris has chosen to take off the morning from work. Wearing a UGA Bulldogs T-shirt and boxers, he luxuriates in this domestic scene. Finally Leah has swallowed enough cereal to satisfy Elise, and she is permitted to go watch *Sesame Street* in the living room. Elise and Chris turn to each other with strange, secretive expressions.

"What?" Elise asks.

"What?" says Chris.

"You go first," Elise says.

"No, you."

"I'm pregnant again," Elise says after a long pause, looking out the window. "Let's hope your news is better."

Chris decides to ignore this last sentiment and lifts her up off her feet, swings her around, inadvertently banging her ankle on the kitchen counter. "That's incredible," he says. "I'm so happy to hear it." He looks at her, concerned. "How about you?"

"Sure," she says, rubbing her ankle. "I just need some time to get used to it." Something in her drains away as she says this. Earlier that morning, making coffee, she had contemplated a new kind of field trip: to the gynecologist's office, to get an abortion, without telling Chris. He would never agree to it, she knows. She forces a smile and allows herself to admit that she is, somewhere, excited about a second child.

"What's your news?" she asks.

"England." Chris says. "I've been promoted. They want me in London as soon as Jason Raleigh retires."

Morning, Broken

Singapore, October 1996

Elise Kriegstein: 42, mother
Chris Kriegstein: 42, father
Leah Kriegstein: 15, elder daughter
Sophie Kriegstein: 13, younger daughter
James Alderman: 45, therapist

Setting: Therapist's office in downtown Singapore. Neutral hues. A few framed watercolors on the wall depict local scenes with a distinctly colonial vibe, including a traditional "black and white" villa (the former residences of British civil servants), the Raffles hotel, and one amateurish botanical print of a Vanda Miss Joaquim orchid. Chris and Elise are seated on opposite ends of a camel-colored couch. Elise is scribbling something in a notebook; Chris is shuffling through papers, reviewing notes for an upcoming meeting. Leah is sitting on an overstuffed chocolate leather chair to their left, with a blanket over her goose-bumped knees (like most interior spaces in Singapore, the air-conditioning is going full blast). Sophie is perched on an office chair with wheels. The therapist is nowhere to be seen.

Sophie swivels around in the office chair, going faster and faster.

There is something slightly wild and desperate about her movements, like those of a much younger child misbehaving to gain adult attention. But none of the other Kriegsteins react. Leah, in stark contrast to Sophie, is sitting incredibly still, holding herself tightly, so tightly she is unconsciously pinching her upper arms with her fingernails. The family's silence is interrupted by the hurried entry of a slightly portly British therapist in a light blue shirt and a mint green sweater vest, who looks badly sunburned.

Therapist: Thank you all for waiting. Apologies on my part for the interruption—a client was confused. Thought it was Wednesday.

(Opens his notebook, composes himself.)

Well, let's not waste any more time, shall we?

(Pause in which none of the Kriesgsteins speak. Therapist glances around, trying to gauge the mood.)

Let's continue where we left off before the doorbell rang. Elise, you had just brought up the subject of your pregnancy with Sophie and the family's move to England three years later. I would like to hear a bit more now from Leah about that time. Leah. What would you call your... most salient memories of England? You would have been five at that time, correct?
Leah (guarded): Yes, that's right. You mean, what can I remember?
Therapist: Precisely.
Leah (considers the question for a beat): Not much. The raspberry

bush out back. The plum tree. Lavender everywhere, leaning over sidewalks. Liverwurst. Ribena. Picnics with taramasolata. Pizza Express.

Elise: And what about your friends? Edith Norrell? Nigel Slater?

Leah: Nigel Slater? Mom, that's the famous cook. I obviously wasn't friends with him.

Elise: Nigel Saunders. That's who I meant.

Leah: No, I don't remember them. I remember trees in bloom in the park, and learning to read.

Therapist: Learning to read?

Leah: I kept mispronouncing "island" as "iz-land." And fish and chips. And... the feeling.

Therapist: Of?

Leah: Of living in England.

Therapist: And what are your memories of Sophie from that time? How do you think she liked it there?

Sophie (jumping in): *I can't remember England at all.*

The therapist does not react to Sophie's response but continues waiting on Leah, intent on her answer. Oddly, his manner is not that of a therapist ignoring a client who has spoken out of turn (as Sophie just has), but rather that of someone who has not heard the client at all. It becomes apparent that Sophie's presence is invisible to everyone else in the room, and her voice is equally undetectable.

Leah: My memories of Sophie? (Blanches.) I don't know how she liked it there.

Sophie: *I was just a baby, really.*

Leah (voice overlapping): She was just a baby, really.

At the coincidence of their having said the same thing at the same time, Sophie looks at Leah in joyful astonishment and laughs out loud.

Sophie (shouting): *Jinx! Personal jinx! One, two, three, four, five!*

At Leah's continued silence, Sophie rises from her chair, suddenly looking much older, graver, and goes to her sister, puts her arms around her neck, leaning her cheek against Leah's. It is a consoling, sisterly gesture, yet one that Sophie never would have performed when she was alive: it is the gesture from one adult sister to another. At Sophie's touch, tears begin flowing silently from Leah's eyes.

Therapist: What is it?

Leah shrugs a grumpy teenager shrug, furious that her emotions are on such gaudy display for her parents and the therapist. Her voice, when she speaks, is heavy with sarcasm.

Leah: "What is it?" What do you think? Why do you think we're sitting here? Because we miss London or Philadelphia or Atlanta? No. We're here because Sophie's dead. Or, to be more precise, that's why they're here (gesturing at Chris and Elise). I'm here because they made me come.

Sophie, sensing that her touch is overwhelming Leah, withdraws slowly and goes back to her chair. Leah shivers at Sophie's departure and draws the blanket around her shoulders, calming herself. She looks out the window. Her face goes numb, distant.

Therapist (turns to Elise): What do you remember of the girls in England?

Elise (eager to speak, to smooth over the awkward silence): That's where Sophie refused to wear anything but dresses. Every day. She would throw a fit if we tried to put her in overalls. And then, two years later, as soon as we moved to Atlanta, she was a tomboy who would have thrown every last dress in the trash if I'd let her. Those beautiful Laura Ashley patterns...

Sophie (looking at Elise): *I can't remember...*

Elise: That's where they both learned to ride a bike. Sophie nailed it in two seconds. And Leah, you took a lot longer, but you never gave up. You just picked yourself up again, and—

Leah (still looking out the window, her voice cold): I get it. I lacked coordination. I wasn't "a natural."

Elise: It was a compliment about being persistent, for God's sake!

Chris (nearly growling, but with a note of pleading): Leah, come on.

Therapist: Chris, what do you remember of England?

Chris: The rain. My boss—he was a real asshole. Jordan Bark.

Sophie (looking around with a wide grin): *Whoa! I can't believe he said the A word!*

Elise: Chris—please.

Leah: Mom, after everything we've been through in the last six months, I think I can handle a little swearing. In fact, I think it's a good idea. (Turns to therapist.) How do I remember England? How do I remember Sophie there? I remember it, and all of us, as pre-fucked. As opposed to now. As opposed to all of us now being profoundly fucked.

Elise and Chris (in one, horrified voice): Leah!

Meanwhile, Sophie is laughing her head off at Leah's display of rebellion—for any thirteen-year-old, even a dead one, hearing someone swear, particularly her straitlaced older sister, is hilarious.

Therapist (obviously made nervous by Leah's dangerous mood): Elise, you haven't mentioned which memories from London stand out to you in particular, aside from what you remember of Sophie and Leah there—

Elise (glares once more at Leah before speaking): Where do I start? England always felt right, even when it was raining, even when the woman at Harrods snubbed me because of my American accent. I was worried that I wouldn't like London as much the second time, but instead it was even better. I was working part-time at a health food store. I was ecstatic. People assumed it was because I was American, the cheerfulness. They should have seen me on my worst days in Philadelphia.

Chris (mutters): Or here.

Therapist: Chris, please. Let her continue.

Elise (folds her arms tightly across her chest, petulant): Now I've lost my train of thought... Right, the co-op. Rainbow Foods. I was the only one who regularly showered. I don't even think the other workers there liked me that much. But I was so happy I didn't notice.

Therapist: What do you think the root of this happiness was?

Elise: Being back in England.

Therapist: But didn't you miss the United States?

Elise: Philadelphia? Those stuck-up, preppy moms looking down on you for not having the right kind of pram? See? I even say "pram," like the British. What's the American word for it?

Therapist shrugs.

Chris: Baby carriage.

Elise: What a horrible word. Sounds like a baby dragging a carriage behind it. Why was I so happy? I was out again! Free! Free from gossip at the playground, free from the Mississippi guilt trip. Free from trying to save everybody.

Therapist: But last session, when we were discussing your time in Philadelphia, you had already begun this journey—

Elise: Then I got pregnant. I got pregnant, Mama came to visit for a week, and then I woke up and I was the old me all over again: addicted to prayer group, checking up on Ivy and Mama with long phone calls every other day, staying at home building Play-Doh castles with Leah.

Chris: I was relieved.

Leah: Me too.

Elise: You were two years old, what did you know?

Leah (quietly): I remember.

Sophie: *That's when you had me!*

Elise (sadly, overlapping): That's when I had Sophie. I wish—

Therapist: Be careful.

Elise: I wish I hadn't. I wish I hadn't had all that pain.

Leah: Nice, Mom.

Sophie (to Elise): *I don't mind.*

Leah (to therapist): She just said she wished Sophie had never been born.

Sophie (to Leah): *No, that's not what she said.* (To Elise.) *Don't worry, Mom, I understand.*

Elise (overlapping with Sophie, to Leah): That's not what I said. You don't understand.

Therapist (now piqued and defensive, with an air of a kinder-garten teacher speaking to a misbehaving class): Look, I feel we've gone quite off topic. I'd like to remind each of you that I'm leading this discussion, that you came to me, after all, for assistance. Any revelations, insights, moments of forgiveness, etcetera, will be bro-kered by me; otherwise, they don't count, is that clear?

The Kriegsteins (Surprised at his violent outburst, the three fam-ily members nod sheepishly and respond in a jumble of voices, Elise and Leah avoiding eye contact.) Yes. Okay. I guess so. All right. Clear.

Therapist (clears his throat): Good. Where were we before all of that? Ah yes. Elise, you say you were profoundly happy in En-gland. So, Chris, while Elise was skipping around the co-op aisles, replacing sacks of millet and giving out free barbecued tofu sam-ples, how were you feeling?

Chris: Fine. It was fine. I like England. Nice pubs, great history.

Therapist: Oh, come on, Chris. You can do better than that.

Chris: What do you want me to say?

Therapist: Were you satisfied?

Chris: I was hungry. And sometimes that's a good way to be. I saw how I needed to bust my ass to get higher up the food chain. And that's what I did. I was successful. That satisfied me.

Therapist: I'm not convinced.

Chris: Well, I'm not convinced this session is worth four hundred Sing dollars an hour.

Therapist: Interesting that you bring up money at this moment. Do you often estimate how much something is worth? How much is it worth that you're discussing Sophie again, for example?

Chris: That's low. Is that what they teach you in grad school? Low blows?

Therapist: What would you say to Sophie now, if she were in the room?

Sophie looks pleased at this.

Chris: What?
Therapist: Why don't you let her know how you feel, Chris?
Sophie (to therapist): *Oh, shut up.* (To her father.) *It's good to see you, too, Dad. I miss you.*

Chris, to everyone's surprise, including his own, begins weeping, cannot speak. Elise puts a hand on his arm. Leah looks away. As with Leah earlier, Sophie now moves to the couch, snuggles in between her parents (there is ample room between them to do so), and puts her head on Chris's shoulder.

Leah (softly, nearly to herself): Does that mean you loved her more? The way you're crying now? Would you have cried like that if I had been the one that—
Therapist: Leah. I believe you know the answer to that. After all of our work together over the last two months.
Leah: Still, I—
Therapist: Let it go. Let's return to England. Leah. You were very small. But later, when you thought of London, did you and Sophie have any sense of . . . how should I put it? Home?
Leah: It's hard to remember . . .
Sophie (overlapping): *It's hard to remember . . .*
Therapist: Yes, I know, you were young—
Leah: . . . being five.
Sophie (overlapping): . . . *being alive.*

Therapist: Take your time.

Sophie: *I liked going back to London. We went back there some summers, after we'd moved away, and we took those funny taxis.*

Leah (to Elise): Remember the red line museum?

Sophie: *Yeah!*

Chris and Elise (confused): The what?

Leah: The museum, with a red line through it, that would lead you through different exhibits.

Sophie (exuberant): *I remember!*

Elise: The natural history museum. It was their favorite. Yes, it did have a red line to follow that you girls loved.

Sophie: *The stuffed boar. The big dinosaur skeleton, right when you walked in.*

Therapist: Splendid. Now. Who of you wants to go back?

Leah: You mean, hypothetically?

Therapist: I don't think that's important to clarify at this point.

Elise: Go back, as in, to that time? Or go back, as in, go visit?

Chris: I have a business trip there next week, actually.

Sophie: *No.*

Leah: Yes.

Sophie: *I don't want to go back.*

Leah: I do.

Elise: In which sense?

Leah: In every sense. I want to go back and be British.

Therapist: What about you, Elise?

Elise: No, thank you. For years, yes. For years I did. But now? (Shrugs.) I think leaving Singapore would feel like leaving Sophie behind, losing her even more. (Turns to Leah.) What do you mean, you want to become British?

Therapist (irritated): That was *my* next question, actually.

Leah: Oh, I don't know. You know. The way I want to be Chinese, and German, and—

Elise: Why?

Sophie: (overlapping) *Why?*

Leah: To fit in.

Sophie: *Look, you were already kind of weird in Atlanta. I hate to break it to you—*

Leah: I never knew how Sophie did it.

Sophie: *How I did what?*

Leah: The normalcy. The steadiness.

Sophie: *I'm normal.*

Elise (overlapping): She was…more normal. But that—

Therapist (exploding): Again, wildly off track. We are, so to speak, off the highway, off the county road, off the dirt path, plunging willy-nilly through woods, running over rabbits and small pines, our Navi on the blink, hoping we will wind up where we need to be. No. No. Not in my office, not on my clock.

Chris: Which is ten minutes fast, I noticed.

Therapist (ignores him): Now, Leah. If you really want to go back to London, I'm going to have to hear a believable accent.

Leah: Seriously?

No response.

Leah: Okay. Well, how about this (in passable British accent): I can't seem to find my Wellies anywhere!

Sophie (eager, competitive, the shrill voice of a younger sister desperate to win): *How about this? Digestives! Smarties! Bobs!*

(Sophie's British accent is terrible; she is merely listing British things in an American accent.)

> **Therapist**: Mediocre. Okay. Can I make a request? Let's all take a deep breath together. Ready? Good. One, two, three— (Everyone inhales deeply.) That's right. And out: three, two, one... (Everyone exhales deeply.)
>
> **Sophie** (stands on the couch, shouts at the therapist, panicked): *I'm running out of time!*
>
> **Therapist** (glances at his watch): We just have a few minutes left. But before we close, Leah, let's return to the garden in London, since it seems like it's such a strong memory for you.

Sophie reluctantly sits back down.

> **Elise** (sighs): English gardens are the loveliest.
>
> **Leah** (exhausted): I don't know what else to say. It was messy, and beautiful in its disorder. That's what English gardens are like, right, Mom?

Elise nods.

> **Leah**: But I don't remember the names of the flowers...
>
> **Therapist**: And that feeling you mentioned, that "living in England" feeling.
>
> **Leah**: The best way I can explain it is that it comes when I hear that Cat Stevens song, "Morning Has Broken."
>
> **Elise** (smiles): That's what you sang every morning at preschool.
>
> **Therapist**: And what is the feeling that comes with the song, exactly?
>
> **Leah**: Belonging. No, that's wrong. Peace? Also wrong.

Sophie begins humming the song.

Leah: Something like what I used to feel sitting with Sophie in the backseat of the Volvo—that's the car we had in England—giggling at the passengers facing us in the cars behind us. A feeling like that, but I'm alone. But not sad.

Therapist: You know, it was originally a hymn. Cat Stevens didn't write it.

Leah: Okay.

Therapist: You loved singing that hymn.

Leah: What are you getting at?

Therapist: I don't know... (Suddenly cheered.) But I think you are all doing well.

Chris: That's the first thing he's said that makes any sense.

Elise: Should I write that down? Can you please repeat that? I just need to find my pen... (Shuffles through her purse.)

Sophie: *He's not incorrect, exactly...*

Leah (in a perfect British accent): England is the only place abroad where I spoke like everyone around me.

Therapist: Leah, we have to wrap this up.

Leah (stubbornly): I went to a British preschool, I wore Wellies...

Sophie suddenly vanishes. At her departure, the other family members and even the therapist suddenly slump; the brief optimism from a second ago seems to have departed with Sophie.

Therapist (struggling to keep his voice buoyant): Wonderful to see you again, Elise, and you, too, Chris. Leah, I'll see you next week, Tuesday at eleven.

Silence.

Elise: I felt so close to her, just a second ago—
Chris: I know.
Leah: And whenever we went back to London we would eat hot buttered toast for hours.

Chris and Elise gather their things.

Elise (turns to Leah): Ready?
Leah: I think I'll just walk home. You guys go ahead.

Elise nods, trying to hide the hurt. Chris wraps an arm around her and the two exit.

Therapist (takes his notebook and stands, goes to the door): Take your time, Leah.

He turns off the lamp on his way out. The room falls into shadow. The door closes with a soft click. Leah sits in the darkened room for a second, eyes closed as though trying to summon a word or a specific memory. She can't. It's gone. Outside, it begins to rain, gathering the strength of the tropical thunderstorms that characterize late afternoons in Singapore.

The Good Years

Atlanta, Georgia, 1987–1992

What is there to say about the Kriegsteins' good years in Atlanta, aside from their goodness? Had Chris and Elise earned the breather, the blossoming spring, the soft-pillowed sofa, after their respective adolescent struggles in Indiana and Mississippi, all those hours spent yearning for broader, more flattering horizons? After the bumps in Hamburg, the roaring pain of childbirth, the wandering through the wilderness of early marriage, of turning from each other in dismay? Had so many homes in so many years— London for two, Hamburg for one and a half, Philadelphia for four, London again for one—forged a bond such that now, back in Georgia, where Chris and Elise had first met, they were able to stand unquavering and go about building a quietly faithful middle-class existence? With Palm Sundays at First Presbyterian (a compromise between Elise's post-London liberal theology and Chris's homegrown Lutheran habits) and brunch at Houlihan's, the restaurant across the street from the church, complete with crayons and kids' menus and Bloody Marys?

❧

Elise had hit her stride, working as a science teacher in a public middle school, away from the expat wives, back with southern women, some of whom were tough single moms. These were females she admired and feared, with their set jaws and their tight schedules and their brittle smiles; when they came in for parent conferences, she wanted to ask them what had happened, how they had survived, but instead she stuck to the script and solemnly presented the naked woman Evan had drawn on his photosynthesis worksheet or repeated the cruel rumor Jean had spread about the new girl from Vietnam.

⁂

Did it help that Chris had quit his job? That he was casting around for what to do, shooting baskets in the driveway while the girls and Elise were in school, calling up old college friends and attending UGA alumni events, hoping to make connections? Did it help that he "cooked dinner" sometimes, Chris's euphemism for ordering pizza, encouraged Elise to have a girls' night out with her fellow female teachers? Did it help that their bank account had shrunk, that they now drank frozen orange juice from cans and that the girls, who had worn Laura Ashley in London, now wore Kmart? If not for the collapse of the Soviet Union, Chris might have fallen into a significant depression. But perestroika had perked his ears, he had a few ex-colleagues who were talking about expanding energy markets, and Chris spent days at the kitchen table sketching elaborate plans for joint ventures across Siberia.

Elise was proud of him for quitting and for sleeping in until eleven. She'd known Chris only as ambitious and eager to please, and his refusal, one foggy November morning in London, to put up with his boss's insults anymore had been touching, like watching Sophie speak her first words. It was Elise who had hatched the plan to return to Atlanta, found herself a teaching job through her old college roommate, and spotted the white brick house as they were driving through Little Five Points. They still had a little bit saved, and Chris's parents, relieved their son was back in the States, offered to help with the down payment. Elise relaxed back into her southern accent, visited her mother and Ivy once a month in Mississippi, dropped in on her brothers now and then in Little Rock, where the two had opened a hardware business together, and could hardly remember being anywhere or anyone else.

⁂

For five years, the four of them were inarguably American. The girls lost their British accents over a two-week trip to visit their grandparents on the Kriegstein farm, where they ate sugar snap peas from the vine and jumped in hay. What is there to say about a state of normalcy, other than its wondrous comforts? After they moved to China, the Kriegsteins would privately meditate on each of these unnoticed luxuries in Atlanta, like the opposite of a Buddhist exercise, pinpointing and sharpening their desires for back then, back there.

Over their five years in Atlanta, the following pleasures were freely available and routinely taken for granted: Fat bagels with slick white cream cheese. Car trips up to Athens, for basketball games at UGA. Braves baseball games. Front lawns. Laughter. Chilled white wine on plastic chairs in the driveway with the neighbors. Driving alone. English. Anonymity. Sunday school. The neighborhood gang. Four square. The dogwood tree in the front yard, on the strip of grass between the sidewalk and the street, just right for climbing. The shady, overgrown, ramshackle alleyway. Hiding places. The honeysuckle vine, bending over the driveway, fragrant, offering a faint, near-imaginary nectar when you sucked on the blossom's stem. Unpolluted air. Chocolate chip cookie dough milk shakes. Family members in the same time zone. Large libraries, full of English books. Buttercups in the backyard. Citizenship. Country stations. Oldies stations. The greatest hits of the seventies, eighties, and today.

⁂

Over the five years in Atlanta, the girls grew, became people. Elise stared at them each morning, astonished. At Leah's furrowed brow over a book, at Sophie's white-blond curls, clipped back with red barrettes. The screaming fury that had characterized Leah's first eight months in Hamburg had subsided into a quiet watchfulness that occasionally broke out into a private fit of giggles with Sophie. At seven, then eight, then nine, then ten, Leah was every inch the older daughter, tall like Chris, conscientious, hesitant to join games or other children until she felt secure. The girls' respective complexions spoke to their personalities. Leah had delicate, pale skin, and straw hair. She burned easily, with freckles that spread over her face at the first hint of sun in early spring. Sophie had olive skin, dark eyebrows. When they went to Florida, to the beach house that Ada rented each summer, Sophie wriggled out of her mother's sunscreening grasp and turned a gingerbread gold. Leah, pouting her disapproval, was made to wear a T-shirt over her bathing suit and still got feverish at night, as Elise rubbed aloe on the spots she'd missed. Leah, having no older sister, needed more protection. Sophie was less shy and wanted badly to win, coaxed Leah into races down the street, her taut tan body coiled and desperate to overtake.

⸎

Five years in Atlanta: 1987: Leah in the backyard, frowning with concentration, weaving purple clover chains. 1988: Sophie sprinting after a fading neighborhood friend in the early dusk, letting out a sharp laugh of triumph when her finger reaches his shoulder blade: "You're it!" 1989: Leah gathering piles of books in the delicious cool of the air-conditioned library: Nancy Drew, Hardy Boys, the Boxcar Children: careful not to pick any books with a copyright date later than 1960, because they were more likely to have sad endings. 1990: Sophie building a fort in the backyard with her best friend, Ana, dragging ferns over the stick frame and sweeping pine needles off the floor. 1991: Leah watching *Look Who's Talking* at her best friend's house and asking Elise the next day how babies are made. 1987–1992: The sisters' twenty-two-month distance, their opposite natures, bind them to each other like sun and shade. This pleases Elise, who always wanted a sister closer to her own age. Since she was a child, the seven years separating Elise and Ivy have felt like a gulf she couldn't quite bridge, like the ravine the Ebert kids used to fling themselves across on a rope swing, holding on for dear life to the fraying twine.

Elise knows that Ivy's band has gotten good—very good—from the newspaper clippings that Ada sends her in the mail. When Choked by Kudzu comes to Atlanta in 1988 and plays at Chastain, Elise strains to love the music but recoils from the gravel in Ivy's voice, the obvious fury of the guitar wail. Sometimes Sophie or Leah asks to hear one of Aunt Ivy's tapes on a road trip to Indiana, to visit the Kriegstein farm, and Elise is always relieved when the tape is finished, the same feeling she gets when the credits finally roll after a particularly violent film.

❧

What is there to say about the good years, aside from their goodness? Was it a mistake to leave the comfort of Atlanta, to presume that struggle abroad would be better, more interesting, build character? How different was that celebration of hardship from the farming philosophy practiced by Chris's father, waking up at four every morning to work the land? For that matter, how different was it from Ada's Southern Baptist soft spot for suffering?

Chris and Elise stay up late into the night discussing the potential move to Shanghai. They are on their fifth year in Atlanta. It is a sultry summer night, and thunderstorms are rolling in. The girls are in bed. Sophie is asleep; Leah is watching the storm tear across the sky, feeling safe under the covers and behind the window. On the front porch below, a little spray from the rain catches Elise's arm and she moves her rocking chair back. "You and the girls would be able to come back each summer for vacation," Chris is saying. "There's an American school there where you could teach and the girls would go to school."

Elise thinks of Janice Wong, a single mother who teaches language arts at Elise's middle school, who stayed in Atlanta when her husband went back to Taiwan. That's how it happens sometimes. But the idea of a move to Asia also excites Elise. She pictures herself walking through fresh produce markets, fingering silk, exploring bamboo groves. "I want to go there and see it first," she tells Chris firmly, trying to sound ambivalent.

"Of course," he says. He takes her hand and moves her rocking chair closer to his. A flash of lightning lights up the street and they both shiver. "China would be so much fun with you," he says. She nods and snuggles into his sweater.

∽

Let's say they had stayed in Atlanta. Elise keeps teaching at the middle school, has a brief affair with the art teacher, an amateur photographer who seduces her after a photo shoot of Elise leaning on trees in Piedmont Park. Chris begins working as a consultant for a firm expanding its operations to Siberia; begins learning Russian on tape during the long transatlantic flights. Leah joins the less nerdy of two nerdy cliques in high school, gets an adorably dorky boyfriend, suffers a secret abortion at seventeen, and afterwards breaks up with said boyfriend and starts performing at a lot of poetry slam events. Sophie becomes a popular athlete, remains best friends with Ana, and surprises everyone by choosing a beat-up red pickup truck for her first car, her first sign, at eighteen, of any latent eccentricity. She drives out to Pomona with Ana, who will be studying at UC Santa Cruz.

If they had stayed in the States, would *it* have happened? Was Sophie's death a foregone conclusion in any geography, a heart failure built into her system that would have struck her down on any continent? Later, the doctors would say, "There was nothing you could have done. Undetectable heart conditions are just that: undetectable. You mustn't blame yourselves." But because the death will happen in Singapore, its occurrence will be unimaginable anywhere else. Thus, in the parallel (irrational) universe, where they stay in Atlanta, where the good years never end, Sophie never dies.

∽

What remains to be said about the good years, aside from their goodness, is the following: they were unsustainable, and in that sense, never safe. In other words, staying in Atlanta was never a distinct possibility. It was too late for Elise and Chris, having lived in Hamburg and London: by the fifth year, Atlanta had begun to feel boring. They saw it as a particularly pleasant rest stop, a quiet chapter in their cumulative adventure. Even Leah, with eleven-year-old pretentions of grandeur, craved a "next," though her memories of "before" Atlanta were limited to the backyard in London, fish and chips, and falling blossoms in a British park. Still, Leah grumbled that they always went to the airport to pick people up but never went anywhere themselves. Sophie also longed to fly somewhere far away, because then you got toiletry kits with slippers and toothbrushes, which Chris always brought back for the girls after his trips to Russia. Also, the one time Sophie and Leah had flown to Wyoming for their babysitter's wedding (visits to Indiana and Mississippi were always limited to road trips in the van), they had been allowed to drink Coke on the flight, which Elise forbade otherwise.

⚭

In Atlanta, Elise is a science teacher. In Shanghai she will be an expatriate mother, then a guidance counselor and a self-appointed disciplinarian who chases the Chinese American and Filipino boys from the basketball court into math class.

In Atlanta, Chris is an out-of-work husband, a dreamer, a regular at the local deli, where he always orders club sandwiches with fries and tries to avoid chatting with the overfriendly waitresses, something he hates about the South: how much you have to talk. It is twenty years too early for smartphones, so Chris brings along biographies of Gorbachev to make him look preoccupied. In Shanghai, Chris will again be a front-runner, a deal maker, a man who gives speeches and unsuccessfully refuses traditional Shanxi grain alcohol, a man in charge of five hundred Chinese American factories without knowing a full five words in Chinese.

In Atlanta, Leah is a fourth grader who curls up in corners, always reading, oblivious to Elise's calls to supper; who is still not unconvinced that Santa Claus exists (despite Sophie's pragmatic assertions to the contrary); who wants to become her mother, flaxen blond and beautiful; and who resents Sophie for being poised to assume Elise's legacy, given the honeyed color of Sophie's curls and her ease with strangers. In Atlanta, Leah reads in her own closet, hangs upside down with Sophie on the monkey bars, and lets out a scream, sledding down the hill in Piedmont Park the one day a year that it snows. In Shanghai, at twelve, in one year, Leah will be taller than most Chinese men.

In Atlanta, Sophie performs in the talent show alone when Ana suddenly drops out. Sophie dons her black turtleneck and leggings and white gloves and does an interpretative dance to Enya while Ana stays at home with a fake headache. In Atlanta, Sophie is secretly pleased when Leah comes in to sleep in her room, snuggling into the bottom bunk, even if Leah talks too much when Sophie wants to fall asleep. In Atlanta, Sophie collects baseball cards and never wears dresses except to First Pres, the only time Elise puts her foot down. In Shanghai, Sophie will politely reject the advances of a gawky British boy in her class, except for once at a school dance, when she feels sorry for him. She will lose Leah, a little, to Leah's own teenage loneliness, a territory Sophie will swear to herself never to enter, and which she never will. In Shanghai, Sophie will always order lemon chicken when they go to their favorite restaurant.

⚭

When the Kriegsteins leave Atlanta for Shanghai in 1992, with a six-month layover in Madison, Wisconsin, where Chris's company headquarters are located, they are desperate to be overseas again. After three months in Shanghai, they will be desperate to return home. Like Persephone's annual permitted return to her mother aboveground, by the gods in Olympus, the powers that be at Chris's company will grant the Kriegstein women "home leave" once a year, each summer, when they will stay with friends and relatives, the flights covered by the company. In September they will be forced to leave again, back to China. This habit of home leave will cement Atlanta as "home" in their minds, since they always fly back to the Atlanta airport. In other words, the oblivion of the good years will become dissected, memorized, fossilized, and neatly placed in a glass jar with the label "home." Years later, as an adult, when asked where she is from, Leah will always say "Atlanta," as if we come from our joy, as if, aside from their goodness, there was anything to say about the good years.

The Six-Month Layover

Madison, Wisconsin, 1992–1993

After several years in Asia, the Kriegsteins will grow accustomed to long layovers in airports, and Sophie and Leah will rank their favorites. Tokyo is number one, for the Oreo cookies you get in the business-class lounge. Any domestic Chinese airport is a nightmare, where you better pray you don't have to pee. The Seoul airport is number two, for its emptiness, which allows for races down travelators and hide-and-go-seek among the potted plants at midnight, fluorescent light bouncing off the tiled floor, tired Korean flight announcements echoing in the halls. Singapore is ranked number three, for its excellent gummy bears. The Atlanta airport is actually a million times better than all of them, because it means they are back home for the summer.

But for now, the Kriegsteins' six-month stint in Madison, in between Atlanta and China, is their first and longest layover, a pregnant pause in a spotless midwestern state before heading off to a Communist one. It resembles spending a good while in the shallow end, trying to gather courage before advancing to the deep part of a chilly pool. Their months in Wisconsin are meant to build up their collective confidence, to reassure themselves that moving isn't a big deal.

We can do this, they think, in September, unpacking boxes in their temporary suburban abode, and then, in April, telling themselves the same thing, as they pack them up again. But moving to Wisconsin in order to prepare themselves for China is about as effective as training for surfing in Hawaii by boogie boarding in the Gulf of Mexico.

⸙

Over the six months, as Leah takes up the trumpet, as Sophie learns to play ice hockey, and as Elise becomes self-conscious of her southern accent, they forget that they will soon be leaving again. The only reminder of this is their biweekly Mandarin lessons at a local Chinese restaurant, the Golden Dragon, where they struggle, unsuccessfully, to remember the Chinese words for one another: *Mama, Baba, Mei Mei, Jie Jie, Nu er, Qi zi, Lao Gong,* and console their clumsy mouths with sweet and sour pork and fortune cookies.

In Madison, unlike Atlanta, snow never means you can stay home from school. Oddly, Sophie and Leah spend the six white months eating copious amounts of Dairy Queen Blizzards: Leah orders hers with Nerds, Sophie hers with M&M'S. Elise had anticipated dismissing all midwestern women as repressed robots but is both annoyed and relieved to discover that many are voracious readers and some don't even shave their legs. Chris, at Logan's corporate headquarters, being groomed for his upcoming Chinese assignment, looks like a golden retriever who finally, after an agony of searching and frantic paddling in the water, finds his stick and swims back, proud and fully himself. Chris is relieved to be back behind a desk, giving and taking orders, overachieving, and as reticent to talk about more than the weather as all the other German American Lutherans around him.

❧

On April 17, the date of their departure, there is still snow on the ground. Sophie and Leah receive "Good Luck!" cards with signatures from all their classmates. Elise's new girlfriends throw her a luncheon with no fewer than ten casseroles. Chris's secretary shyly presents him with a certificate to Chili's, which Chris irrationally packs to carry with him to Shanghai, even though it will be three years before a McDonald's comes to Shanghai, let alone a Chili's.

The Kriegsteins wave good-bye to Wisconsin with studied ease, board the Northwest plane, and snuggle into business class feeling like celebrities. It is only midflight, four hours from Tokyo, that Elise panics about not having put Ada's quilts in storage, Leah has a nightmare about getting her period the first day of school, Sophie can't get warm under the thin Northwest blanket, and Chris stares at his blank yellow legal pad, trying to come up with a stirring speech to give his new employees on the first day. The plane soars serenely over the Pacific Ocean.

Part Three

Mechthild

Outside Hanover, Germany, 1885

hris's great-grandmother, Mechthild Mayer, left her village in northwest Germany at the tail end of summer, as winter's hard red berries popped onto bushes, as the *Septemberkraut* began to brown. She wept on the train to Hamburg, wept as she boarded the ship that would take her across the Atlantic. She wept across the pitching, aching passage, pausing only to vomit overboard, wipe her mouth with her sleeve, and continue where she'd left off. At first, the other passengers tried to comfort her. When she did not respond, but simply wept harder, they began ignoring her. Her sobs continued, and they grew irritated. They made fun of her or yelled at her to shut up, depending on their moods.

Only a little girl, Katha, seven years old, whose mother was too busy taking care of her brothers and sisters to notice her absence, was kind to Mechthild. For Katha, the crying woman, who sat immobile, aside from her shaking shoulders, was like a giant doll. Katha combed and braided Mechthild's hair, told her stories as she stroked her hand, and bossed her around, telling her she should find a husband, repeating what she'd heard her mother say about Mechthild to the other women. And Mechthild wept, beautifully. It was what Katha liked most about her.

Just one month earlier, Mechthild had laughed at sentimental women, the kind who cried when the bread came out wrong, or when their sweethearts forgot their birthdays. That was before she had rounded the corner in her small house, where she lived with her parents and her older brother, having forgotten coins for shopping in the village market, and entered her parents' bedroom, the midmorning sun falling gloriously on the entwined bodies of her mother and Mechthild's fiancé.

That image, so stunningly, unquestionably lit, like the stained glass scenes of Christ in the village church, which Mechthild had loved to stare at as a child as the preacher droned on, would not leave her vision now. The gray, choppy sea, the rough pine of her bunk, Katha's large blue eyes and grave gaze, taking her in, merely framed the other image, the horror. When the ship reached New York and the passengers stepped, shakily, onto land, they were so consumed with the details of their new life in the new country—counting offspring, practicing English words, sniffing the air expectantly—that they didn't notice Mechthild had stopped crying.

Mechthild never returned to Germany, though she spoke German with Gregor Kriegstein, the man she wound up marrying two years later, whom she chose for his doglike loyalty and his toughness. Gregor would make it in America, she could tell. He was a thick branch hanging above her, as she was being swept down a cold current, which she grabbed and held on to. It was she who would have affairs, later, while Gregor was in the fields, after they had moved to a German community in Indiana and begun a small farm. It would occur to her, picking hay out of her hair, lying in a square of hot afternoon light in the barn, in the arms of a neighbor, that her decision to emigrate, the moment she left her parents' bedroom, had been a melodramatic one. It had just been lust, after all. The long voyage, the years of hard labor and loneliness, the foreign taste of English on her tongue: her mother probably wouldn't have slept with her fiancé again, after being caught, and Mechthild could have kept her place at the table at Sunday dinners.

Mechthild did not have a child until she was forty-two. She had assumed she was barren until the sperm of the Polish handyman, traveling through town, repairing broken farm machinery in return for a warm meal, was lively enough to rouse her lethargic eggs, and she gave birth to a black-headed screamer the following February, to her blond husband's resigned suspicion and to her great joy.

❧

What would Mechthild Mayer have said, watching the four Kriegsteins climb out of the airplane in Shanghai after a mere twenty hours (as opposed to her twelve-day sea voyage), stretching from the flight, searching for their baggage on the carousel, Chris trying to assume a manly knowingness, Elise looking after the girls, Leah taking Sophie's hand, the four of them walking to the taxi that would take them to their new home? Mechthild would have laughed. Laughed and laughed, just as long and hard as she had wept on the ship to America. To think that her descendants, after all her struggles as an immigrant, would have the arrogance to simply up and relocate, to another continent, another culture, with no thought of the consequences of their actions. Or perhaps their relocation was the very consequence of her own actions? At this point, Mechthild would have stopped laughing and concentrated all of her energy on wishing them well.

The People's Square

Shanghai, China, 1993

Those first days, we were awoken by the sounds of ballroom dance music at dawn. Old tunes from the fifties, like "Jailhouse Rock," along with waltzes and tangos.

"This is exactly why I said I'd never live in an apartment building again," Mom told Dad on our third morning in Shanghai. "Remember the Schmidts in Hamburg? The parties they would throw?"

"You were just mad they never invited you," he said.

"They ruined John Denver," Mom said, ignoring him. "You could always tell a party was winding up when 'Country Road' started playing, over and over."

"Hey," Sophie interrupted. "It stopped."

We all listened. She was right. The apartment was silent, except for the refrigerator whirr and a distant whine of traffic. Then "What a Wonderful World" started up.

"That's it," Mom said, and stormed out. Five minutes later, she came back, mystified. "It's not the neighbors," she said. "I think it's coming from outside."

We all crowded onto the balcony. It was just after seven, and the sun had barely risen. I stayed close to the door because I didn't like heights, and our apartment was on the thirtieth floor. Mom was right—the music was coming from the street. It had to be deafening down there, because it was still loud by the time it got up to us.

"Over there maybe?" Mom pointed vaguely across the street.

"I can see it; there, in front of the big building!" Sophie's voice was shrill with triumph. Of the two of us, she always spotted things first, but only because she was obsessed with winning. Technically, I had the better eyesight, a fact proven each time we went to the doctor for eye exams, which drove her crazy. "Down there!" she yelled, even though we were right beside her. "They're dancing!"

We had already begun to say "they" to refer to "them," i.e., the locals, the Shanghainese, the not-us. Those first weeks were full of "What do you think they're yelling about?" and "Are they pointing at us?"

Dad looked at his watch. "I need to run."

"Can we go down there, Mom?" Sophie asked. "I *have* to check this out."

Mom looked at me. "I'll keep an eye on her," I said.

"Like I need it," Sophie scoffed, and went after her sneakers.

"Take the swipe card to the apartment building," Mom said, fishing through her purse in the living room. "Here's the apartment key. If they look upset that you're there, come back up right away. Maybe it's closed to foreigners."

"Mom." I rolled my eyes. "Come on, it's a public square. The *People's* Square, remember?" We'd learned that much from a short tour around our neighborhood the previous day, led by one of Dad's employees. Sophie and I had spent the half hour giggling and poking each other whenever we saw stuff like the neat rips in Chinese toddlers' pants, so they could do their business anywhere; or how people spat on the street as casually as if they were blowing their nose into a Kleenex. Back in our neighborhood in Atlanta, Sophie had been something of a spitting legend: she could spit as far and aim as well as any of the boys. "This is my kind of country," she had whispered to me, watching an elderly lady let one sail across the sidewalk, prompting Dad to turn around and shush us.

"Yeah, the People's Square!" Sophie called now, from the hallway. "As in, all people, including Americans: *helloooo!*" That elongated "hello" was a new tic of hers, something she had picked up during our six months in Madison that I wished she hadn't. "Come on, Leah! Before they're gone!" She was out the door. Mom smiled ruefully at me.

"Careful crossing the street," she said.

I laughed obligingly. It was our family's first inside-China-joke, since we'd nearly gotten run over every time we'd attempted to cross the street in the past two days. "Deal," I said. I liked my new wise-older-sister role, which had somehow fallen on me with the move. I gave Mom a tired, grown-up-looking smile in return.

I dropped the smile as soon as I left our apartment. Sophie was in the elevator, holding the doors, which had begun to squawk in protest. "What took you so long?" she demanded. I hurled myself inside just before the doors shut.

"Ha!" I said.

"Ha yourself," Sophie returned, and we both started jumping up and down as if we were on a trampoline, acting on a recent discovery. If you jumped right before the elevator stopped on a floor, it "shielded" your stomach, as Sophie said (a word she had made up but pretended she hadn't), like being on a roller coaster, or going over hills fast in a car. Back when we had a car, that is, back when there were hills.

❧

The Shanghai air hit us as soon as we left the lobby of our apartment building. Dusty and smelly. We giggled at it, like one of us had farted.

"Let's *go*," Sophie said, all urgency, and grabbed my hand. We tore down the sidewalk. There was something about being stared at in China that made you want to either go hide under the covers or do something crazy, like scream and sprint down the street. When Sophie was there with me, I often had the latter impulse.

We managed to cross the street, dodging raging bikes and honking cars, and reached the People's Square, where we slowed down, suddenly shy. We were in a sea of senior citizens. Most of them were dancing to "Twist Again," but some of them were off to the side, doing random moves with swords. Another pack, farther to the back, looked like somebody had pressed a slow-motion button on them. I punched Sophie in the arm and pointed, but she didn't even turn around, she was so caught up with the dancers.

Thankfully, nobody was crowding around us, saying "Hello!" or shoving their babies into our arms to take pictures, as they had the few other times we'd left the apartment. "Let's dance!" Sophie said, and took my hands. I didn't really feel like dancing, or doing anything to draw attention, but Sophie was already spinning away from me and spinning back, singing "Like we did last summer," at the top of her lungs. Some of the couples gave us thumbs-up signs, but most seemed to be so intent on the rhythm that they didn't want to bother with us. They were astonishingly good dancers, didn't miss a beat. The majority were old married couples, I guessed, but there were also quite a few women dancing together, who looked like they'd gotten fed up with their husbands stepping on their toes and had asked their best girlfriends to be their partners instead.

The only time I'd done any dancing, aside from tap lessons in fourth grade, which I'd done largely to appease my best friend, was at a school dance in Madison, four months before we moved to China. A boy from my grade, Robby Chestnut, had approached me during an R & B song. We began the awkward seesawing step so beloved of middle schoolers, like standing on a rocking boat. "Let's waltz!" I'd suggested, when the chorus hit. "I don't know how to waltz," he replied, probably already regretting he hadn't approached someone less weird. I didn't know how to waltz either, but I grabbed his right hand and placed it on the small of my back, took his left, and started moving like I was Scarlett in *Gone with the Wind*. He shuffled along for a few steps before muttering "Sorry," and fleeing back to his friends. My cheeks burned now, thinking of it. My first day at Shanghai American School was in three days, and I was anxious for a fresh start, determined not to commit social suicide anymore.

After the song, everybody clapped, including Sophie and me. I wandered away from her to get a better look at the geezers in slow motion, until I heard an outraged "Hey!" behind me. I whirled around. Sophie was holding the back of her head like she'd been hit. "What happened?" I demanded, pulling her to the side, as the old people around us began a slow tango. We kept getting knocked by elbows and hips, and received multiple annoyed looks and old-people mutters of disapproval.

"That lady just came up and touched my hair," Sophie said, jerking her head back in the direction we'd come from. "Let's get out of here. It's dumb."

"Hold on a second. I want to check out those slow people over there."

"I said, let's go!" I had never seen Sophie cry, except in photos when we were really little. But it was in her voice now, all right.

"Okay, okay. Take a chill pill." I scanned the crowd, looking for a path through the spinning bodies. "You first."

Sophie began moving towards a narrow gap between the dancers and the sword swingers, charging through like she was Moses. I hurried after her and linked arms. "Follow the yellow-brick road," I sang, and we started doing the yellow-brick skip through the square, not caring now if we collided with the dancers. Some of the old people even tried to imitate us, and I flashed them a smile. Sophie kept her eyes on the ground, singing faintly. But by the time we were back in the elevator, she seemed fully recovered. She didn't say anything about the lady touching her hair to Mom, so I didn't either.

⚘

The next incident occurred three weeks later, on a trip to Suzhou with Dad's company. Mom had conned us into going by saying that we could have a sleepover the following Friday with our new friends from school. It was a bizarre bribe, since she would have happily said yes if we'd asked for the sleepover ourselves. Not that I had any friends that I wanted to come over, except for maybe Evgenia, this Russian girl who was the only person in my grade I felt normal around. But something about Mom's asking looked so desperate, like she didn't want to be stuck on that trip without us, that I said yes, and knocked Sophie in the ribs when Mom went to the kitchen, and Sophie said, "Yeah, okay," too.

It was a disaster from the beginning. Dad's colleagues picked us up in a van, and the driver put in a Michael Jackson CD before we had even left the parking lot. One of the most annoying things about living in Shanghai, I had already discovered, was how Chinese people always expected you to be in love with everything American, just because you came from there. I had always hated Michael Jackson, and hearing him now made me hate him even more. We got stuck in traffic, so what was supposed to be a two-hour trip took three hours. When the CD was through, the driver just played it from the beginning again. "Torture," I mouthed to Sophie, and she mimed dying a slow death in the backseat, which made me laugh out loud, and Mom shot us a *quit it* look.

Meanwhile Mrs. Li, the wife of Dad's joint-venture partner, who didn't speak English but still wouldn't leave us alone, kept plying us with disgusting local snacks. First she tried feeding us prunes covered with salt and a sourish orange powder, as if prunes themselves weren't gross enough. Barf. I spit it out in a tissue, to Mom's everlasting embarrassment. Next up was a packet of tiny dried fish, bones and eyes still intact, which stank up the whole van like a pet food store. Double barf. When Mrs. Li finally brought out the bananas, which looked like Twix bars in comparison to all the other crap, Sophie and I readily agreed to one, our first mistake. Between the driver's twisting his head around, looking for us to sing along to "Billie Jean," and Mrs. Li stuffing more bananas in our hands, Sophie and I looked like a low-budget circus act. I glanced at Mom, staring out the window absentmindedly, enjoying the rice fields flying by, and suddenly felt furious. Now I saw why she'd wanted us along: to be deflectors, so she wouldn't have to deal with Mrs. Li. Convenient. "I think my mom wants a banana," I told Mrs. Li politely, and turned on my Walkman, as the translator translated my words.

After that, Mary Chapin Carpenter drowned out Michael Jackson, and I relaxed, transported back to my bedroom in Atlanta, where I'd listened to *Shooting Straight in the Dark* a million times. With the headphones on, the translator couldn't ask me about my favorite school subjects or whether I agreed that Chinese food was the best food in the world. I could see Mom mouthing "teenage moment" to Sophie in the backseat. But it wasn't a teenage moment. I didn't mean to act like a teenager; I didn't feel like a teenager. I didn't like band posters or lipstick or making friendship bracelets for other girls. I didn't think listening to your Walkman fell into that category. It was all about survival, about not feeling awful. Mom and Dad had moved us halfway around the world; the least we deserved was the right to take personal timeouts, until we were ready to go back in the game. And sure enough, three songs later, I felt a little bit better, and even finished my banana like a good foreigner.

❧

When we arrived in Suzhou we piled out of the van and went straight to a restaurant, even though we were already stuffed. Dad was the only one of us who ate the "drunken prawns" at lunch, which are exactly like they sound, and which turned me vegetarian, at least for the rest of that day. Dad would do anything to make his Chinese business partners think he was a good guy. Even eat an innocent, flailing, boozed-up shrimp.

Then it was time for a tour of Suzhou in the rain, with a translator who could barely speak English, his accent was so thick. Mom would say I wasn't being fair, or sympathetic of "cultural differences," but I honestly tried listening at the beginning and I couldn't make out a word. I put my headphones back on and avoided eye contact with Mom. Sophie came over to me in the middle of the Suzhou Museum and tried to get me to give her a listen. No way.

It was in the next room, full of long scrolls of Chinese characters, that it happened. We should have known better when we saw the room fill with Chinese kids, all decked out in bright red scarves and blue baseball caps, like they were going to the World Series. Basically, when they saw Sophie they freaked out. I guess I was too tall for them, above their sight lines or something. But they went for Sophie like yellow jackets to strawberry jam. They all wanted to touch her hair. Mr. and Mrs. Li were smiling and laughing about it, like proud grandparents, and Dad was looking at them, smiling too, but I could tell Mom was worried, and suddenly Sophie screamed, superloud, "Get off me!" and booked it out of the room.

I ran after her, and had to run for a while. She sprinted out of the museum, down the road, people pointing and laughing, and then headed for a small park, where there was a pond with no one there, because it was still raining. When I got there she was crying, and I mean, crying crying. I didn't really know what to do. I put an arm around her, and she shoved me away. "You let them come," she said. "You were laughing."

That wasn't true, and I told her so. It unnerved me to see Sophie so upset. Between the two of us, she had always been the braver one, even though I was older, which was embarrassing. If we went to camp together, it was she who hung out with the popular kids and braided the counselors' hair and gave them back massages, while I sat in the shadows of the campfire, burning my marshmallows. If we went to our parents' friends' houses for dinner, something I always dreaded, it was Sophie who would suggest that all the kids play army dodgeball. It was Sophie who told me that Santa Claus didn't exist, and it was Sophie who could read scary books before going to bed, and watch Indiana Jones without running out of the room, unlike yours truly. So this was a new side to her, and even though it pained me to see her so down, there was a tiny part of me that was thrilled to finally be the tough older sister.

"I hate them," she said.

"They're just dumb kids."

"Why didn't they go after you?"

"I guess because I don't have your perfect blond curls," I said, which came out a little more bitter than I'd intended it to. I'd always been jealous of Sophie's hair. It was the same shade as Mom's, especially in pictures of Mom as a kid at Grand Ada's house (that's what we called Mom's mom, who lived in Mississippi). But now I felt pretty smug about my iron-straight hair.

We stood there for a while, just watching the pond. There were a couple of ducks paddling around, looking depressed, surrounded by paper cups, cigarettes, and plastic wrappers.

"China sucks," said Sophie. I knew she was waiting for me to agree, but for some reason I held back and stayed quiet.

"What's the first thing you would buy at Kroger's?" I finally asked her.

"A Butterfinger," she said immediately. "You?"

"A box of Honey Bunches of Oats."

"Weirdo."

We walked back, me humming the Honey Bunches of Oats theme song. It made me feel invincible, as though by summoning up the memory of the cereal commercial—a cartoon farmer walking through his wheat field, singing, birds flying down to join him—everything else—the rock gardens, the heavy museum doors, the echoing rooms, our parents, frowning—was only half-there, only half-real.

⚬

I always assumed it was the Suzhou incident that prompted Sophie to cut her hair. According to Mom, who went with her to the hairdresser's, which was just the master bathroom of a French lady in our apartment building, Sophie kept telling Madame Claude to cut it shorter and shorter. Mom let her do it, something she wouldn't have done in the States. That was one thing in China's favor; it had really relaxed Mom's policies. Before China, we were stuck with one measly hour of TV a week, on Saturdays, which always spurred big arguments between me and Sophie. She wanted to watch Garfield; I wanted to watch country music videos. Now we were free to watch as much as we desired, although it was mostly crappy Australian TV, with emu puppets, and 1970s shows like *The Stunt Guy*, which just featured some dude crashing cars, falling off cliffs, and getting back up with a crumpled smile, saying "No worries." We were also allowed to have any kind of cereal, including Cap'n Crunch, which had been reserved strictly for grandparent visits in Indiana or Mississippi before. Mom had even agreed to let us get a Nintendo, a sign that she'd truly broken down.

When Mom and Sophie came back from the fourth-floor French-lady hair salon, I nearly spit out the Sprite I was drinking. Even though Sophie had always been tomboyish, playing sports and shunning dresses, she had also been extremely vain about her hair. Those long curls were the first thing everyone commented on when they saw her. As opposed to what they said when they saw me, which was inevitably how tall I was. (I didn't really consider that a compliment. It was like the difference between calling the flowers of a rosebush beautiful and remarking on how tall the bush is. Who cares if it's two feet or four? Everybody knows it's the Christmas red of the petals that counts.)

I don't think Sophie had really thought the whole boy-look thing through. She had to put up with a little bit of teasing at school, but like I said, she had a knack for being popular that saved her, and, before you knew it, two other girls in her grade had whacked their hair short, too. It was only when we were around Chinese people, on our Sunday walks through Shanghai with Mom and Dad, or during company banquets, that it was an issue. If anything, Chinese people touched her sheared curls even more now than before. "Your son has a beautiful hair," they would tell my parents, and Sophie would fume. She took to wearing sweatshirts, hood up, even in the hottest weather, walking as fast as she could, her eyes on the ground.

Banquets were even worse because she couldn't wear a hood. Back then, it seemed like we had to go to banquets at least once a week. Dad's Chinese joint-venture partners would throw them in his honor, or to celebrate some contract they'd signed that week. They lasted forever and consisted of about a million courses. Sophie and I would sit there chugging coconut milk or sugary orange juice, picking at the stuff on our plates. Some of it was delicious, like the shrimp dumplings or steamed ginger fish, but there were a lot of unsavory mystery elements involved with most of the dishes. Back in Atlanta, one of our favorite games had been taste tests, where one of us would blindfold the other, and then go in the pantry and spoon out Worcestershire sauce or sesame seeds, or shave off the top of a Pop-Tart, and put it into the other person's mouth. The only rule was you couldn't mix things, on our babysitter's insistence, because she didn't want us to puke. Back then, we had known everything in the pantry, so the whole blindfolded business was a challenge but not inherently scary. But in Shanghai, at the banquets, you had no idea what you were getting into: was it jellyfish or tongue or liver something? The translator didn't usually help, though he tried. "Bearded scrounge dipper," he would announce, or "pearl imperial abalone." Mom said we should try a little bit of everything, but after a couple glasses of wine she would stop checking on us and we could eat whatever we wanted, which usually meant multiple courses of fried rice.

Anyways, during those dinners, there was a lot of Dad's Chinese colleagues and their wives patting Sophie's head and calling her a lovely boy. In the States, if Mom or Dad had corrected such a mistake, the offending party would have apologized and said yes, how silly of them, Sophie was a beautiful girl. But in Shanghai they would just argue back, as though maybe Mom and Dad had gotten it wrong. I was used to Sophie getting more attention, even before we moved to China. She had always possessed something that drew people to her, including me, as much as I tried to ignore that pull. But in Shanghai I suddenly felt lucky to be the one who escaped notice. I had a new feeling of needing to do something to rescue her, to help her out. I had always been the sensitive one, but I could sense the dynamic was changing. She would make up excuses so she wouldn't have to go for family walks on Sundays, and she grew quieter in general.

I wanted my old sister back. I didn't want to be the one to chatter brightly at dinner about everything I'd done that day. That was her turf. I didn't know what to say when Mom and Dad trained their gaze on me, desperate. That's the only way I can explain why I went along with Sophie's scheme.

⚘

It was about a month after she'd cut her hair, in the late spring. I heard a knock on my bedroom door, really soft. I was working on impossible math homework. Things had gotten a lot harder in math and science since coming to Shanghai, because the Korean and Taiwanese kids in my class were a million times better than the rest of us, and our teacher, Mrs. Ng, who was Singaporean, said we should all be at their level. I was totally lost, and making Cs and Ds on tests for the first time in my life. I hadn't told Mom and Dad yet, although Mom would probably find out soon, since she taught fourth grade at our school and had lunch with Ms. Ng every day in the teachers' lounge. Sophie opened the door a crack. "Hey," she said, and entered without asking, which I let slide. Her voice had an urgency to it, and some of her old excitement, like when she would be in a huddle with the neighborhood kids in Atlanta, hatching a plan for how to steal the flag from the other team. Those games had always been pointless to me, I could never summon up any kind of caring for a stupid old flag, and it had been exhausting to pretend that I did. But Sophie lived for that kind of thing.

"I have a plan," she said.

She unfolded a wrinkled piece of notebook paper, onto which she'd scrawled long lists in pencil with headings like: "Supplies," "Tickets," and "Important Phone Numbers." Basically, the plan was to run away from home. Or, as Sophie argued, when I put it that way, the plan was to run *back* home, since Shanghai was not our home and never would be. The heart of the scheme entailed going to the airport, buying tickets with one of Dad's credit cards, and moving in with Sophie's best friend in Atlanta, Ana. "Go for it," I said. "I'm staying here."

"Come on," she said.

"Forget it." I turned back to my homework.

"Pleeeeease."

"Get out of here."

"I need you," she said, and I softened a little but didn't say anything. "I don't look old enough," she said. "With you, it'll work."

That hurt, but I also knew that Sophie would never admit that she really just wanted me with her. That's how she was. "You'll never pull it off," I said.

But her excitement was infectious. She slept in my room that night, in the other twin bed, and we stayed up late talking about "the plan." Pretty soon I could picture it too, being back in Atlanta, enrolling in Piedmont Middle School, where all my friends were now, not having to be around all the weirdos at Shanghai American School. I still felt awkward around everybody there; my plan to be wildly popular hadn't really panned out. I'd never been very outgoing, but I'd always had a best friend in Atlanta, plus the neighborhood gang. Now I just had Sophie.

The next morning, we went downstairs with our backpacks and hid in the mailroom instead of waiting with the other kids for the bus. Through a crack in the door, we watched Mom come downstairs and take a taxi to school. Then we hurried back up to our apartment, giggling like crazy in the elevator. I should point out that normally Sophie and I never did anything wrong—never disobeyed Mom and Dad, I mean. It's hard to explain why. Aunt Ivy told me that one time, when she was babysitting us, when I was six and Sophie was four, she heard us fighting in the bathtub, and she came in and asked us what was going on. Apparently, we told her we were "pretending to have an argument." So to go from never being rude at the dinner table to running away from home was a big step. But it didn't feel like that. It felt like the adventure we'd always wanted China to be, ever since Dad had told us we were leaving Atlanta.

We didn't know where Mom and Dad had put our suitcases, so we just started shoving clothes into our backpacks. I found Sophie in the kitchen, filling plastic bags with food. "What are you doing?" I asked.

"For the trip."

"They feed you on the airplane, dummy."

She looked sheepish but kept out a can of Pringles. "Just in case," she said.

We went into Mom and Dad's bedroom and into the closet where we knew Dad kept a bunch of change, candy bars, and a few fifty-yuan bills. Sophie stuffed it all into the front pocket of her backpack.

"We forgot the credit card!" I cried at the door, secretly relieved that the plan would be foiled.

She whipped it out of her back pocket. "Sneaky," I said, impressed and a little disturbed that she'd suddenly gotten so good at stealing. I could feel Mom's disappointment leaking into me. So much for the wise-older-sister routine. But I reasoned that I was helping Sophie. We needed to get out of here. Shanghai was good for Mom and Dad but not for us. Had anyone asked us if we'd wanted to move to China? No. They'd just informed us we were going. And sure, back then we thought it was going to be great. All the kids had treated us like celebrities, and I'd figured Shanghai would look like the inside of the Golden Dragon Restaurant back in Madison—red lanterns, big fish tanks, fortune cookies. I hadn't counted on what we had found here, where I felt lost and not really myself at all. I told myself that leaving was the adult thing to do.

I wrote something to this effect in a note to Mom and Dad and stuck it on the refrigerator. Then we hauled everything downstairs, got in a taxi, and told the driver to take us to Hongqiao Airport.

Everything went according to plan until we got to the Delta counter. An older white woman, who reminded me of Aunt Beth, peered over the counter dubiously. "Where are your parents?" she asked when I presented the Visa card.

"They're divorced," Sophie suddenly piped up. "We haven't seen our mom since Christmas five years ago. Our dad said we should come here and buy tickets with his credit card. He's going to join us soon."

I gaped at Sophie. The Delta attendant looked unimpressed. "You'll have to wait until your dad comes," the woman said.

"Okay, ma'am, thank you," I said, and took the card back. We stepped out of line.

"She was about to buy it. Why'd you give in?" Sophie demanded.

I didn't answer and walked briskly to the airport exit. "Where are you going?" Sophie yelled at my back. "Leah! I know you can hear me!"

Outside, on the curb, I hailed a taxi. "Get in the car," I told Sophie.

She shook her head.

"Get in."

She threw her backpack on the sidewalk and crossed her arms. "Forget it. I'll go by myself." She tried to snatch the credit card from my hand. That did it. I took her by both arms and shoved her in the taxi. I was bigger than her, and it took her by surprise. I'd never pushed her around before, aside from playing basketball or wrestling in the backyard in Atlanta. "*Shanghai Shangcheng,*" I told the driver in Mandarin, our apartment building. Sophie tried to get out of the car, but I held on to her arm. "Ow, you're hurting me," she wailed. "Let go!"

I wouldn't, and I reached over her and locked the doors. I was furious. For lying so smoothly, for dragging me into this. I shook her roughly and she cried out in protest. "I can't believe you lied like that," I said. " 'We haven't seen Mom since Christmas five years ago.' What is wrong with you?"

"You're such a goody-goody," she said. "I wish I hadn't told you my plan. I should have gone alone."

"Yeah, right," I said. "Your plan. Like that would have ever worked." We were heading onto the highway, back towards the city. Everything that I'd seen on the drive to the airport an hour ago—the dirty streets, the unfamiliar faces, the Chinese characters I couldn't read, thinking, I'll never have to look at any of this again—crowded my vision now, and I closed my eyes. I couldn't remember ever feeling worse. I didn't want to stay in Shanghai, but I didn't want to get on a plane back home either. That's what I'd realized at the ticket counter. I'd been relieved when the woman refused the card. I'd discovered, yet again, that I wasn't as brave as Sophie.

I thought Sophie might cry a little, which would have made me feel better, but she just sat in stony silence, looking out the window.

"Your brother has beautiful hair," the taxi driver said to me in English, as we paused at a red light, and I said, "Yes, he does."

⤬

Back in the apartment, Mom was waiting for us. She hung up the phone when she saw us and ran to us, crying and mad like I'd never seen her.

"What were you thinking?" she kept saying.

That's when Sophie started sobbing, conveniently. She fell in Mom's arms and wept. I stood there awkwardly.

"I counted on you, Leah," Mom said.

It made me want to stalk out of the apartment again, for good. But instead I went over to the sofa where Sophie was lying in Mom's lap and sat down on Mom's other side. I put my head on her shoulder and closed my eyes.

"I hate it here," Sophie was saying in little gulps and hiccups. Mom was smoothing her short curls.

"We're going home in a month, for the whole summer, sweetie," Mom said. "Just think about that. All the Kroger's and soccer camp and time with Ana that you want."

That made Sophie cry harder. "But it's just a visit," she finally said, once her breath had turned raggedly even. "It's not home."

"Home's here now," Mom said firmly, and something in me plummeted. I had hoped she'd say, "We'll see about going back, or staying after the summer."

"We can't just abandon Dad, can we?" Mom continued.

"Why not?" Sophie sniffled.

Mom seemed to think about it for a second.

"Shanghai will grow on you," she said finally, not answering the question. "You'll see. I promise. It happened to me both times, in England and in Germany." She sighed. "I wish you girls had told me how you'd felt, instead of just running away."

Neither of us said anything, but I held Mom tighter.

⚭

Mom was right: it did get better. Kind of. At least, Sophie started to love it. She found a bunch of expat kids from our apartment building to play hide-and-go-seek with, except in Shanghai they called it manhunt. I would play with them too, halfheartedly; I felt lame sitting in my bedroom alone. But once I got outside I always missed the quiet calm of my desk and my books. I loathed crouching in the bushes, and the haunted, lonely feeling I got looking for people when I was it. Sophie, of course, adored the game and liked nothing better than ambushing me, screaming like a banshee, laughing her head off at my cry of terror, and sprinting away. She even concocted a manhunt uniform for herself, to maximize invisibility: her ubiquitous black hooded sweatshirt, black leggings, and black sneakers. We played with Jillian, a Swedish girl from the fifteenth floor; Nan, the daughter of the marine sergeant, from the ninth floor; and Ji-Mun and Seok-Jin, Korean twins from the sixth floor who always hid to-gether and were easy to find.

Outside our apartment complex, on Shanghai's streets, Sophie still got mad when people touched her hair and called her a boy. But she had learned how to say saucy things back in Chinese, which always impressed them. Then they would launch into an elaborate speech about how brilliant her Mandarin was, which Sophie couldn't get enough of.

And I had finally found a best friend, or at least something close to it. It turned out my instincts had been right about Evgenia, and we started hanging out together at lunchtime. She had the same sense of humor, and it made the days less lonely. But her father was really strict and wouldn't let her go anywhere on the weekends or after school.

I had a strange feeling I was getting younger, not older. I knew my friends back in the States weren't playing hide-and-go-seek any-more. But it wasn't like there were movie theaters we could go to in Shanghai, aside from the marine's apartment, where they would screen American films every now and then. There were other kids in my grade who got together on the weekends, but I'd hung out with them a couple times and it horrified me. The first time, we'd spent the whole Saturday throwing eggs at Chinese people from a taxicab. I'd sat in the middle seat after throwing one egg and hitting a lady on her bike, messing up her dress. Everyone had given me a high five and I'd wanted to die of shame. I knew those kids (Joan, from the States; Zara, from New Zealand; Brad, from Australia) went out to bars and clubs on the weekends—if you were white, the bouncers just let you in—but that sounded worse than manhunt to me.

In fact, contrary to what Mom had promised, the longer we were in Shanghai, the more I missed the States, maybe also because I felt like I'd lost Sophie as a partner in crime, now that she had turned so enthusiastic about the city. Or maybe she'd just decided that she couldn't talk to me about it anymore. I wondered what would have happened if we had made it onto that plane. I pictured us on the flight, holding each other's hands tightly, hugging each other out of excitement when we landed in Atlanta. The shock in Ana's voice when we would call her from the airport, getting into her parents' Volkswagen, the worn leather seats, seeing Atlanta come back to us from the highway. With every new day in China, I felt like I had to put on a face of okayness, of tough survival, with Mom and Dad and even Sophie, too, the same way I put on my clothes every morning.

⁂

That was the first year. The second year, after we got back from summer vacation in the States, I found that Shanghai had grown on me. I was happiest during family excursions, just the four of us. Walks around the city on the weekends. Sunday brunch at the Hilton, where you could tell the chef how to make your pasta, and pick out tiny cups of chocolate mousse, a string quartet playing in the background. Or sometimes, a private, delicious feeling when dusk came, when I was on my own. In the gathering dark, nobody could tell I was foreign, and I could watch the city without anyone noticing me. What I saw was beautiful: the lick of flame under an enormous wok; old people sitting on the stoop in their pajamas. My favorite thing to look at, however, was still the people moving in slow motion, like the ones I'd seen among the ballroom dancers on our third day in Shanghai. I'd since learned these movements were called tai chi. I felt sure that if I could learn to move like them, I could also slow everything down enough for it to feel good. Their faces were both focused and absent. They were so intent on their exercises that they didn't seem to see me on the park bench, watching them, and I, too, wanted to lose my self-consciousness like that.

That was the year I turned thirteen, a real teenager. I didn't know it then, but Shanghai was in an adolescent phase too, unsightly construction sites everywhere, in the midst of a crazy growth spurt. I've thought sometimes since then I must have felt some kind of empathy from the city, which was as clueless as I about how to hide rapid development, as embarrassed about its razed neighborhoods and disappearing rice fields as I was my new breasts and my monthly period.

Aunt Beth visited us that year from Indiana. She brought Butterfingers and Honey Bunches of Oats for Sophie and me, mustard-covered pretzels for Mom, and Good & Plenty candy for Dad. Before she came, we had been worried about how she would handle all of the pointing and general foreigner frenzy; after all, she was six feet tall and had dyed red hair. But she pointed and stared at the local Shanghainese as much as they pointed and stared at her. She'd always wanted to be a movie actress, she told us, so she liked the attention. "I didn't know you wanted to be an actress," Dad said. "I always thought you wanted to be a librarian." Aunt Beth gave a kind of snorting laugh and took a big sip of wine. For some reason, she winked at me as she put the glass down, and I gave her a conspiratorial smile back, even though I hadn't really understood what the wink was about. After that, I saw her differently, as someone more glamorous and more mysterious than I had initially given her credit for. In Indiana, I'd always read her relative silence as boring, but now she seemed intriguing, and, oddly enough, more at ease in China than I'd ever seen her in Chariton.

We'd been expecting a lot of sympathy from Aunt Beth about how tough it was to live in Asia, but instead she went on and on about how good we had it, pointing out things like our driver, the vacations to Phuket and Thailand, and our apartment building's humongous swimming pool. Mom told her that she should apply for a job at the American school, but Aunt Beth said *somebody* needed to be close to Grandma and Grandpa, and then it went quiet at the dinner table until Dad jumped in and started talking about how Clinton was worse than Jimmy Carter.

I felt really sad the day we dropped Aunt Beth off at the airport; it was like leaving the States at the end of the summer. With Aunt Beth there, Shanghai felt more normal: I didn't feel so gawkishly tall, all of us laughed a lot more, and America felt close and real, not like some dream we'd just woken up from. Aunt Beth had a way of being in China that I admired. She didn't try to fit in or be Chinese: she dumped sugar in her jasmine tea and, when we protested, told us that that's how she liked it. Yet she wasn't one of those annoying tourists who ask for a fork and a knife and only eat rice; she was the only one of us who tried chicken feet, and pronounced them delectable, a word I had to look up when we got home.

⤸

For a while I tried to act like Aunt Beth, adopting her casual, slightly wild laugh, and the way she lifted her eyebrows in humorous disbelief instead of getting upset. But Sophie made fun of me for copying her, and it was true—it wasn't really me. Aunt Beth's easy gestures and her quick humor were part of the luxury of being a tourist, of nothing mattering, and also a privilege of being grown-up. None of the tricks helped when you were in the seventh grade, and it was the spring dance show, and you were in a black leotard, and the guys were scoring the girls' bodies. I got a six, which was better than Clara

Park (four) but worse than Evgenia (eight). At those times, when the drowning feeling started, I pictured being back at Grand Ada's mountain home in North Carolina, sitting on the porch. I remembered the air that smelled like pinecones, and drinking Swiss Miss hot chocolate with lots of Cool Whip on top, sitting on the warm beams of the porch, and stretching my legs out, not feeling like I needed to slouch or suck my stomach in.

Home Leave

Great Smoky Mountains, North Carolina,
1993–1995

E ach year, mid-June, the expatriate women and children of Shanghai abandon China as if it is the *Titanic*, sinking fast. They stuff their suitcases with gifts for the folks back home: fifty-cent fans from the local market that make their clothes reek, deliciously, of sandalwood; stuffed panda bears; brightly colored sets of chopsticks for relatives who only use forks and knives, and calendars featuring "China's Awe-Inspiring Classic Best Tourist Attracts."

Looking at these families, these moms turned single for the summer, checking in at the airport, brandishing passports and boarding cards for Spain, Brazil, France, Canada, the US, and Germany, you would think they were all going back for good, given the size and quantity of their luggage. *But of course we need all of these suitcases!* the mothers, shocked at such ignorance, would point out to you. How else will they have enough space for everything they need to survive another year in China? Colgate toothpaste (their kids refuse to use the Chinese kind), jeans and dresses for Mom (Western women can only fit their big toes into Chinese women's clothes), shoes for their teenagers (who've already outgrown local sizes), and boxes of cereal that will admittedly be consumed over the first week back in Shanghai but are essential in maintaining the illusion that everything you need from back home can be tucked into a corner of a suitcase, even if it means you have to stand on said suitcase while your kids zip it up.

For Elise, Sophie, and Leah (like most other expatriate men, Chris stays in Shanghai, working most of the summer), home leave feels like trying to watch two movies with one VCR. Early on in the middle of the first film, you eject the tape and slide the second one in, watch that for a while, and then go back to the first one, in the middle of the scene where you stopped the tape. The advantage of such a system is that you can watch two movies, nearly simultaneously. But the choppiness of the viewing experience speaks against it, not to mention how annoying it is to repeatedly get up from the sofa.

China and America are two such completely separate films. When the Kriegstein females fly back to the States each summer, they re-enter their American selves, interact with other Americans, against an American backdrop. For most of the summer, this is the mountain cabin in North Carolina that Ada bought after Charles died, two hours from the Atlanta airport. But back in Shanghai, in the fall, it is as though North Carolina never happened. How can Leah explain, to Evgenia at Shanghai American School, the simple comfort of being covered in your grandmother's quilt, drinking hot chocolate on the cabin's front deck, hearing the bells from the town chapel tolling in the valley, knowing you have a whole day of reading ahead of you, and nothing—no sidewalks full of twelve million inhabitants; no giggling gaggles of Shanghainese schoolchildren, pointing; no menus listing indecipherable dishes—to remind you that you don't belong?

On the other hand, in the States, how do you explain (to aunts, old school friends, former neighbors, your brothers) what it feels like to live in Shanghai? "Bless your heart," Elise is told repeatedly. Then, as if what she is enduring is too unbearable to voice aloud, the listeners put a hand on her arm (in solidarity?), close their eyes, presumably imagining the horrors of living in China, and shake their heads quickly, as if rousing themselves from a nightmare. Of course, Elise, Leah, and Sophie can always take out the Shanghai photo album they have brought along, but they find that they don't really want to look at themselves back there, preferring to fall into the rhythms of American life and forgetting that there is any other way to be.

This works best at Ada's mountain home. In Atlanta, they sleep on friends' pullout couches since they no longer have a house in the city. Spending the night at her friend Rina's house, Leah tries to feign interest in the latest gossip about kids she hasn't seen in two years. At soccer camp, Sophie is heralded as the camper who has come the farthest to participate, and suddenly, the stares that meet her from the other campers feel as uncomfortable as the gawking she has learned to ignore on Shanghai's streets.

Such discomforts disappear in the mountains, where the TV never accuses them of having missed episodes for the last nine months, and Grand Ada is just as soft and snuggly as Sophie and Leah remember, baking the same blackberry cobbler that she always has. For Elise, her mother's predictably passive-aggressive remarks and thinly veiled disapproval of Elise's leaving Chris to "fend for himself," as Ada puts it, in China, hinting that such long stretches of time apart are not healthy, particularly for men, do not faze Elise as they would have before. Instead, the motherly barbs feel reassuringly familiar.

That they meet in North Carolina is also part of the deal: Elise has no desire to spend weeks on end back in Vidalia. If her mother wants to see her, she can come see her in the mountains, on more neutral turf. To Elise's large relief and slight apprehension, Sophie and Leah seem to enjoy a relationship with their grandmother that resembles what Elise shared with Ada before everything went so wrong. But with Paps gone, there is nothing Elise needs to protect the girls from, no further tests of Ada's allegiances. Elise sees her mother's kindness to the girls as an extended apology, one that, after so many years, Elise is too tired not to accept. Having the girls there lightens the atmosphere: they keep Elise from sinking into bad memories, not unlike the water wings Elise had insisted Sophie and Leah wear in the pool, long after they had learned to swim. When Sophie and Leah leave the house to build forts in the yard or pick blackberries near the pond, the temperature in the room drops considerably, Elise's tone with Ada grows harsher, and it is always a relief to hear the door slam, have Sophie run in with their spilling, juicy bounty, see the tension drain from Ada's face as she takes the berries from her granddaughter's sticky hands to wash in the sink.

Sometimes Ivy drives up from Vidalia, and Dodge and Grayson and their wives from Little Rock, and there are long meals with cheese squash, catfish, corn bread, fresh tomatoes with mayonnaise; Dodge doing imitations of all the folks back in Vidalia; Grayson's twin boys sitting with Sophie and Leah at the kids' table; all the grown siblings raising their eyebrows about how much Ivy is drinking, so they won't have to worry about how much they're drinking.

♺

Over the course of their two and a half years in Shanghai, the Kriegstein women perfect the art of home leave. Elise, in particular, develops elaborate coping strategies: don't try to visit too many people; don't go to Indiana without Chris; make sure you have a week for yourself, in Atlanta, in New York, wherever, without the girls; don't expect phone calls with Chris to be points of reconnection. (The time difference, the odd echo that often creeps in, and their two separate surroundings conspire in making Elise feel more alone after she's hung up than before, even though she can hear, in Chris's voice, that he is lonely, that he hates the summers by himself, that he misses them and the US.)

⚜

Home leave, for all of its glorious familiarity, is always confusing. Which film—the one taking place in the US, or the one taking place in China—is the real one? In the American film, Leah is tall, but not exceedingly so; Sophie's blond curls garner smiles but not shrieks; and Elise is never asked her age and weight by anyone except her gynecologist. In the American film, on their third summer in the States, Leah kisses Lane, Sophie's best friend's older brother, and spends the summer with a racing pulse, blushing and stammering, sneaking off to make out in the woods, unaware of Sophie and Ana spying from the rhododendron bushes—whereas in the Chinese film, Leah is never once asked to dance at school dances. In the American film, Leah's old school friends have received their learners' permits, while Leah has never so much as sat behind the wheel. In the Chinese film, Leah can cross Shanghai alone, bargain for oranges in Mandarin, and describe the distinct cultural pressures her friends feel, depending on whether they are Brazilian Catholic or Korean Protestant. The only things the two films have in common are Leah, Sophie, and Elise—and, to a lesser degree, Chris.

When they first moved to China, Chris assured them that Shanghai would just be two and a half years, and then they would be back in the States. No more leave, just home.

Then Chris is given an offer he can't refuse, in Singapore.

The girls are bribed into moving to Singapore with the promise of a dog. Elise isn't so easily bought. For some reason, one that even Elise cannot articulate to herself, she adamantly does not want to leave China, despite the air pollution, and the apples you have to peel, and the anxiety about your weight that being surrounded by tiny Chinese women inspires.

Like nowhere else before, except perhaps London, Elise feels captivated by Shanghai. The city is like a gorgeous boyfriend who treats you badly but always leaves you wanting more and, when he wants to be nice, melts you. Elise never really had a boyfriend like that, but she always fantasized about having one. Or maybe she is just sick of saying yes to Chris. "Sure, honey, why not?" like some simpering fifties sitcom housewife. Like Ada.

Chris is shocked at Elise's resistance to the move. He begs and pleads, pointing out that there is no job back home anymore. Elise calmly explains that she doesn't want to go "back home"; she wants to stay in China. "*Wo bu yao zou*" (I don't want to go), she tells Chris in Mandarin (she's been taking lessons for two years now), which leaves him unamused.

"Why don't we ask the girls what they think?" Chris shrugs, the courteous diplomat. (There is a reason he is such a successful business negotiator, and even beats his Chinese colleagues at their own game.) Sure of victory, Elise does not pause to consider that Chris has never suggested such a democratic procedure before. For years to come, Elise will regret agreeing to the "referendum," as she comes to think of it. She hasn't felt so ganged up on since the ninth grade, when tenth-grade girls spread a rumor that she was on the varsity cheerleading squad as a freshman because she'd let the football coach kiss her. It also stings because Elise presumed she knew their daughters far better than Chris. There was no way Sophie and Leah would choose a new foreign country in Asia over staying in Shanghai, she thought. But she underestimated their desire for a puppy, American movies, and decent cheeseburgers, all of which are on offer in Singapore. Elise is outvoted, three to one.

During the two months before the move to Singapore, Elise moves around in a daze, going on long walks alone after school, not coming home for dinner. Chris leaves work earlier, takes the girls to restaurants, and the three of them are often giggling conspiratorially on the couch when Elise returns, which doesn't help her feeling of intrafamilial exile.

Then the day comes to leave Shanghai, in early August. Elise, like Mechthild, weeps the entire trip. Sophie and Leah, no longer giggling, hug her on either side, and Chris keeps her supplied with a steady stream of white wine and antianxiety medication. Elise doesn't inquire how he conjured up the pills. She swallows them gratefully and avoids looking out the window as the plane takes off, and shuts her eyes, again, when the plane touches down at Changi Airport.

The Heat

Singapore, November 1996

Back at therapist's office, one month later, near the end of a fifty-minute session. Family is seated in same chairs as last time. Noticeable tension in the air. Only Sophie seems serene.

Elise: I knew it. I had a bad feeling about the move from the beginning—

Therapist: But surely you grasp, Elise, that Sophie's cause of death, the heart condition, was a chronic one, something she had at birth. It had nothing to do with Singapore—

Elise: The heat!

Chris: The doctors told us, over and over, it had nothing to do with the temperature that day—

Elise: Sure they told us that. With their Singaporean smiles, giggling out of nervousness, the same way they would laugh at sad parts in movies. I remember watching *Philadelphia* in Singapore— the audience erupted in laughter when Tom Hanks died—

Chris: Elise. Listen to yourself.

Elise: We should have stayed in Shanghai.

Therapist: Chris?

Chris: It's not rational. It's cruel. She blames me for it, you know? Not out loud, but whose fault was it that we moved? Mine. And therefore... you do the math.

Sophie: *I was always going to die.*

Leah: She was always going to die.

Elise: How do you know?

Sophie: *I didn't know until the day it came. I felt strange when I woke up. I thought, I bet today I'm going to get my period. (Rueful laugh.) But it was something bigger.*

Leah: I don't know... I didn't know. I was with her the whole day. I didn't sense a thing. I wish she could have given me some sort of sign, communicated somehow—

Sophie: *I was embarrassed. I thought about asking you how to use a tampon, but I didn't know how to bring it up. And it wasn't like I was even bleeding. (Softer.) We never talked about that stuff.*

Therapist: Leah, what do you think Sophie would have said to you that day? Or, wait, I take that back. What would she say to you now? Why don't you pretend she's in this chair? (Gestures at the chair where Sophie is indeed sitting.)

Sophie (to Leah, in pig latin): *Ust-tray or-yay own-hay eaths-day.*

Leah (looks away, then turns back to the chair, concentrating, listening; she speaks slowly): Trust your own deaths.

Sophie: *That's right. Yes! You got it, Leah!*

She rushes up to give Leah a high five; then, at Leah's nonresponse, Sophie remembers the rules, slouches back to her chair.

Elise: What? Trust your own—that doesn't sound like Sophie. That sounds a little scary, sweetie. What do you mean by that?

Leah (to the chair): "Trust your own deaths," yeah right. What are you now, some kind of back-from-the-dead psychic? I bet that's a line from *Star Wars*.

Sophie disappears.

Leah (senses Sophie's leave-taking, breathes in sharply): Sophie!

Therapist looks nervous; his role-playing exercise has pushed Leah to a place he didn't intend.

Elise (to herself): Trust your own deaths.
Chris: See? It wasn't because we moved to Singapore. It wasn't the heat. Leah just said as much.
Elise: She wasn't talking about that, Chris. Jesus! You're so literal.
Leah (to Sophie's empty chair): You see? Here they go and there you went. Fuck that. I'm out of here too.

Leah climbs up on her chair, straddling the two arms, as though she is on the ledge of a tall building, contemplating a fatal leap.

Therapist: Leah, will you please take a seat?

Leah obliges, with adolescent resentment. Chris and Elise continue bickering in the background.

Therapist: Guys, I'm afraid we're approaching the end of the session. Chris? Elise? (Clears his throat.) Chris! Elise! Time to wrap things up.

Silence. Elise comes over to Leah's chair, hugs her. Leah flinches. Chris comes and circles his arms around his wife's waist.

Chris: Let's go.
Therapist: Leah, can I speak to you for a second, alone?

Chris and Elise depart.

All four Kriegstein voices, including Sophie's (from offstage): *Gute Nacht, oyasumi nasai, buenas noches, bonne nuit, wan an, anyon, ood-gay ight-nay!*

Leah is clearly listening to these voices, which the therapist cannot hear. It is "good night" in seven languages—including pig latin—something that the Kriegsteins, up until Sophie's death, always said to each other after prayers at night.

Therapist: Leah, you're making progress, trust me. But I'm a little concerned about how the session ended. How are you doing?

Leah nods, not answering, shrugs on her sweatshirt, dreamlike, walks slowly to the door, pauses.

Leah: Why did you ask me to listen to her if you didn't want me to see her anymore?
Therapist: It's hypothetical, Leah. I asked you to consider what she *would* say.
Leah: Did you ever lose a sister?
Therapist: I don't think it's appropriate for me to get into my personal—
Leah: No, you didn't. So don't try to kill mine a second time.

Safety

Singapore, 1995

Singapore's torrential downpours make the thunderstorms Leah and Sophie loved in Atlanta look like light rain. They come out of nowhere, clouds gathering suddenly, inexplicably, with the fury of a borderline personality. From a bright blue sky outside and intense, unremitting sunlight, the room is abruptly cast in deep shadow, and rain descends with the finality of a stage curtain, the angry pounding distracting Leah from Mandarin class and, if lightning is present, calling a quick end to Sophie's soccer practice.

Shanghai's storms had been moody, whole-day, drizzly affairs that occasionally gathered enough momentum to actually rain, at which point garbage flowed freely in the streets. Ponchos blossomed in every color on the city's millions of bike riders, and the dirt of construction sites turned to sludge. Even the brightest of Shanghai's blue fall days had been compromised by a thin line of haze, like the giveaway bloodshot eyes of an alcoholic. Nature, throughout the city, had been subdued and beaten to an unrecognizable pulp. The Suzhou Creek had run black and reeked blocks before you arrived. The leaves of plane trees in the French Concession were gray with dust.

Singapore, by contrast, is verdant everywhere the Kriegsteins look, even in the city center. Fuchsia bougainvillea tumbles from pedestrian crossovers, sidewalks smell of the lemony gardenia trees towering above, and the sprawling grounds of their colonial villa boast papaya, mango, and jackfruit trees.

Shanghai's dirty air had caught in their throats and given them perpetual colds. In Singapore the air is warm and moist, rich with the oxygen of the island's exhaling trees. Singapore is the safest city in the world, they are told, over and over, by the real estate agent, when they look at apartments, before settling on the villa; by the school counselor, when they first check out the American school; and by Chris's colleague, who takes them all out to dinner with his two daughters, who are Sophie's and Leah's ages.

But black spitting cobras are also endemic to Singapore, which was an island covered in virgin rainforest less than two hundred years ago. At night, in the bedrooms of their colonial villa, the Kriegsteins hear the remains of the jungle, shouting, creaking, arguing with itself. By day, the sounds disappear, aside from the clicking of a gecko in the kitchen and the grumble of thunder outside.

After moving to Singapore, the family quickly falls into the rhythm of American expatriate life like somnambulists, dressing in blue and white uniforms for the American school; playing soccer, basketball, and softball for the American Eagles; swimming in the body-temperature water of the American Club pool. Only Elise remains leery, put off by the city's gleaming surface. English is the national language, but Elise finds the hidden meanings in polite Singaporean speech harder to decode than the broken English in Shanghai. A month after their move, Elise begins working as a science teacher at the American school, grateful to abandon herself to the periodic table, or to explaining the water cycle to sixth graders. It's the only time of day that the foreboding lifts.

In Singapore, Sophie is overjoyed that no one is trying to touch her hair, and Leah is relieved that the boys at school are generally taller than her. True to Chris's promise, the girls quickly acquire a yellow Lab puppy imported from Australia, who waddles up and down the small strip of sidewalk with Sophie and Leah in the mornings. Elise mysteriously christens the dog Robo Cop. The rest of them are so relieved to see Elise enthusiastic about something that they don't question the choice of naming the dog after a cyborg.

⁂

They all undergo small, barely noticeable changes. Their white skin burns and turns darker. Sophie goes from being a tomboy to painting her toenails and hanging out by the American Club pool with her new friends. Their mouths catch fire as they sweat through bowls of fish-head curry. Their consciences sting, a little, now that they have a live-in maid: a smart, beautiful Filipina woman named Myla, who irons their laundry and cooks and then cleans their dishes. But all the other expatriates around them are doing the same thing, so they silently tell one another to relax. Relax.

After the chaos of Shanghai, Singapore feels easy, and they rely on one another less than they did in China. They are lulled into a feeling of security, despite the occasional news story of a python found lurking in a swimming pool, looking like a hose.

August 22, 1996

Singapore

The day Sophie dies the sky is perfectly clear. No hunching clouds, no uneasy breeze. Just a hot, late August afternoon.

Part Four

Sophie and Leah

Singapore, 1996

Before they moved to Singapore, before they moved to Shanghai, before they moved to Madison, back in Atlanta, Leah and Sophie played four square on the porch in front and basketball by the garage out back. They pulled onion grass up from its roots in the yard, stuck it in microwaved water, and tried to sell onion soup on the sidewalk. They invented games with ghost runners and unlimited points, then taught the rules to their babysitter. When the neighborhood kids decided to put on a production of *The Princess Bride*, it was Sophie who got to be the princess because she had blond curls. Leah got cast as the giant.

When Leah misses Sophie now she tries not to think about things like that, things like wanting Sophie's curls so bad. Leah tries to remember safer things, like Atlanta summer nights, nights she stayed awake, with Sophie asleep in the other twin bed. And even though it's been five years since they left Atlanta, Leah can still picture her floral comforter bunched at the foot of the bed; she can still see nine o'clock shadows stalking the purple street outside. But she can't picture Sophie's face on the pillow. Only the memory's noise remains whole: the hum of an old attic fan through the house. The summer heat trying to quiet the hum and the hum keeping Leah awake.

☙

One week after Sophie's funeral in Indiana, Leah boards the first leg of the flight back to Singapore. The flight attendant leads her to an aisle seat. A few minutes later the same woman appears with a blanket, slippers, a kit containing toothpaste, a toothbrush, mouthwash. Two seats away, Chris and Elise are taking their own kits from a different flight attendant, already removing the plastic wrapping from their slippers. Leah accepts the toiletries wordlessly, stuffs them under the seat in front of her.

The plane lifts. A swift jerk in Leah's stomach reminds her of what happens now, of what has happened. The plane is diagonal and she watches the aisle angle irreversibly. She turns on her Discman, finds the songs she has listened to since Sophie's death. She closes her eyes against the cabin's sickly tilt.

Later, the stewardess pushes a cart slowly down the aisle, smiling. Leah picks at her chicken. In the front of the cabin, a movie begins. Leah glances up from buttering her roll to watch. Suddenly the plane is filled with jungle, soaked deep in green light. It reminds Leah of the Botanic Gardens in Singapore, of *Indiana Jones and the Temple of Doom*, of watching HBO with Sophie this summer at Grand Ada's, glassy-eyed. Curly haired. Glassy-eyed.

Curly haired. Leah lays the dinner tray on the seat beside her, unfastens her seat belt. She stumbles to the toilet through slight turbulence, sits on the toilet seat, and sobs until she thinks the German man waiting outside might hear her. She bites her fist to keep from screaming. She looks at the mirror for a long time, then lets the hot water run over her fingers. When she returns to her seat the movie has changed colors from jungle to expensive hotel room. She falls asleep amid heavy beige curtains, late afternoon light.

♔

Three hours later, Leah wakes and holds herself in the rent of remembering. The screen now displays a simple map with a small white airplane moving pixel by pixel across fake blue sky. Leah shudders to see the airplane like that. It is terrible to watch the plane not move.

Snores gather around her like barking dogs. Across the aisle, a man in headphones is laughing out loud in abrupt, three-second peals. Leah glances at her mother. The blue light from the screen falls on her mother's cheek gently, like sun resting on warm brick. Leah's father's back is to her, and she watches it jolt like a kid's ride outside of Kmart. The day that Sophie died, Chris had collapsed on Leah, a seven-foot human skyscraper demolished in a single blow. She had leaned into his weight, like trying to prop up a crumbling cliff.

Five hours pass. Leah reads the in-flight magazine. What to do for twenty-four hours in Seattle; how to stay hydrated midflight. She dreads her family's return to Singapore. She remembers how the other Americans descended on 59 Cairnhill Road the day after Sophie died. The smell of their lilies filled Leah's lungs like water. Trying to sleep now, Leah thinks she can already hear geckos clicking in the storage bins above.

The intercom announces that Tokyo is one hour away, just as day breaks through the greasy airplane windows. Breakfast comes from the same stewardess who gave Leah the blanket. Leah orders cereal, like her father, and her mother asks for an omelet. When the food comes they all smile weakly at one another and rip their cutlery from its plastic wrappers. Her mother holds up a little cream packet.

"Remember how Sophie used to drink these?" She laughs, tipping the unopened packet to her lips. Leah looks away, clenching her fork tightly in her hand. On her left, she can see clouds flecking the cobalt sky outside, which grows hazy as they land.

⚬

Their layover in Tokyo lasts two hours. Leah leaves her parents by the gate and walks through a long, gaunt hallway. She watches an old Chinese woman in a blue *chipao* waiting in line with her husband, gripping his palsied hand tightly. Leah meets five uniformed officers at the security check. The two women have pale hidden faces and slight frames. The three men stand erect, unsmiling; they wave her through silently. The fluorescent light throbs overhead and Leah steps onto the travelator, moves to the beat of the bilingual flight announcements, walks towards the United Airlines terminal.

She remembers the Seoul airport at midnight, where she and Sophie sprinted down empty travelators, when there was no one else but their parents in the giant hallway and the lighting was dim, orange-yellow, economical. Leah on the travelator in Tokyo now walks faster and faster and faster until she is nearly running again, racing no one, no body, no sister, no thing. She slows down after catching looks from a French couple dragging their toddler behind them.

At Gate 73, Leah watches a Japanese family fall apart. The daughter is leaving for San Francisco. The father stands by, looking at his watch. The mother and daughter cling to each other: the teenage girl sobbing, the mother holding her. A little boy quietly plays a handheld video game near the father's feet. Other passengers brush by the family, brandishing their tickets and passports, ending cell phone calls.

⸎

Leah nearly cannot board the last leg of the flight to Singapore. She pauses outside of the plane and touches the surface of it, recoiling at the memory of a tradition that Sophie started on the family's first trip home from Shanghai three summers ago. "Touch the plane for good luck!" Sophie had said, slapping the white metal as if it were her hundredth time. Unthinking, utterly confident: that was what Leah had always envied the most in Sophie, what she had wanted so badly.

Now Leah's mother, waiting behind her, taps Leah on the shoulder, then touches the plane. "Touch the plane for good luck!" she says, and behind them, Leah can hear her father's hollow laugh. Leah takes a large step forward to lose her mother's grip. She feels the hand fall away accusingly. Leah walks onto the plane, holds out her boarding pass to the next smiling stewardess.

Twenty minutes before the plane lands in Singapore, as the movie is ending, Leah closes her eyes and sees Sophie splayed on the ground again, under the frangipani trees.

⸎

It is mid-August, the first soccer practice of the season. Leah and Sophie are with the rest of the high school team on a soccer field in Singapore, midafternoon. Along with a few other promising middleschoolers, Sophie has been asked to join the high school tryouts. The sun beats down on the girls' ponytails. The air is thick with newly cut grass and pig manure. The girls stretch in a circle and then break into pairs to warm up. Leah and Sophie sprint to the end of the field and begin passing the soccer ball they brought from home. The ball comes at Leah fast from the inside of Sophie's cleated foot. Leah kicks the ball back, watches it go wide, sees Sophie sprint after it, performing a smooth turn to reverse direction.

The coach blows his whistle and the girls gather around him again in the center of the field. They tease each other, gossip, suck on plastic water bottles. Sophie stands slightly apart from the others, her foot tapping the top of the ball impatiently. The coach points to the cones set up around the field, orders four laps.

"One whistle means jog, two means sprint," he yells as the girls take off. Leah runs to catch up with Theresa. Sophie falls back to join Ang-mi, a friend her age. Then two long whistles. The coach's faint shout from the other side of the field. "Sprint!"

Leah passes Theresa, Heather, Joon. She nears the first corner of the field alone, then runs past the goal, watches the coach flash through the orange net. She stretches her stride a little, enjoying the pull on her calves. As she nears the second goal post, Leah sees a circle of girls and the coach standing under a cluster of frangipani trees by the sideline. Then Leah sees the rest of the girls behind her breaking away from their laps, running to the sideline. Leah follows at a cautious jog. Under the trees a girl lies on the grass, gasping. Her familiar face foreign with spasms.

"Move Sophie to the shade. Don't worry, Leah, it's just sunstroke, she just—"

Blond hair splayed over thick jungle grass. Sophie's jerking face.

"Get back. Come on, Leah, we need to—"

Sophie.

"She'll be fine, Leah, don't worry."

Under the branches. Sophie.

"Back up, girls, so she can have some room."

Under clotted braches of frangipani sky. In the middle of their whispers, an ambulance wail. Then out of the burning afternoon into a freezing hospital iron white lips no smell Sophie.

Leah's mother. "Sweetie, come here for a second."

⁂

It was a mistake, Leah knows. She was the one who should have died. Leah with her stumbling hesitation, her heavy thinking, her uncertain smile. She was always nearer to death than Sophie, who was not afraid of other people or of living, like Leah was. The worst part: before her death, Leah was sick of Sophie. Her perfection, her lithe body, her effortlessness. Leah wanted her gone and then she was.

When Sophie sank to the ground on the soccer field, most of Leah lay down, too. She had always been a good older sister. Sophie died and Leah followed, assuming that the dark shape in front was Sophie. They had always traveled to foreign places together, relying on each other to navigate Shanghai's alleyways, Phuket's roiling surf, Singapore's tangled vines. Death would be no different.

The silent figure ahead of Leah now looks like Sophie, but she never speaks. Her motions are smooth, methodical. Where Sophie ran, this figure glides. Where Sophie laughed, this figure purses her lips, assumes a haughty, distant look. Leah does not pause to consider whether the figure in front might be her own death, a new sibling. In life, Sophie had always been there to remind Leah of her shortcomings. In death, Sophie's shadowy shape, always just out of reach, reminds Leah that she does not deserve to survive.

⁂

The Singapore airport is empty when the flight from Tokyo arrives with Leah and her parents at two a.m. The three of them go to separate customs officials, who whisk through their documents. They drag their suitcases to the taxi queue. Leah's father gives the taxi driver brief directions; then they all fall silent. Each winces privately at the bougainvillea on the overpasses: too familiar, too tiny a detail to have steeled themselves for.

When they enter their home, a moldy old smell coats the walls. It is the house's smell, nothing unusual for an old colonial bungalow, but it seems to have strengthened in their absence. The odor gets in Leah's clothes even as she unpacks. She removes T-shirts mechanically, taking long steps across the pale rose-colored carpet. She puts all of the shirts in drawers, doesn't fold any of them. She falls asleep sweating, unaccustomed to the tropical climate after four weeks in autumn America, after the cool nights that followed Sophie's funeral.

Leah remembers the weight of her grandmother in the bed beside her in Indiana. Moonlight leaking past faded curtains onto her grandmother's pale wrinkled skin, onto a blue silk nightgown cut for old women. Her grandmother's careful grasp over Leah's horrified clutching one. Words falling from her grandmother's mouth, dropping slowly to Leah like sinking coins. Words that wouldn't fall during daylight, with her grandmother dressed, midwestern emotional restraint keeping her face as tidy as the daily-vacuumed living room.

But in the dark, the words came quiet, slow, with an understanding born of bitter farm winters and of other lives cut short. Words that Leah's great-great-grandmother, Mechthild, would have whispered to her son, Tomas, in Plattdeutsch, which slipped out to Leah that night in Lutheran-American English. The sturdy old bed barely holding both of their pain.

❧

At breakfast the next morning on the veranda, black-and-white shutters drawn up for the day, Myla, the family's maid, comes behind Leah and squeezes her shoulder tightly.

"Leah, I—"

Myla holds a plate of sliced mangoes and papaya. Myla did not leave Singapore with the family after Sophie died. She stayed in the house and threw away the broccoli casseroles when they grew moldy, the lilies when they rotted. Myla grew up in the countryside in the Philippines with nine other sisters. She is twenty-six and beautiful, with an old woman's kind gaze. She has straight black hair that falls near her waist, small hands.

Leah twists in her chair and looks at Myla dumbly, stock still.

"It's really terrible, Leah," Myla says, wiping her eyes with the back of her hand. Leah's mother comes and sits down across from Leah.

"Good morning, ma'am," Myla says, crying, and leaves.

"I forgot how nice it was out here at this time of day," Leah's mother says tremblly, looking over the lawn. Leah nods, looking at her plate. Her father arrives at the table dressed for work.

"Hey," he says gently, and sits down next to Leah's mother, who places two elbows on the glass tabletop and begins to cry, making snuffling, gulping sounds. Leah stares stonily into bougainvillea that pours onto the porch tile.

❧

At tenth grade that day, Leah shows up wearing navy blue pants and a white polo shirt, like everybody else at Singapore American School. The air-conditioning drones in English 10 like a hurricane, and chill bumps rise on her skin. She writes *Sophie* in her notebook and feels grief steal over her like cold winter sunlight. It keeps her apart and she trusts it as though it were a small child leading her through the crowd to a candy shop. At lunchtime, the cafeteria is noisy and Leah orders rice with beef and broccoli, takes it to a seat beside her friend Arna. Arna squeezes Leah's hand and goes back to speaking to the girl on her left about upcoming student council elections.

⁂

Two months pass. Singapore in November looks the same as Singapore in September. It rains every day at four o'clock, and waxy angsana leaves shade the same sections of the sidewalk. When Leah waits for the school bus, the morning air is always tepid. Every sunset begins at seven. In Madison, the days grew shorter with winter's approach. On nights when the sky turned pink, Sophie and Leah stayed awake on Leah's bed, peering out the window, placing bets on snow.

At soccer practice after school, Leah runs hard. Words ring in her head as her cleats pound the ground. Sprint Sophie dead sister done. After an hour, Leah jogs away from the field, back to the school building. She finds a corner of concrete in one of the open-air stairwells. She sits down on the pebble-paved surface, folds herself up, and cries. Dies. Rain falls lightly outside.

Leah walks through the drizzle to food stalls across the street. She watches Indian curry thick with steam brought to smoking men. She passes by a little Chinese girl with Down syndrome squishing ants by the stairs of an apartment complex. She walks around a small pond and yellow petals float by like dead bird feathers, next to trash. She sits down and picks a scab.

Back at the American school, as Leah is closing her locker, she hears heavy steps echo in the hallway. She turns to find David LaSalle from journalism class hurrying towards her, slowing when he sees her looking. Leah puts her books in her backpack and waits.

"Hey," he says. He is tall, red haired. "Where are you headed?"

"Bus."

"Oh yeah? Me too."

They trudge silently for a while, down the stairs to the school's front entrance.

"How's volleyball going?" Leah asks him when they reach the parking lot.

"Awesome," David replies. "We've got some really good freshmen this year, and the team feels really tight. How about soccer?"

"It's okay." They reach Leah's bus and she stops. "This is me."

"Hey, Leah—" David stops too. He jingles change in his pocket. "I was wondering if—"

He looks at her directly and she looks away, turning her attention to a group of primary school kids getting on the bus.

"I was wondering if maybe you wanted to go to dinner or see a movie on Saturday?"

Leah keeps watching the kids, half smiles when one boy hits another with a papier-mâché turkey. *Boys liked me, not you,* Sophie's voice reminds her. *Now you think you can have that too?*

"Leah?"

She looks back at him. "That sounds great," she says finally. "See you soon, David." And gets on the bus. She feels Sophie's narrowed eyes.

⚭

Myla makes adobo for dinner that night. Leah's father is working late, and Leah lights candles while her mother helps Myla bring in dishes from the kitchen. After the prayer, Leah ignores her mother's worried look from across the table and silently begins spooning herself adobo. A Handel CD whines from the living room, interrupted periodically by an invisible gecko's clucks.

"Do you want some bread, Leah?"

"No."

"You know, I saw Mrs. Kedves at Tierney's Gourmet today."

Leah cuts a piece of pork and stares at her plate.

"She said you were doing great work. Do you like that class?"

Leah takes a sip of water and looks at the clock.

"Leah?"

"What?"

"I asked if you were enjoying your acting class."

"Um, I don't know. It's okay."

The gecko clucks again, louder. Myla appears from the kitchen.

"Great adobo, Myla," Leah's mother says.

"Yeah, Myla, this is awesome," Leah echoes faintly.

"Thank you." Myla looks at both of them and hurries back to the kitchen. Leah and her mother don't say anything. The Handel CD starts skipping, one high violin note chirping until Leah goes to the living room and stops the music. She collects her plate and glass when she returns to the table. "I've got a lot of homework," she mutters, clanging her fork and knife against the china to cover up the sound of her mother alone at the table, beginning to weep.

Leah goes upstairs, shuts her bedroom door, and sits down at her desk. She starts English homework and waits for David to call. He doesn't. Angry, Leah tries to remember what it was like when she wasn't alone. She remembers, re-sees herself walking into Sophie's room, Sophie's back to her, Sophie at her desk doing homework. Leah watches herself picking up Sophie's little basketball from the floor and aiming at the basketball goal on the back of Sophie's door. Leah sees Sophie put her pen down, turn around, start playing defense, both of them laughing as they fall over the laundry basket.

Leah looks at another memory after that one, where Leah is passing Sophie in the hallway, shocked to see Sophie's typically messy, ponytailed hair carefully styled. Sophie walks to the door with painted toenails, *Seventeen* magazine, sunglasses.

Leah laughs. "Where are you going?"

Sophie is defensive. "The American Club."

"To do what?"

"Hang out. I don't know. Sit by the pool with Lynn and Gina."

"Well, aren't you Miss Teen USA?"

"It's not like I'm going there to tan or something. We're just going to—"

"Sure. Have fun. Tan well."

Leah watches the back of Sophie's calves down the hallway, a determined exit, then Sophie's black silhouette when she opens the door and white noon glare floods in. How did she know how to do it? When Leah hit puberty they were living in Shanghai and she felt her body change like some foreigner's disease, as the rest of her mostly Asian classmates at the American school remained flat chested and petite. Before she died, Sophie's body hadn't developed but she had begun to do the teenage-girl things that Leah always avoided nervously, or performed sloppily. Hanging out at malls, sitting by the pool. Jealousy rises like bile in Leah's stomach. But how can you be jealous of a dead sister? How dare you? Sophie's voice is low.

Leah shifts uncomfortably now in her seat at the desk, trying to turn away from memories of Sophie, but once they've started, separate recollections blur into a mob of voices, and soon Leah is staring at Sophie's face twisting on the grass again. Little pearls of sweat beading on Sophie's forehead and Sophie's eyes fluttering open, not recognizing Leah at all.

It feels good to cry when the crying starts. Leah moves from her desk to the bed and clutches the covers. Her mother knocks on the door lightly and then lets herself in, sits next to Leah sobbing on the bed. "Cry, Leah," her mother whispers, holding her head. Leah feels her mother's silk shirt against her right cheek, feels her head being lifted into the linen sea of her mother's lap. Her mother's thighs and stomach start to shake, as the borrowed grief flows from her mother's eyes onto Leah's own bare neck. Leah stiffens. Her mother loses herself as she finally finds her own sadness. Leah grows old and stares at the oriental carpet on the floor. Her mother rocks and tumbles against her, sucking in air like she is coming out of the ocean, drenched in it, her sadness slapping against Leah's ankles. Leah wrenches her head from her mother's lap, then silently places her mother's wet, shaking face against a pillow and leaves the room.

❧

"I even grieve for silly girls who cry when their nails break," Mrs. Kedves says from her stool. Mrs. Kedves is the Acting I instructor. She lost her husband in Turkey ten years ago and then lost her baby to a miscarriage a few months after that. Mrs. Kedves wears generous amounts of bright blue eye shadow and holds on to the ends of words like she is sucking on hard candy. Sometimes after class she talks to Leah about death. Today Leah is seated a few feet away from her on a plastic chair, next to a long white table with a pen-scratched surface. Kids' yells from outside rebound quietly in the hallway.

"It's still loss, you know, Leah," Mrs. Kedves continues. "Everyone feels loss, and it's that understanding that brings compassion, that can bring you closer to Him. Mmm." Mrs. Kedves closes her eyes and moans lightly. She shakes her head and soft tangles of dark brown hair swirl around her like a mussed doll. "You must trust in Him, dear. That's all we can do. I am so thankful for that. And for you."

Alarmingly, Mrs. Kedves moves from her stool to wrap her arms around Leah. "You have talent. And you can use that sadness. Put your grief in your characters. Trust me. He wants things like that to happen."

Leah lays her head on the table. She can hear hollow thuds coming from its insides like construction work. She pictures Sophie on the trampoline at their uncle's house in Arkansas this past summer, bouncing up and down.

"Who do you like?" Leah asks Sophie, mouthing the words to the long, empty table.

Kyle, maybe, Sophie says to her, as Leah watches Sophie's yellow hair flying across her eyes.

"Would you go out with him?" Leah mouths to the table. Maybe, she hears, along with the hammering. Kyle was the most popular freshman in Leah's high school. Of course Sophie would like him. Of course he would like Sophie. That day, Leah had told Sophie about Lane, the brother of Sophie's best friend in Atlanta. "Why didn't you tell me earlier?" Sophie had asked, a funny hurt look on her face. An honest sisterly demand. Leah didn't know why not. She and Sophie had never really confided in each other. They made fun of their mother's stir-fry and ballroom danced with each other in one of Shanghai's city squares, surrounded by hundreds of Chinese couples. They had hardly argued, unless you counted a few loose elbows thrown during one-on-one basketball. They were too close to talk like that. It would be like trying to correct a mirror's reflection.

But now we're even closer, the new Sophie says to Leah, or is it Leah saying it to Sophie? Sophie and Leah. Sophie-Leah. Sophea. Neither here nor there. Leah's body is in Singapore and Sophie is buried in Indiana but in Leah's mind the two of them flit all over the world, everywhere they've ever lived: Philadelphia, Atlanta, London, Madison, Shanghai, Singapore.

Mrs. Kedves stops talking and begins to rub Leah's back in circles when the crying starts. "There, there," Mrs. Kedves says. "There, there. I know. I know just how you feel."

⚜

As Christmas approaches, decorations appear in the city's main shopping districts. David and Leah walk hand in hand by Santa's bulls peeking out from potted palms. "Rush in for a Bullish Christmas!" David reads out loud, and laughs.

"What do you miss the most about Christmas in the States?" Leah asks him.

"The snow in Chicago," he says, tightening his grip around her sweaty palm. "What about you?"

She stares at the sidewalk and forces her tone to remain even. "Probably family, like my grandparents. I used to love being in Indiana or Mississippi for Christmas."

Leah wants to spit as they walk past a hotel and hear carols pouring out of the door. She bites her lip hard instead. Wealthy Singaporeans pour past them with wrapped presents, and a group of Indian migrant workers waits at a bus stop with pink plastic bags. David takes out a bus schedule and points to the 88 bus.

"Awesome, it's a double decker," she says, grabbing his hand, running with him.

"Slow down, soccer girl," he laughs. They get on the bus and he kisses her forehead lightly. Leah looks for a long time at their reflection in the bus window. David, a foot taller than her, looks straight ahead in a rust-colored button-down shirt, tapping his fingers on Leah's knee. Leah wears a blue paisley blouse she bought in Little India. When she starts to see Sophie's face in the reflection, Leah stops herself, turns to David, and starts talking loudly about music.

⚘

At St. George's Anglican Church the next day, Leah and her family stay only for the announcements and the beginning of the first hymn. After the second verse, Leah hears ragged breathing to her right and sees her mother's white knuckles pressed against the pew in front of them, her head bowed in defeat. Leah's father looks at Leah across her mother's back.

"Let's go," he mouths, and they hobble out of the pew. It is only eight thirty but already sweltering. Leah's sandals catch pebbles from the parking lot. She slides into the car, disgusted.

"Can you turn the radio on?" Leah asks her father.

"I just need quiet right now, Leah," her mother says.

"Where are we going, guys?" her father asks.

"Maybe we could do the Botanic Gardens all together," her mother says, drying her eyes with lipstick-stained Kleenex.

"I'd rather just go home, but you guys should do that, before it rains," says Leah, looking at the thick clouds sitting on skyscrapers.

"Leah, can't you..." Leah's mother trails off.

"What?"

"I just wish we could still do things together, as a family."

You call this a family? Leah thinks, but says nothing, and her father drives home.

⚘

That night Leah sneaks out to go for a walk in the Botanic Gardens, across the street. She has to climb the fence, and she scrapes her shin on the way down. Crickets groan on either side of her. The night air is heavy, the smell sour and musky. Leah walks fast. She stalks up the hill past the empty tourist center, and around the lake. The birds that chatter by day are silent. Through the fence she can see small cars on the highway. She removes her shoes for the Chinese reflexology path. Before she leaves the gardens she runs around the lake four times, each time faster, ready to fall.

Catch me! Sophie screams. Leah is too old for manhunt, but she pretends to like the game for Sophie's sake; she runs for her life. She crawls back into bed with dirt on her knees.

⚘

Leah is grateful the next night at dinner when for once her parents talk animatedly to each other, their chopsticks dripping with strands of Filipino noodles. She basks in their back-and-forth about work, old friends from Atlanta, plans for Christmas. She even volunteers something about David when they ask.

Later, Leah and Myla laugh in the kitchen about François, the French man with gray teeth whom Myla has begun dating. They chew on soft, fresh, sugary buns from the Chinese market. It is only when she plays her favorite Indigo Girls album as she is about to sleep that Leah remembers Sophie's face. Not under the trees now but in the soft folds of a casket. Leah sees her family at the undertaker's two days before Sophie's funeral. The undertaker chewing gum silently, out of respect. Going from Sophie's face twisting on a yellow silk pillow, to her face on a pale blue puckered cushion, then white linen. Sophie's head flailing, knocking against dark oak corners.

❧

"You don't love me anymore," David says to Leah, two weeks later, from her bed.

They are in Leah's room studying for a history exam.

"You only care about your sister. You're so wrapped up in your fucking grief."

Leah carefully kneels to the floor, as if she means to scrub a stain out of it.

"I love you so much," she hears, as she carefully closes her eyes, waits for it to come. There. The soccer field glows neon green. Then Leah is shouting, screaming on the floor, kicking, and there is Sophie jerking too now, grabbing at bits of grass, spit running, the sun beating, tearing at the carpet, the soccer girls hovering, Leah's parents coming into the room, David trying to explain what happened, Sophie lifted and taken by six arms to the ambulance, Leah left writhing on the bedroom floor, alone.

❧

"How are you feeling about Christmas coming, Sophie?" At his error, the British therapist colors and checks his notepad. "Leah—I'm sorry. Are you anticipating—"

Leah looks out of the window. A week has passed since David was in her room calling for her parents to come, pointing at Leah on the floor, Leah's mother shaking her—"Leah, Leah, Leah"—as Leah shook.

In the therapist's office now, across from her, Leah's mother sighs loudly and her father growls. "Leah." She ignores them and replays a memory with Sophie and her father in Indiana, walking through the cornfields at her grandparents' farm.

Sophie had asked, "How does an airplane work, Dad?" Leah's father, the former engineering student, had explained excitedly. Leah had walked behind the two of them, stroking the cornstalks, feeling the soggy ground beneath, watching dark liquid dribble up onto her sneakers with each step. She hated the practical questions Sophie loved to sort out, hated the wooden brain puzzlers Sophie adored, and especially hated how much her father admired these things in Sophie.

Leah had run up to join the two of them, interrupting her father's explanation, shouting her own question: "If you guys could be anywhere in the world right now, where would you be?"

"Leah!" Sophie had exclaimed, exasperated.

"Leah! Sophie!" Leah mouths to herself, feeling her mother's worried look on her, her father's frustration, the counselor's impatient smile, the edge in Sophie's voice.

⁂

The day before Christmas vacation, Leah performs in Mrs. Kedves's winter play. The audience in the high school theater is packed tightly, but when she looks out, all Leah can see is white light. In the last scene, she moves towards the slain Romeo and carefully steps across the white line of the soccer field onto the masking-taped *X* marked for Juliet's breakdown. Leah begins to sob. She kneels over the body. She bites back the scream so the next actor's line will not be interrupted. The audience claps loudly at the end, and Leah accepts flower bouquets.

Sophie narrows her eyes. You're using me.

It's not like that, Leah insists. I miss you. I'm nothing without you.

Then why are you smiling?

⚛

The following day, Leah's family boards the plane to Koh Samui, where the three will spend the Christmas holidays. Each of them touches the outside of the plane, and they silently take their seats. Leah speaks first.

"Hey, look, Mom, the guy that you love is in one of the movies they're showing."

"Really?"

"Yeah, look at your magazine. Dad, can we switch seats so I can show Mom?"

"No way, I want to see this guy too."

"Dad! Seriously, can we switch—" The three of them have become adept at playing merry, although they often collapse in exhaustion, midjoke, and can't finish the act.

"Slippers or socks?" Leah's father pokes her and points at the waiting stewardess.

"Slippers, please."

❧

Two hours later, when her parents are asleep, Leah remembers Sophie's head on her shoulders during flights back home. It always fell in the worst places, the round shape somehow pointy and hurting Leah's shoulder. Leah sits up and adjusts the blanket. She lies back and remembers those flights before. She would tell Sophie her leg had fallen asleep, prompting Sophie to cackle maniacally and start kicking Leah's dead leg.

"Ow! Stop it, Sophie, I'm serious." Both of them dissolving into hysterics that would make whatever couple was in front of them turn around.

When they went camping for the first time, Sophie and Leah left the site every five minutes to pee in the woods. "Isn't it fun to do it out here?" Sophie would ask, crouched over pine straw as their mother had demonstrated, Leah squatting under a maple tree nearby.

"Yeah, it's great, but I can't go anymore."

"Just think about waterfalls," Sophie had suggested.

Warm tears on her cheek, on her neck. Through the plane window, the goddamn stars.

❧

"That's when I cry about Sophie the most, I guess," Leah's father says to Leah, midflight. He whispers, so as not to wake up Leah's mother, sleeping in the seat beside him. Throughout the cabin, as dark as forest, thin beams of light pool onto the pages of sleepless passengers' novels. Stewardesses float down the aisles noiselessly like restless spirits.

"There's something about being alone in the plane on a business trip by myself. When it's dark and I have a window seat." He sighs misshapenly and pats Leah's hand. Leah twists her mouth. "What about you? Are there any times like that for you?"

Leah looks up at the movie screen. It is a slapstick comedy set in rural America, midwinter. Bill Murray screams silently at another actor and lunges at him with a snow shovel. "Leah?"

"Oh. Um. Well—no, I don't know. No, not really. No specific times that I can think of right now, anyways." She can feel herself retreating, taking Sophie's hand, going underwater where the sisters sit together, silently. Her father's voice bounces off the water's surface above.

"I understand," he says, hurt.

She forces a yawn. "I'm going to try and get some sleep, Dad."

"Sounds good. Good night, Leah."

"Good night."

Through half-closed eyes, Leah watches her father pull his seat back and take her mother's hand. They lie there together, sweetly shrouded. After a few minutes, he begins snoring.

Leah turns to her side and turns on her Discman. She pulls the blanket over her head and closes her eyes. An hour later, she is still awake. If she could only... Leah shifts uncomfortably in her seat and tries to find the best sleeping position. She is nearly asleep, clutching her pillow, beginning to dream, when a noise rips the sleep. An airplane noise, nothing more than a rattle somewhere in the bags overhead, but to Leah it sounds like broken machinery inside.

Sophie? The shadow of a nod, but no human head lays itself on her shoulder; there is no even breathing from the other bed. Only the noise, which Leah stiffens against like a wounded animal, half-alive, tensing in the jungle for the tiger's return. What is a paw step and what is a birdcall? And what is only the echo of the mauling in your ears?

I'll Be Home for Christmas

Koh Samui, Thailand, December 1996

Sophie never would have gone for it. Thailand? For Christmas? *It's way too hot there,* she would have protested, and would have kept on protesting until she got her way. She was a traditionalist: she wanted burgers on the Fourth of July and a chill in the air on Christmas Eve. That's one reason we wound up here on Koh Samui on December 21: to get as far away from her as possible.

Of course, as soon as our plane touched down, despite the bamboo flute playing in the airport arrivals lounge, and the rambutan welcome drink when we showed up at the Four Seasons, it was obvious that she was just as present—by which I mean painfully absent—as she had been in Singapore, if not more so. I could see it in the slouch in Leah's shoulders, the forced smile on Chris's face, the tightness in my own voice.

You could nod smugly and say, "Of course—what did you expect? That running away to a tropical paradise would solve everything?"

And to that I would say: it was worth a shot. After eight moves in eighteen years of marriage, Chris and I had gotten pretty good at getting out of Dodge when the going got tough. But it had never been this tough.

In the breezy, rattan-flavored lobby of the Four Seasons, I finished my welcome drink and downed another, didn't say a thing when Leah went for the non-kids cocktail. Cheers. You lose your sister at fifteen, you're automatically older than twenty-one, in my book. Plus, I didn't have the energy to oppose her. If a little rum helped her lose that look of horror, even for five minutes, it was worth it.

The three of us drifted down to the pool area, as porters in glimmering Thai dress spirited away the luggage. I gave them a pained *I'm sorry it's so heavy* smile, as Chris gave them a tip.

I wondered how we appeared to the other vacationers lounging on deck chairs beside the infinity pool, reading various European issues of *Vogue*. They regarded us furtively behind sunglasses and large straw hats. *Americans,* they probably thought, taking in Chris's blinding white sneakers. *Spoiled single child,* they might have decided next, regarding Leah's black mood. And me? *Professional expat wife,* logging my French manicure, the dark tan I'd gotten walking around the American school track with Jeanette Lawless (another southerner, a middle school math teacher, and my latest best girlfriend), as I tried to keep an eye on Leah at soccer practice, trying to look like I was absorbed in what Jeanette was telling me about her son's ADHD.

Since losing Sophie four months ago, I'd experienced an urge that I hadn't felt since Leah was a newborn: to keep my eldest close. It was driving Leah crazy, I could tell. Even now, as she cleared her throat and told us that she was going on a walk and drifted off, her lanky frame far too lanky these days, I wanted to call her back, rock her to sleep, scream that she couldn't leave us now too. As anyone who's had a teenager knows, that was the one thing I wasn't supposed to do.

Yet in between impulses to suffocate Leah and to burrow into Chris like a baby marsupial, I also badly wanted to do the opposite: I wanted to run away from both of them.

Specifically, with Bernard Pinker. I know, I know, a stupid name. And a horribly stupid idea: How on earth could anyone even consider nursing a crush after losing their daughter? In many ways, Chris and I had grown kinder and more tender to each other in the months since Sophie's death than we had in years. And yet. Bernard Pinker was the only reason I wanted to get up in the morning. I'd met him at the new faculty orientation when I'd begun teaching at the American school. He'd led an afternoon session on stress management. Afterwards, I had stuck around the classroom to introduce myself as the others filed out. So much moving had taught me to sense, within about thirty seconds, who I did and didn't like, which strangers I would or wouldn't be friends with. I didn't waste time talking to those I didn't like right away, and I made sure I got to know the ones I felt compelled by. Mama would have died of shame to hear me say such an unchristian thing. Then again, her own mother had sworn by rules that were even worse: don't trust people with green eyes, for example, or avoid lending things to people with small ears. After Sophie's death, my own screening criteria had become more extreme, and a lot of my old friends no longer passed. Anyone who said it had been Sophie's "time to go," for example, was immediately out.

Everyone at the Singapore American School was surprised that I hadn't quit my teaching job after returning to Singapore from Sophie's funeral in the States. The high school principal tried to talk me out of coming back. But what was I going to do at home all day? Start a mah-jongg club? Harmonize with the clucking geckos? Build a Buddhist shrine to Sophie with her soccer cleats and favorite Redwall books? Develop a full-blown alcohol and drug addiction? No, thanks. I was back in school a week after we came back from the States, same as Leah.

Bernard was a high school counselor (not Leah's, thank God), and the only colleague who didn't duck his head when he saw me in the teacher's lounge, or tell me that Sophie was an angel. Bernard was a British atheist who believed only in Lacan. Bernard was thin and frail, as though he'd had a childhood illness (he hadn't). Bernard loved art-house movies. Bernard was also spending Christmas in Koh Samui, staying at the same hotel with his ratty wife, Rebecca, who worked for BP, or British Pollution, as Bernard called it.

Chris and I had already contemplated spending Christmas in Koh Samui, long before I overheard Bernard telling Dan Fawcett, the chemistry teacher, about his and Rebecca's plans. But I must admit that I began petitioning for the Four Seasons in earnest after learning that Bernard and company would be staying there too. Chris held out for a safari in Tanzania for a few weeks, then gave in. Leah didn't care where we went, she informed us icily, staring out the living room window, as though willing us to disappear.

I hadn't yet divulged my thing for Bernard to Jeanette. But I knew what she would say. It was laughingly obvious, wasn't it? I was using Bernard as an escape from my grief, just as we had fled to a Thai island to try to shake Singapore's sadness. But the difference with Bernard was that it worked. Not that I didn't feel sad about Sophie in his presence. But I didn't have to fight it.

We'd started having lunch together sometimes, since we had the same hour free on Tuesdays and Thursdays. One of those first lunches, when my crush was still a dim, nascent affection, I'd burst into tears out of nowhere. The cafeteria was serving *roti canai*, a dish that Sophie had hated. A smile came to my lips, imagining Sophie's exaggerated grimace at the fried pita and curry, and then the smile froze as I remembered that Sophie was no longer around to hate *roti canai*. It didn't make sense—it wasn't as though it had been her favorite food, a dish that prompted a bittersweet memory of her enjoying it at a restaurant—the pain stemmed from the fact that I had forgotten, for a second, that she was gone.

I numbly paid for my *kway teow* and walked straight through the cafeteria doors, instead of taking a left into the teachers' lounge. I headed downstairs, holding my tray, nodding to the kids who yelled "Hey, Mrs. Kriegstein!" I walked to the bleachers bordering the soccer field, put down my lunch tray, and sobbed.

Bernard had followed me. He quietly sat beside me on the metal bleachers. He didn't tell me about his mother's death or his father's cancer; he didn't tell me that Sophie had lived a full life, or describe her smile to me as though I hadn't seen it before. He just sat there. Eventually, when I'd stopped crying, I told him about the *roti canai*, and he gave my hand a squeeze, and I gave a tiny squeeze back, and then we let go and stood up and walked around the soccer field where Sophie had collapsed.

He was just a good friend. A good friend I put on makeup for, a good friend whose presence made my heart race when he gave me a wave across the school parking lot. A good friend I imagined at night, lying next to Chris.

⸎

I had set my alarm for six, for a seven a.m. tee time. I didn't have anyone to play with—Elise hated golf—but I didn't care. I'd never been as good at golf as the other sports I played in high school and college—basketball and baseball—and so I always looked forward to nine holes alone, without anyone to witness my mistakes.

The hotel breakfast area was an open-air affair, covered with a traditional Thai thatched roof. It was practically empty, just a couple of cute yoga moms who were getting in their mango shakes and snake fruit before classes on the veranda overlooking the bay. I could hear from their broad accents that they were Americans (midwesterners, if I had to bet) so I said good morning to them, and they smiled back cheerfully, with that extra kindness you grant a compatriot in a foreign country.

They hunched together as I walked to my table, and I overheard them negatively comparing their husbands' physiques to my own. I smiled to myself and stood a little taller. I considered myself lucky: as my colleagues' and college roommates' bellies had ballooned, I had stayed slim—thanks to my genes and my daily twenty-minute workouts, which I stuck to regardless of where I was: Moscow, Abu Dhabi, Buenos Aires. The only day I had missed for the last ten years had been the morning after Sophie died, when I could barely have told you my own name. But the following morning I was back at it. From the look Elise gave me, when she saw me doing push-ups in the bedroom, I could tell she considered it callous, crude. She didn't understand that I had to hold on to something. She and Leah had the luxury of falling apart. I, for all of our sakes, did not.

Both Elise and I had aged well: people told us all the time that we looked like we were in our thirties, when we were both in our early forties. Nobody had said that to us in the last four months, of course: you don't comment on how fresh the bereaved look. Elise looked different, I thought, although it wasn't what you'd expect: she didn't have baggy eyes and hadn't gained or lost weight. If anything she seemed more vigilant, more vivacious, although it had a dangerous edge to it, in my mind. The way her eyes shone looked unhinged. And she was hardly sleeping. She came to bed after me and was often up before I woke. I felt guilty about how well rested I was, by contrast. How could a PowerPoint presentation I'd been assigned at the annual board meeting last year have made me lose more sleep than my younger daughter's death?

I had to wait on a Japanese couple to tee off, and then it was just me and the smell of freshly cut grass. It was a gorgeous course. Koh Samui gets insufferably hot in the afternoon, but right now the temperature was perfect. Below, to my left, the sea sparkled like Crest toothpaste, and, to the right of the driving range, lime-green rice paddies glowed.

I missed Sophie. Out here, alone, it was a pure missing, much different than the convoluted sadness and anger I felt when I was with Leah and Elise. I knew that wasn't right, that I should be spending more time with those two now than I ever had, that Sophie's sudden departure should make me appreciate them more. It did, in some ways. But I had lost my buddy. I'd never explicitly wanted a son, unlike some of my guy friends, but I admit that I had been pleased and proud when it turned out that Sophie had an affinity for math and science, that she excelled in sports, that she was desperate to know how everything worked. What made a car engine run? What made an airplane lift off the runway? One of my favorite memories with her was buying a physics kit in Atlanta—she couldn't have been older than nine—and wiring up a lightbulb, watching her excitement when we finally got the circuits correct.

Leah and Elise didn't care about that kind of thing. It wasn't their fault. But I felt increasingly unsure of myself around them, without Sophie's steady camaraderie: outnumbered and insufficient. I was working longer hours now, disappearing into the office. It was a slippery slope, I knew. That's partly what this trip was for: getting back together, spending time with one another. And here I was on the golf course, alone. Nice one, Chris. I tried to call Sophie to mind, to think of something she would have said, how she might have teased me.

"Aw, come on, Dad, lighten up!" But it was just me, saying it in her voice to myself, and it didn't even sound like her.

Then, as I was practicing my swing, the rare thing happened: a fresh memory surfaced. One nightmarish consequence of Sophie's death was how quickly memories of her had become stale: how her smile, or the image of her in a softball uniform, became as familiar and meaningless as the picture of my long-deceased great-grandmother, which I'd passed every day in the hallway as a child.

But this memory of Sophie hadn't occurred to me since it had happened, three years ago, in North Carolina. All of Elise's family were up at Ada's mountain house. The girls had said they wanted to come along with Elise's brothers and me to play golf. I'd said no at first, then given in: I was never as tough as Elise when it came to setting rules. I'd even let Sophie drive the cart, after giving her careful instructions. On the ninth hole, she had suddenly gunned the engine when we were in reverse, and before I could say a word, we were headed for the pond as fast as a golf cart can go. I managed to lean over and slam the brakes, and we came to a shuddering halt on the seventh hole, as the golf clubs clattered out of the back and scattered on the grass. Leah was laughing her head off in the backseat. Sophie looked up at me, pale and wide-eyed. I rarely saw her unsure of herself. I think she was surprised when I wrapped her in a big hug instead of scolding her. When we got back to the house, she was already bragging about it, claiming she'd meant to do it, which Leah fiercely contested. But here, in Koh Samui, on the third hole, I suddenly felt touched again, remembering that look of panicked vulnerability, her stark need, in that second, for me, and my own relief, knowing what I could do for her, and doing it. All gone now.

"Sir? You going now?" A Thai caddy honked the golf cart horn behind me. I'd been standing next to the ball for some minutes, and a group of Italians were waiting impatiently. I hit horribly, as I always do when strangers are watching, and got on my cart to chase the ball down. I was relieved to feel tears in the back of my eyes.

⁂

I lay just inches from Bernard, my body tingling. We were discussing the weather in England, of all things. A topic fit for two Austen characters chatting chastely in the parlor. It was our second day in Koh Samui, and circumstances had conspired such that he and I were alone together on the beach. Rebecca the Rat was getting a mud massage. Leah was off on one of her punishing morning runs. Chris was golfing. I was sprawled out on one of the hotel's generous terrycloth beach towels, abandoned by my family members, feeling like a woman in one of those Dove Bar ads, on the cusp of indulgence: *Go on, you deserve it.* The fact that I had not invented an excuse to seek out Bernard, that I had simply been on the beach by myself, sulking, when he'd shown up, seemed to exempt me from any ill doing. He was just keeping me company, and we were talking about the weather, for God's sake. How much more G-rated can you get? But the feverish feeling I had, lying next to his towel, was not harmless at all.

"Sleety and slushy," he was saying.

"I remember that," I said. "But I always felt that the Brits did Christmas quite tastefully." I never said things like "quite tastefully" to anyone else. I hated how chameleonlike I'd become, how I immediately took on a drawl with Jeanette, spoke clipped Singlish with our gardener and faux British now with Bernard. It was subconscious, which made it all the more impossible to avoid. Where had my own voice gone? The only voice I had managed to hold on to, through all our moves, was my singing voice, but when did I sing? In the car, on walks alone in Singapore's Botanic Gardens, when there was no one in sight. It had been suggested, when I was a girl, and even later, during the Jericho! years in college, that I could have made a career out of my clear soprano. That's what Mama had wanted more than anything, I knew. She had always been pleased with Ivy's singing success, but equally frightened of it, too, like we all were. I suppose she trusted that I would remain just as well behaved and boring were I to rocket to stardom as I had been in the church choir, a thought I'd always found incredibly depressing, largely because it was probably true. Of course I had envied Ivy her years of semi-fame, but what did she have to show for it now? Three CDs, the occasional fan letter, the surfacing memory, in a silent kitchen in Mississippi, of crowds shouting her name. These days, Ivy mostly sang backup vocals for car commercials and country demos. Singing had always been my greatest talent, the thing I loved most, and that's why I had decided, ultimately, to keep it to myself. I never wanted it tarnished by failure or near success.

Bernard was nodding: as always, with him, my inner monologue had spilled out.

"Sing something," he suggested.

"No, no." I was already beginning to blush.

"Please?"

"Another time."

"I'm not going to let you forget that."

This partial promise of another meeting, where something intimate would be revealed, seemed to simultaneously terrify and calm both of us, and we fell silent.

I knew we should move to the shade, what with skin cancer and the hole in the ozone layer, but I didn't want to. In Singapore, the unrelenting tropical glare felt like a hindrance, another foreign obstacle; but here, in Koh Samui, with nothing to do but bask in it, no groceries to haul across the parking lot, no soccer games to watch, it felt good to burn a little.

"A hot Christmas reminds me of home," I told Bernard, returning to safer ground. "Not hot like this, but I can remember a couple of Christmases in Mississippi where we didn't even need to wear jackets outside. And some years we would go down to my grandmother's for Christmas, in Florida. So in that sense, Koh Samui feels just about right."

"I'm writing a poem about the bizarre feeling of Christmas here, the disjuncture," Bernard said. "The sound of carols interrupted by parrots, sand castles instead of snowmen…"

I didn't like it when Bernard talked about his poetry. It sounded desperate to me. I preferred him as a startlingly articulate guidance counselor with a formidable vocabulary, not an amateur bard. This past semester, he had even taught a creative writing class after school, which Leah had made fun of at dinner once.

"He writes poems, too, along with the students, and reads them out loud, can you imagine?" Leah had gasped. "David told me that one was about Bernard's mother, and how she once caught him—"

"That's enough," I'd said. I had secretly been relieved that Leah had shunned the class; I harbored a terror that he might fall in love with my younger version. But Leah hated any kind of creative writing: she liked facts. On Sunday mornings, she and Chris devoured the *Herald Tribune* and then debated the latest current events. My own views were dismissed as sentimental.

I just wanted to touch him. It was torture to be freed from the school grounds, to spend time together on what was arguably one of the world's most romantic islands, and to remain politely platonic. As if to reinforce this fact, Rebecca the Rat bounded up to us, all ribs and bad teeth.

"Elise, what a lovely surprise!" she said, balancing an enormous plate of fish and chips. She spread her blanket next to mine and chattered on about her fabulous massage. "I *must* give you the name of the masseuse," she gushed, and offered us fries. She seemed utterly unthreatened by my presence, which I found insulting.

Ten minutes later, Chris and Leah showed up. Chris shook hands with Bernard in a stiff, businesslike manner, and then talked rising commodity prices with Rebecca before pointing down the beach, where he and Leah had laid their towels. "We're going to jump in," he said. Leah hadn't even come over to us; she was already in the water, bodysurfing. I had a sudden urge to be with them, with her. I was grateful for it.

"I'll leave you two alone," I said. "I need to cool off." *Cool off?* As soon as I said it, I kicked myself inwardly. Why was I talking like I was on *Baywatch*?

"See you later," Bernard said.

"We should all do dinner one of these nights," Rebecca suggested, mercifully, so I didn't have to.

"Sounds great. I'll check in with those two and give you guys a call."

Bernard gave me a smile and a wave, one that felt so private and so close that I walked away wrapped in it, dazed. It wasn't until I laid my towel next to Leah's and Chris's that it hit me, like a kick in the stomach: how badly I wanted Sophie's hand now, how much I still expected her to be here, to run with me into the waves, to laugh at their cold slap.

☙

I hadn't always minded losing basketball games, back at Chariton High and UGA. If we were better than the other team, sure, losing was embarrassing. If it was a close game and we couldn't sink enough shots in the last five minutes, I'd be pissed along with everyone else. But a game where the other team was obviously better was a different story: I wasn't one of those guys who came in the locker room afterwards and started kicking things. I almost liked those clear-cut losses, because the outcome was assured from the beginning. Not that I didn't try. I ran as hard as anyone out there: it wasn't in my German genes to slack off. But to humbly accept your fate at the buzzer, your inevitable failure: I didn't mind it.

I felt something akin to that now with Bernard Pinker. Of course, on the face of it, most would agree I was the superior male specimen. More attractive, taller, in better shape, without Bernard's nervous tic of playing the piano on the table when he got agitated. But that is also to say: I lacked Bernard's adorable eccentricities, or at least any eccentricities that were easily recognizable. Nobody knew that I often shampooed twice in the shower, for example. But even that habit wasn't fascinating; it was just silly and wasteful. I always felt like showers went by too fast. I didn't want to start using conditioner—too feminine—but I felt like I deserved a long shower. Standing under hot water doing nothing felt like wasting time, hence the double shampoo. Every now and then Elise would point it out, on the rare occasions we showered together. I always pretended I'd forgotten that I'd shampooed already.

But I did not have a British accent; I did not have one thousand Monty Python scenes at the ready, to reenact; and I was not the opposite of myself. It was painfully obvious to me that Elise was attracted to Bernard, in large part because he represented everything I was not. On a rational level, I didn't mind: I could even sympathize. After eighteen years of marriage, you start to gravitate towards something different: in my case, it seemed to be effusive Latin types. The furthest

I'd gone was not far at all: I maintained a strict no-sex policy, which did not preclude taking attractive women to my hotel room on business trips and driving them crazy by pouring wine and talking, and talking—kissing at the end, maybe, a little bit of fumbling around on the bed, but no penetration. Most guys couldn't have managed it, but I've always enjoyed the triumph of discipline over bodily needs; it's what made me keep running sprints in practices, when the other guys were bent over double. And there was nothing keeping me from satisfying myself once the women had left the room.

And so, with Bernard, I'd decided to just let it happen. I saw it as a foregone conclusion, and, I'll admit, it was a good excuse for me to tune out even more. Elise was the one who had insisted we needed this vacation together, the three of us, so if she wanted to spend it drooling over some balding community-theater type, more power to her. It took her off my hands.

Yet even thinking such a thing felt cruel, and lazy, something I've never been. I could tell that Elise was waiting for me to intervene, as she chatted about Bernard, getting dressed for dinner; as she informed me that the two of them were going for a walk; and later, as she filled me in on the hilarious things Bernard had said on the walk. But I didn't have the fight in me. I could see her slipping away, and I wished her bon voyage.

Then came Christmas Eve, the night we all had dinner together at the hotel.

Halfway through the meal, we were all fairly tipsy. Rebecca left soon afterwards, to do something quintessentially boring and British, like watch the Vienna Boys Choir sing "Silent Night" in her hotel room. Leah was drinking wine like it was Gatorade, while Bernard and Elise were giggling over something the Spanish teacher had said to the principal at the faculty Christmas party, leaving me responsible for refilling Leah's water and making secret signs to the waiter to skip my daughter's wineglass. Then Leah got up from the table, swaying a little, and told us she was going to bed.

"I don't want to catch Santa Claus in the act," she said. "If that happens you don't get any presents." It sounded like a veiled accusation, but we all laughed obediently.

She wasn't going to bed, I could tell. If Elise noticed, she didn't say anything.

"You think she's all right?" I asked Elise about fifteen minutes later.

"I don't know, honey," Elise said. "I hope so."

"Chris." Bernard leaned in, his lips all ruddy and purple from the Malbec, like he'd been making out with a packet of grape Skittles. "I would give her some space. Not that I have a teenager, but from what my students tell me…I think kids this age know what's good for them more than we give them credit for."

Elise nodded emphatically. "Cheers," she said. "To giving them credit." She lifted her glass.

Give me a break. I pulled back my chair. "Well, you two can stay here, but I'm going to check on her," I said, ignoring their hovering glasses. As I walked away, I heard the crystal clink. For some reason, I took my wineglass with me and crossed the lobby as though it were my living room. Up on the fifth floor, I removed my keycard and opened the door. We were in a suite, but Leah had her own room. I tapped on her door.

"Leah?" Nothing. I opened it hesitantly. I'd never been an intrusive parent, and I didn't like reversing that precedent now, but then again, I wasn't going to ignore my niggling nervousness. I flipped on the switch. As I had suspected, the bed was empty. No note, of course.

I pondered my options. I didn't feel like enlisting Bernard's help or putting up with his and Elise's conspiratorial smirks. I would do a quick search myself, I decided. Where would I go if I was her age? Was she at one of the other bars? Had she met a boy? The last thing I wanted to do was find my daughter making out with some pimply Belgian teenager behind tropical ferns.

I put my wineglass down, changed into sneakers, and began the search. A quick half-hour sweep of the hotel grounds revealed nothing. She wasn't by the pool, the bar, or the garden that stretched to the end of the cliff, overlooking the bay. I checked my watch. Ten thirty. Maybe she was in the hot tub, I thought. They had separate spa areas for men and women in the locker rooms of the gym. Maybe she had gone there to relax. But how was I going to check? Ask a female hotel staff person to run in? I decided I would figure it out once I was down there.

And that's where I found her. Not in the locker room, but in the gym itself, a possibility that had never occurred to me. She was on the treadmill, running fast, on a steep incline. I walked over and pressed the emergency stop button. She stumbled a little as the treadmill suddenly slowed, and she whirled around. I had never seen such a raw wreck of feeling on a person's face. Ever since Sophie died, aside from the occasional panic attack or violent outburst in therapy, which I had always let Elise or the therapist handle. Leah had remained removed, distant, numb. Right now she looked humiliated, furious, and caught. Her face, which should have been red from the exercise, looked frighteningly pale, like she was about to pass out.

"Just thought I'd get in a run, so I could sleep better," she said between gasps of air, trying to sound casual.

Elise had mentioned Leah's overexercising to me, but I'd always dismissed it. I'd actually taken pride in the idea that Leah was just as committed to being in shape for her soccer season as I'd always been for basketball. But this was something different. I steered her to one of the weight machine benches and sat her down. She was shaking. I saw, for the first time, in the garish light of the gym, how skinny she'd grown in the last few months. I went to the cooler and got her a cup of water. She downed it and I retrieved another one. I wished it was that simple, that I could just keep bringing her cups of water until she was hydrated, until she was no longer hurting.

"Why don't we take a stroll?" I finally suggested, once her breath had evened out. It sounded corny, even to me. But she nodded. We skirted the restaurant and walked down the path to the bay, lit now by flaming torches. There were honeymooners and swooning gay couples; I hoped it didn't look like Leah was my underage girlfriend. I glanced at her. Her face was, once again, set, stony, numb: all evidence of the molten emotion from the gym vanished. "You've got to go easy on yourself, Leah," I finally said. "Don't go overboard."

She nodded.

"You want to sit?"

She shrugged. We sat. The sand was surprisingly cold.

"I couldn't stay there," she finally said.

"Where?"

"At that table. With Mom and Mr. Pinker. And you just sitting there, like, I don't know, some sad old dog."

I had never felt like hitting my daughters, but at Leah's words, I had to struggle not to smack her.

"Some sad old dog," I said, my voice strange and shaking.

"Yeah. Just letting her go for it. Just letting this ugly, stupid British dude flirt with her the whole night, while you order more rice. Disgusting. That's why I left. That's why I went for a run. To try to get all of you guys out of my mind."

"You have no idea what it's like," I said. "You are so spoiled." As the words came out, I was already willing them back.

"Screw you," she said, and glared at the ocean like she hated it, too.

She had never come close to cursing at me before now, and I was overwhelmed by the injustice of it. I didn't trust myself to speak. I stood instead and, at her unrepentant silence, walked away and left her there. Senseless, I knew: not good parenting. What had been the point of the entire exercise? To go find her, remove her from danger, and then leave her there, alone, on the beach? But I was angry. I never got angry, and I was angry. I marched up the path back to the hotel. I looked back and saw Leah sitting there, a sad little statue. Obscurely, Bernard's words comforted me, and I believed them, in that second, maybe because it was convenient: kids know what's good for them. I should have left her in the gym in the first place, I thought. Let her run it out.

I went to the restaurant. Elise and Bernard were still sitting there, like idiots, listening to a crappy Filipino band play "Rockin' around the Christmas Tree." I strode over to them.

"Everything okay, Chris?" Bernard said.

"Shut up," I said. "Come on, Elise."

"What do you mean, come on?"

"I mean, come on. Enough."

She sat there, her arms crossed. This wasn't going exactly as I'd pictured, which had involved punching Bernard and Elise melting into my arms, whispering that she was sorry.

"Where's Leah?" Elise asked. "Was she in bed?"

"No," I said, taking near pleasure in the worry that came over Elise's face now. "She was in the gym. Running. Looking like she was about to collapse."

Elise looked as horror-struck as I'd hoped. "And now?"

"She's on the beach." That was a bit harder to explain.

"Alone?"

I nodded. Elise rose swiftly, throwing me an appalled look for abandoning our daughter, and headed towards the path to the beach. Bernard and I maintained an awkward silence until he asked if I wanted to get a scotch at the bar. Somehow, in light of everything else that had gone down, it seemed like the fitting thing to do.

⁂

I followed the path down to the beach, where I quickly spotted Leah: the only one who was there alone, a huddled spot not far from the waves. I had been trying to figure out what I would say to her, but now that I was there the words fled, and even going up to her seemed like too great a task. So I positioned myself fifteen feet behind her and sat down to watch the ocean and my eldest, my only.

I wondered if she was crying. The crash of the waves and the rattling palms in the wind made it impossible to tell. I realized, now that I was sitting here, how much I craved the act of doing just this, every day: watching her, making sure. Shadowing her. I could devote my life to that, I thought. Ducking behind columns, wearing wigs and fake mustaches, hiding behind bushes, sitting two rows behind her and her friends in the movie theater. It was a way to not have to live anymore, while making sure she stayed alive. An affair with Bernard would have been good for me, I knew. Against all commonly accepted mores, a fling with him would have been the safer thing at this point, the kinder option. I could feel, strongly, how the three of us—Chris, Leah, and I—were becoming our own solar system, establishing a gravitational pull on one another. Bernard would have drawn me away from that, would have made me feel beautiful, made me want to wash my hair.

Over the past few months, flirting with him, I had been trying to save myself. If things had gone a little differently tonight—if he and I had played things more subtly, if I hadn't sabotaged it by overdoing the flirtation in front of my husband and child—it might have been Bernard and me on this beach, kissing, doing whatever forty-plus-year-old lovers do when they are finally alone, at night, on the sand. It would have been much healthier than this overly protective, guardian-angel routine. But now that I was in the role, I didn't mind somehow: I felt relieved to be assigned to the task.

Thirty minutes later, when Leah rose, I did too. I followed her to the lobby and hid behind a man-size Buddha head, watched her safely inside the elevator. I saw the buttons light up until it reached our floor. Then I walked slowly back outside. I headed to the pool and lay on a chaise longue, where I could see Bernard and Chris at the bar, having a man-to-man talk, of all things.

At some point, I fell asleep. Later, I was woken by Chris, and I sleepily put a hand to his face as he stroked my shoulder. His cheek was scratchy with a five-o'clock shadow, and it was Bernard. He led me, with determination, back down to the beach. I wondered which of my family members were watching me now, as I'd been watching them. I had an irrational desire to give a wave, and suppressed a private giggle. We passed the spot where I'd sat behind Leah, and stumbled over boulders to a smaller beach. Then farther, over more boulders, until we got to a beach that was barely bigger than the two of us, and Bernard laid out the pool towel he'd been carrying and produced a minifridge bottle of champagne (although, at that point, I honestly would have preferred straight gin), which I sipped as he removed my dress.

And it was for my own survival that I abandoned my family that Christmas Eve, including Sophie, and let his caresses bandage me and allowed his long-imagined touch to let me drift back to myself, and to him. Afterwards, sitting naked, Indian style, on the towel, watching the phosphorescence gleam green on the waves' white froth, I felt fortified. He felt as close as a childhood best friend in a tree house. We walked back silently, barefoot, dodging waves: the tide was coming in. We kissed once more on the beach in front of the hotel before he suggested I go ahead; he wanted to sit outside a bit longer. I was relieved to hear he wouldn't be clingy.

For as long as I could remember, physical desire had been laced with (and often undermined by) an unshakable repulsion. Something invisible and insidious, like the smell of sulfur, that refused to lift. Thanks to Paps, I guess. I had had phases with Chris when I was the one who initiated sex more than he did, but it was always part of a larger act, about how I wanted to see myself. It was less desire for Chris, or for sex, per se, and more the desire to be someone who wanted sex, a modern woman who knew her own body. I'd tried talking to Ivy about it a few times, after a couple of drinks, to see what it was like for her, but it turned out that Ivy, the wild child, the black sheep, was as shy as a Girl Scout when it came to discussing the birds and the bees, and it went nowhere. She had had a lot of partners, I gathered, but in the end that didn't tell me too much.

That night with Bernard, the desire felt clean. And—how do I put this?—it ultimately felt like a gift from Sophie. A whisper to come back to life, to stop the endless accusations that I should have been a better mother, should have hugged her more, should have been less strict when she was little. *Go for it!* I heard her say. Sophie always knew how to have fun; it came more naturally to her than it did to Leah, or me, or even Chris.

I'm sure Genevieve, my therapist in Singapore, would have said that this was all an elaborate ploy to evade Sophie's death. That's why I never breathed a word about Bernard to her. Or to Chris. The next morning, as he and I wrapped Leah's presents, I told him that I'd stayed out on the beach alone after Leah had come in; he made no further inquiries.

Back in Singapore, I slept with Bernard about once a month, until we moved back to Madison three years later. Each time, I left feeling like I'd eaten granola or gone to yoga. Weirdly enough, my affair with Bernard also improved sex with Chris: I felt more open, more available. Of course, there were the normal headaches and horrors of cheating: the fear of being found out, the logistics of meeting up, the growing suspicion, towards the end, that Bernard was a bit of a bore outside the bedroom. But strangely enough, the guilt and shame that have accompanied me nearly all my life, the huge waves of regret that have hit me at the most minor things, like a surprisingly high grocery bill, never troubled me with the affair, my greatest transgression. I've never been able to explain, not to myself, nor to any therapist since, how sleeping with Bernard saved my marriage, even if he ruined Christmas that first year without Sophie. Which was arguably already fucked.

Higher Education

1999–2004

W e—repatriated global nomads, third-culture kids restored to our first culture—are happy to be home, by which we mean the United States. We are happy to have graduated from our international schools, happy to have left all our foreign countries behind: Singapore, Indonesia, France, Ghana, Germany, Costa Rica—you name it, we lived there. We are happy to be here, Going to College, with our new pinstriped duvet covers and our glossy orientation pamphlets and that nervous feeling in our stomachs, which we shouldn't have, after switching schools a million times, but still...

We are happy our parents are on flights back to the time zones where they're stationed. We're happy our roommates aren't total weirdos (except for the one who only eats blueberry fruit-on-the-bottom yogurt and never wears shoes, not even outside; what's up with that?). We're happy to pick classes, to finally choose our life's destinations, after being schlepped around the world for eighteen years by our parents ("Your fathers, you mean," our mothers remind us, sternly, in our heads).

We are happy to have our pasts erased. To be neatly, cleanly, American—until we are asked our opinions on politics by cute guys and girls who've grown up listening to NPR and who have invited us to protest with them in support of minimum wage outside the dean's office on Wednesday. (Is it a date? We hope so.) This invitation, and the ensuing late-night dining hall conversation over November's election, during which we are conspicuously silent, intent on shaping our brownie into a human head, reveals to us two things: (1) we know the name of our country's president, are fifty percent sure about the name of the vice president, but have no clue when it comes to the secretary of state; and (2) we know the name of the president / dictator / ruling junta from our former foreign homes, where we lived up until three weeks ago, but not the names of the vice president / opposition party / jailed dissident there, proving us to be hopeless about politics in both locales. We do, however, know where you can find the American cereals and soft drinks that once reminded us of home, back there (the Wellcome store / the army base / KaDeWe) and where you can find authentic local food, which now reminds us of home, here (Jade Garden / Entrez! / Bavarian Lodge).

⚭

Two months into the semester, we puzzle our roommates by developing an obsession (their words) with Halloween and decking the common area with strings of black bats, plastic orange jack-o'-lanterns, and a *Haunted House* CD from CVS, until the only roommate who ever says things out loud, the one with soft chestnut hair, who pointed out a week earlier that we hadn't changed our sheets since the semester began, insists that "Enough is enough" and chucks the CD out the window like a Frisbee. Always cavalier (it was we, after all, who, at seven years old, ignored the taunting of the Chinese / Bolivian / Nigerian kids around us, yelling "Foreigner! White ass!," and neatly scored a goal at our local soccer fields), we shrug non-chalantly and return to our rooms, where we cry for an hour and eat all the Halloween candy we were going to share with our roommates.

⚜

Halfway through the semester, we meet with our guidance counselors, who express concern that we are not doing well in our Mandarin / Spanish / Korean classes. We attempt to explain that our intermediate classes are filled with students whose parents speak these languages. Our guidance counselors interrupt, gently, but with a gleam of triumph in their eyes: "But didn't you live in China / Mexico / Korea for four years? It says on your high school transcript that you studied the language while you were there." We do not attempt to evoke for her the laughable routine of our American school language classes, where the instructors were cruelly teased by the expat students for an hour, in English, before the instructors bowed their heads in daily defeat and assigned homework that nobody did. We do not attempt to explain how college language classes now result in an eruption of memories for us, how hearing those familiarly unfamiliar dialects instantly summons markets with bloody meat / the tang of fresh lime and cilantro / riding up an escalator, nodding our heads to ambient Korean pop music, to buy clothes that will not fit, at a mall in Seoul. We bow our heads humbly and promise to do better.

We do no better, not even close, but after class one day, the teachers ask us to stick around. We sit in our desks as the other students shuffle papers and throw backpacks over their shoulders. We nervously draw little people in our notebooks. You're a terrible student, the teachers tell us, once the room is empty, but your accent is perfect. Why?

And so we tell them about Shanghai / Mexico City / Seoul, and they tell us about Hangzhou / Juarez / Busan, where they grew up. We spend the next hour reminiscing about the odd fact of caged dogs in Chinese zoos / Mexican drug cartels / a Korean game similar to jacks. When the bell rings, the teachers and we look up, startled. Nervously, shyly, the teachers say how nice it's been to think back on their homelands. We agree. The teachers ask what we are doing on Thursday night. Most of us say we are busy. The few of us who are free (and hopelessly naive) go to our teachers' humble apartments for some home cooking. And of these few, two of us lose our virginity to our language professors, who say things, between caresses, that we vaguely recognize, but cannot, when pressed by our best friends the next day, translate into American English.

⚭

When the summer comes, our parents are pleased to hear we've found jobs. They assume it will be in their newly adopted American cities, since they have recently moved back to the States to be closer to us. (We are not convinced that this was the real incentive, considering these cities are also corporate headquarters.) They are startled and disappointed to learn that we will be heading abroad, returning to the countries we lived in as teenagers, to work for a travel guide that hires college students. The editors said we'd be perfect for the job, we explain. How much does it pay? our parents ask, resigned. Nothing, we admit, but it covers travel costs! At the long silence that follows, we hurriedly change the topic. Our parents suggest a part-time job in the fall.

On June 5, we fly to Singapore / Hamburg / San José, reveling in our imminent homecoming. We beam at passengers with

Singaporean / German / Costa Rican passports, who steer their children away from us. In our diaries, midflight, while everyone else is asleep, we scrawl, "Can't wait to be back home!!!" and fall asleep only as the plane is landing.

We take taxis to our high school best friends' houses. It's kind of weird because our best friends are spending the summer on an organic dairy farm in Vermont, but their parents are nice and serve us cookies and ask about college. We oversell it, the way our parents always used to oversell living abroad to relatives during home leave. The next day, we examine our itineraries. "Since you're practically a local, we expect you to come up with several new entries," our editors said. After breakfast, served by a Filipino maid by the pool (we feel new twinges of guilt, picturing what our Socially Conscious Crushes would have to say about this setup), we scrawl down some potential itineraries for the travel guide, consisting of our personal favorite hangouts from high school: Pete's Place, a burger joint; the American Club; and Tower Records. Only once we've written these down do we recognize the fallacy of our suggested entries. Nobody travels to Singapore / Hamburg / San José to go to restaurants they could easily find in Oklahoma. We need something authentic. We're embarrassed to find ourselves stumped, and even more embarrassed to realize that we don't have a single Singaporean / German / Costa Rican friend to call and ask.

⚶

Aside from a near rape in Kota Kintabalu / Munich / Monteverde, the rest of the summer as travel-writer extraordinaire is a success. We hike through rain forest / force ourselves to visit a Holocaust museum / fall off a horse during a carefree beach canter. Throughout our journeys, we shun fellow tourists. Their wild enthusiasm for "exotic" Asia / Europe / Central America embarrasses us, as do the things that the Australian backpackers find it hilarious to tell waitresses. We have developed an unofficial rule for ourselves over the six weeks: speak only to locals. As if every conversation we now have with a stranger in a foreign language will make up for the fact that we never had these conversations growing up. We find the Mandarin / German / Spanish that escaped us on our college campuses coming through in true form now; we feel practically fluent. Our elation at this discovery, our pride at gaining insights into the culture through our newfound curiosity and extroversion, will lead to the near rape mentioned above, when a customer at the restaurant where we are eating one night, a friend of the owner, offers to give us a ride back to our hotels. Like idiots, we happily agree. We are surprised and vaguely alarmed when he turns off the main road and drives into a park. We are downright terrified when he drives into some bushes and turns off the engine. We will try to remember the Chinese / German / Spanish words for "That's inappropriate!" and "I'm going to yell for the police!" When this doesn't work, we will jiggle the door handle and try to escape.

For unknown reasons, our captors and would-be violators, sleepy eyed, sad, frustrated, will abruptly stop pawing us and will back the cars out of the shadows and drive us back to our hotels. We will trip up the stairs to our tawdry, stained rooms smelling of cigarette smoke, with one fluorescent bulb, and feel wildly homesick for the only homes we've ever had: our nuclear families. We'll use the phone downstairs to call our mothers, crying, trying not to frighten them, but needing to tell somebody. They'll urge us to come home. A bizarre sense of duty, which will utterly evaporate in ten years' time, will convince us to keep going.

When we return to the States, we will be ten pounds skinnier, bedbug bitten, and strangely quiet, from so many weeks of not speaking to anyone (we dropped our chat-up-the-locals routine after the aborted amorousness in the park). Our backpacks will reek of green tea / bus stations / the ocean. And as we throw our things into the washing machine, back in our parents' sparkling abodes, we'll realize: we already miss being back there, being foreign.

⁂

Around Christmas of sophomore year, we land Significant Others. They are everything we are not: born and bred in New York City, assured, unambiguous, on the crew team. We do everything with our new loves: homework, sex, eating mountains of cereal, watching *The Simpsons*. Our roommates will roll their eyes when we resurface every two weeks for clean clothes, having basically moved into our new lovers' dorms, sharing a top bunk and trying not to piss off the bunkmate below when the bed squeaks.

With our new loves, we are relieved to have found partners and friends. We tell them everything. But sometimes, we have to lie in bed alone, to be with the old images and objects—palm trees, rotting fruit, oily water, sickening heat, cold hospital—that hover around the edges of our vision. When we go to those places, our boyfriends/girlfriends cannot come along. They sit on the edge of the bed for a while and then leave, or they hold us, or they get impatient and tell us to snap out of it. When we go to these places, we start to shiver, we sometimes scream, we talk to dead siblings / mothers / friends, we whisper we are sorry to still be alive, so far away.

⁂

In the end, we find others who live between these borders. We sense a weight in them, the carrying of two people, and we meet up with them at coffee shops and dining halls and bars. Our dead sisters and brothers and mothers and fathers squeeze into the booths too, demanding more room, just like they always did on long car rides, or airplane flights, or the sofa. It is these friendships that will last, longer than the Significant Others, who, after all, cannot see our Sophies sitting there, plain as day.

♣

The rest of college flies by. We get wasted / get sober / get hung over / get puritanical / go hedonistic / and repeat. We throw ourselves into poetry, only to be told we're precious. We study history and literature, only to be told, at the end of a paper, that we are not the first to theorize about what the British were doing in India and that our evidence is lacking. Despite this minor failure, we are enamored of postcolonial theory and literature; we consume it hungrily; it sheds garish light onto our former lives abroad that we can't tear our eyes from: how different were we in Singapore / Ghana / Martinique in 1996, we wonder, than the French in Algeria in 1890? Absorbed in guilt and self-deprecation, we do not pause to consider the condescending implications of this assumption: namely, that certain modernized, independent nations are as helplessly victimized and subjugated by global business now as they were by colonialism in the late nineteenth century.

Fiery with our new knowledge, unaware that our facial expressions look very much like those of our parents at our age, consumed with their own private causes, we march back home for the summer between junior and senior years. Our parents have since moved back overseas, and we are thrilled to be returning to the Heart of Darkness. (We are quick to explain that our metaphor refers to expat culture, not, God forbid, the local culture; we've come somewhere since Conrad, after all.) We do not have "jobs" until July, when we will fly back to the States for various internships, so we busy ourselves with Feeling Things, Making Art, and Writing It All Down. The first week, this involves constructing a diorama, much like we did when we were ten years old. The diorama consists of an old shoebox, with photos of local construction sites stapled to the outside. The inside of the shoebox contains dirt from the construction site and an abandoned worker's glove that we snatched from the site when no one was looking. On top of the glove—this is what we're really proud of, the real punch line—is a note of local currency. We present it to our parents over breakfast and they react the way they do when the dog drags something dead onto the porch. It dawns on us that we will have to explain our art to them (the greater dawning will happen later: that any art that has to be explained is probably bad art). This is a construction site, we explain, pointing to the photos, and these are the oppressed Sri Lankan workers. This is one of their gloves. Our parents nod solemnly. Where'd you get that cash? our fathers ask casually, and we have to admit we took it from their wallets, since we haven't had a chance to change our dollars yet. We promise we'll pay them back. As the conversation shifts to what English movies are playing in town, we conclude that they just don't get it, and place the diorama at a conspicuous place in the living room after breakfast, so that our parents will have ample opportunity to absorb it. Four days later, we find the diorama has been moved back into our rooms, on our bookshelves, as our mothers work with the maids to tidy the house for a dinner party.

The second week "home," we achieve enlightenment one evening in our backyards. It occurs during happy hour, a ritual imbibing trea-sured by both our parents and ourselves. The harsh realities of the day, the fact that we don't know where we're going in life, the empty malls, the excessive air-conditioning, our friends back in the States, all fade with the dying light, and with our bracing gin and tonics. It's the gin and tonics that clue us in, ring a bell in our heads. E. M. Forster, we think. Eureka! *A Passage to India.* That's what we're dealing with. We cast a glance at our manicured grounds, our panting dogs, our fine silks, our sweating glasses. We've reached the conclusion, we gravely tell our parents, drawing courage from the dark and the drink, that you two are neocolonial alcoholics. We say it with the slightly apologetic air of doctors informing their patients of a serious disease. We do not include ourselves in this diagnosis, although we follow our pronouncement by drawing a long sip of the G and T. Silence. Did they not hear? Then our mothers' voices, weary, hurt, carrying over the lawn: "Don't you think you're being a little melodramatic?"

⚘

We don't graduate with everyone else. We do six-month stints as re-porters in Cambodia, congratulating ourselves that we've found an expat occupation that is honorable, ignoring the fact that most of the male reporters have prostitute girlfriends. Back in college, we join the newspaper staff and begin writing features, which we find much easier than term papers. Our off-campus apartment bedrooms are covered in museum posters with Chinese calligraphy and Nepalese prayer flags. We walk around campus with Cambodian hammocks that we hang from trees in front of the library until the police ask us to take them down and give us a citation.

We have grown up. We do not go to classes in pajamas anymore.

We are applying for journalism jobs, fellowships, anything. After weeks of waiting, suffering through rejections from Cambridge University and internships at *The New Yorker*, we get a packet in the mail that looks promisingly thick. We learn that we've received a scholarship for a year abroad, a language fellowship, in the country where we lived before we went to college. We call our parents. We're going home, we say. But we just moved back to the States, to be close to you again, they protest. You mean corporate headquarters, we remind them.

Three months later, we're on a plane. We're twenty-three, college graduates, determined to live overseas differently than our families did before. After two weeks of intensive language classes (surrounded now, not by kids whose parents spoke the language when they were growing up, but by white kids from Ohio who actually paid attention in college language classes), we desperately miss the American Club.

We drive past the club sometimes now, on our way to other destinations. We're no longer members, and no longer allowed inside, but we cast hungry looks at its gates and imagine the swimming pool and the grounds within: the diving board, the turquoise water, the mango granitas, the nachos. The dining room with hamburgers and spaghetti, blond families with kids looking like drowned rats, fresh from the swimming pool, the shared-sympathy smiles from one American parent to the next, scanning the menu before placing their orders, then leaning back, assured of imminent French fries and unquestioned belonging.

Voice Recognition

Berlin, Germany, 2007–2011

When I moved back to Shanghai after college, for a language-study fellowship, I thought I was going home for good. Eager to immerse myself in Mandarin and certain that my Chinese alter ego, Li Ya, would blossom, I forgot that I was white and that I'd never learned how to use chopsticks properly. The pipe dream that Shanghai could be a permanent home lasted for slightly under three years, and I was gone again.

�֍

Now I was in Berlin, where I had landed via a German boyfriend, Dieter. I had met Dieter in Beginning Chinese Literature classes at Fudan University. We both liked Lu Xun's short stories and had both been scolded for writing "creative" essays. *Try mastering the language first,* Zhu Lao Shi, our teacher, had dryly written on our papers. We had planned on spending the summer in Berlin, where Dieter was from, and returning to Shanghai in August. But when August arrived, I found that I had fallen in love with Berlin and out of love with Dieter.

Moreover, with two months' distance from Shanghai, I realized I was never going to be accepted as a local, no matter how convincing my Mandarin tones were when I ordered *cai bao* from a street vendor. When Sophie, Mom, Dad, and I had first moved to Shanghai, in 1993, I had never tried to belong to the city or the country; all my energies were concentrated on fitting in at the American school. A decade away from the city, in Singapore and the States, had sharpened my missing for it; I had been naive enough, at the end of college, to mistake that missing for homesickness. Only to realize, upon my arrival, that China would never let me call it home, the way some lovers blanch at the word "boyfriend." Case in point: during countless taxi rides through the city, the drivers would ask me where I was from. "Here," I would say, which they treated like the punch line of a great joke. Of course, had I truly been *from* Shanghai, I would have answered in Shanghainese, not Mandarin; I would have been Chinese, not pale and blond.

In contrast, Berlin was the ideal compromise, I thought: it wasn't the States, where I felt like an outsider but looked like everyone else; nor was it Asia, where I felt like I belonged and looked like I didn't. In Berlin, I looked German (until I opened my mouth), and the fact that I'd been born in Hamburg made me feel like I'd come full circle in a satisfying way. Unfortunately, being born in Germany hadn't granted me citizenship, but who was I to complain? There were plenty of second-generation Turkish kids living in the city who had to choose between Turkish and German citizenship when they turned eighteen. This fact hinted at some of the antiquated notions of German blood-belonging that I disliked, but since when had I wanted things to be easily comprehensible?

Good luck with that, Dieter told me on the day he flew back to China, slinging his backpack over his shoulder. Did you ever consider the possibility that you're just terrified of commitment? I didn't answer, and he walked out.

⚹

But of course I was looking for commitment—just of the geographical, rather than the romantic, variety. To put it simply, I was looking to stay put. After years of shuttling back and forth between continents, after the failed experiment of Shanghai, I wanted to try out permanence in the country of my birth, something that customs arrival forms in airports worldwide had been hinting at for years. Germany was also the only country I had ever lived in without Sophie. Perhaps living here again, I thought, would teach me how to live without her again.

But even more than Germany, I felt called to Berlin. The subway sounded like the Tower of Babel. Barely anyone was *from* Berlin. Despite this fact, or because of it, everyone was nonetheless eager to claim some kind of belonging (think JFK's "Ich bin ein Berliner"). The city threw so many multicultural street festivals they put the token Kwanzaa songs found in American elementary school Christmas recitals to shame.

Of course, Berlin's hedonistic cosmopolitanism was complicated by its pitch-black national past. For every all-night dance party there was a shiny copper cobblestone with the names of the murdered dead; for every art installation there was an abandoned lot filled with broken glass (and sometimes they were the same thing); for every mixed-race couple making out on the banks of the Landwehr Canal there was an old German pair walking home with shoulders sagging from memories much heavier than their groceries. Germans have never been accused of being a lighthearted people, and many wore their history like a hair shirt. As it should be, some would say.

I didn't know. But to a certain degree Berlin's schizophrenic struggle was familiar to me. It was another kind of home leave, an exhausting internal commute between life and mourning. The grief and guilt of surviving Sophie were all around me in Berlin—in every sad-eyed statue, empty church, crippled Jewish graveyard, awkward silence. They were not the same, of course. But they spoke to one another.

A place's pain can make your own more bearable. The throbbing ache of Phnom Penh, where I had done a reporting stint during college, made mine seem normal, as did Shanghai's still-gaping sores from the Cultural Revolution. Ann Arbor, by contrast, where I had attended college, was entirely too cheery, too whitewashed, too good-natured, too American.

Coming to Berlin was like leaving a Hallmark store in a suburban strip mall for a walk in deep woods. I left plastic expressions of sympathy for a society with sadness in its marrow. Everywhere I looked in Berlin I saw monuments to nightmares, wars, and walls. But things were growing, too: wildflowers bursting from concrete, blackberries drooping over S-Bahn tracks, ivy coating whole apartment buildings, barely hiding the bullet holes.

⁂

Despite my initial ambitions to conquer the city as an energetic, no-holds-barred Brenda Starr, a series of reality checks had diverted this career goal such that now, nine months in, I had instead joined the invisible, yet very vocal ranks of the city's English-language voice actors. Each week, I filed multiple MP3s, not news stories.

The foreign-correspondent dream had sputtered and died at the realization that there were thousands of others like me, namely, overqualified and underemployed English lit majors who had just gotten off the plane from Brooklyn and Little Rock. (The ones from Little Rock were the ones to fear: they were hungrier for success.) The difficulty of the various tasks I had set for myself after Dieter's departure (the first: forgetting him by becoming a wildly successful reporter) became clear during an unpaid internship at the Associated Press's Berlin bureau.

The other intern and I were like the before and after versions of a journalism school makeover, with me being the before case. I was painfully shy and counted down the minutes to lunch. Kendra was outgoing, winning, well dressed, and constantly pitching stories that ran in newspapers worldwide the next day. She casually called up local police chiefs and, in fluent German, demanded to know why justice had not been served to the neo-Nazis taunting Turkish shopkeepers; I reluctantly dialed the Berlin zookeeper and asked for a quote (in English) about Knut, Berlin's beloved polar bear. Whenever I had to do a phone interview, I typed out all my questions beforehand, including an introductory paragraph at the top with my name spelled out, in case I forgot it. All in all, it wasn't pretty, and I was relieved when the six weeks were over. Kendra, by contrast, stayed on at the AP and is now working for them in Cairo, last time I checked.

※

I got into the voice-acting racket through a friend of a friend, the way most things happened in Berlin. It was astonishingly simple. Show up, read into a microphone for thirty minutes, get paid a hundred euros. I'd always been the dork in elementary school who would volunteer to read out loud from the textbook and obnoxiously continue reading beyond my assigned paragraph until the teacher intervened, so this job was perfect. Occasionally the scripts would be a little bit odd, plagued by my boss's non-PC policies: I would get calls every now and then to do African American accents, and once was asked to read from *A Raisin in the Sun*. "Mama! Sister! There's a white man at the door!" I practiced it for Mom over Skype and she said I sounded like the whitest black person she'd ever heard. I felt squeamish doing the recording, but I needed the money.

It was a strange feeling to let your voice float away from you, to be captured on an English-language instruction CD for bored middle schoolers staring longingly out the window in a hot May classroom somewhere in Bayern. After a couple months, I received my first call to audition for a video game voice-over, and showed up with five other American women in a slick lobby in downtown Berlin. I hadn't known that Berlin had slick lobbies: it seemed the city was driven purely by tourism and shabby coffee shops, where aspiring freelance writers would spend all day trying to come up with a good lead on another euro doomsday story, or the revival of 1920s cabaret fashion. But this lobby was the real deal: black leather sofas so shiny they looked wet, an enormous espresso machine, and modernist art so unattractive you knew it was expensive.

I exaggerated my acting experience in the interview, which was conducted in front of six executives in suits: four men and two women. At one point, after running through my CV, they asked me to demonstrate a dying sound, like I had been stabbed. I groaned obligingly and gasped shallowly. I was also asked to say, with wonder: "Look! On the horizon! The glowing tower of Trenea!" and "This is one bitch you won't mess with, Wrath Master!" I thought I did especially well on that last line. They said they would call me in a week.

I was in German class, reading the lines of a travel agent from Munich in our *Deutsch ist super!* textbook, when they called back: I'd gotten the part. They emailed me the script and said I should prepare to come in four days later. I pored over the lines and read a few of them out loud to my German roommate, Marie, which prompted a long, boring diatribe from her on the misogynistic nature of video games. I could see what she meant with my character's looks, however. They'd sent me a sketch of Lavender Lopez over email: tight black leather pants, high-heeled boots, an eye patch, and light purple hair. Lavender Lopez was not rewriting any heteronormative notions of beauty. But as an imaginary alter ego, she was pretty badass.

I practiced for Mom over Skype, leaving out some of the more offensive lines, and she said I sounded great. Now that I was in Berlin, Mom and I spoke at least three times a week: aside from one or two girlfriends from college, she was the only person I kept in touch with from the States. Mom's and my relationship had gone from a tense, mostly silent standoff in high school and college to a best-girlfriend bond now. After having lost Sophie, after moving around so much, after breaking up with Dieter, I liked that I didn't have to explain anything to Mom; that I could talk about the Botanic Gardens in Singapore or about something Sophie had done in Shanghai, and Mom would know exactly what I was talking about, wouldn't take on a weird pitying tone that even my closest friends back home still did. She could also empathize with what was so maddening about Germans (their nitpickiness) and what was so great about them (their moral aversion to small talk).

The only thing I didn't like, speaking with Mom, was how hungry I was for her approval, for her empathy. Since she was the only one I trusted to *get it*, the times when she didn't would be extremely painful, and I never felt so foreign, or so alone, as when that happened. It usually came up when I would talk about how much I wanted to settle in Berlin. For our family, the notion of living overseas had always been paired with the unspoken assumption of an eventual move back to the States, as certain a belief for most expats as heaven for most Christians. That was the logic behind home leave every summer, to remind you of what you were missing and where you were really from.

But I didn't have home leave anymore. I didn't have the money for it, and even if Mom and Dad were happy to pay for my flights back to Madison, where they were now, what would I do there the whole summer? My work was in Berlin, I told Mom, trying to convince myself.

"Is there a chance they'll hire you full-time?" Mom asked, and her question echoed all the voices of doubt in my own head. How long could I keep this gig going? Then she and I would fall into an uneasy silence, or what I thought was an uneasy silence, until it just turned out to be a Skype delay.

⤲

But the studio was happy with my performance as Lavender, and I was soon assigned several more roles. Biking through Berlin, my head was filled with aggressive, staccato phrases ("Make my day, sad sack!"), and words like "flamethrower," "ballbreaker," and "Geronimo." I thought about starting to play video games myself, to go more deeply into the roles, but I ultimately decided that the worlds I imagined were even more intense, and I didn't want to put up with Marie's teasing.

Around that time, I also joined a singing group. I viewed the group as one of the classic contradictions of German culture, which I loved. Here was a people that would come up with the most complex philosophies and entangled explanations for personal motivations or desires (Marie regularly quoted Wittgenstein when talking about troubles with her boyfriend), yet they were also prone to delightfully goofy behavior, like ordering cocktails with names like "Watermelon Man" (straight men included), wearing Speedos (ditto), or requesting two scoops of the popular ice cream flavor "Smurf." And several of the smartest, most compelling Germans I knew, who had come to Berlin from across the country, from both sides of the Wall, had a weekly singing group, the sort of equivalent of a piano bar, where we would show up each Thursday in one girl's kitchen to sing songs like "Fly Me to the Moon," "My Favorite Things," and "Eternal Flame." The group had originally been formed because one of them had read an article suggesting that singing helped alleviate depression. The fact that it was all so premeditated struck me as hilarious and yet very relatable. Somehow, the earnestness I saw all around me in Berlin, the commitment to trying to make yourself feel okay, because happiness was hardly a given, felt like home, and much more peaceful than the expectation that joy be the status quo, which always felt like an unbearable pressure in the States.

⚭

Between the singing group and my various video game avatars, I started to go a little bit batty. It was around this time that I began losing Mom, or maybe she began losing me, over the phone. "Losing" isn't the right word, exactly. It was more that we weren't connecting in the way that we had for the last couple of years. Her voice sounded distant to me when I filled her in on my day; her responses on a particularly challenging video game scene, in which I'd played a Scottish elf princess, struck me as hurtfully halfhearted. But then again, that's how most things had begun to feel: the sun could be out, shining full blast, and it would seem as paltry to me as weak winter light; the laughter of strangers on the street sounded sarcastic and cruel; and German grammar felt like an elaborate practical joke on my tongue.

I was two years in, and the honeymoon phase with Berlin was over. I realized how wildly alone I was. I'd seen other young expats suffer this epiphany, and show up to dinner parties with shy, secretive looks, as though they were about to announce a pregnancy. "I'm going back home," they'd say, when we were all drunk enough. "I've had it." But which home would I return to? Singapore—to do what? Teach at the American school? Atlanta? What did I know about Atlanta, aside from where the best hiding spots were in my old backyard? My happiness in Berlin thus far, I realized, had involved turning it into a kind of cocoon. Swaddled in foreign anonymity, surrounded by acquaintances but no real friends; the memories from my former homes—ballroom dancing with Sophie in Shanghai, petals falling in a London park—were as present as the Soviet architecture lining Karl-Marx-Allee, or the bakery down the block. The calls with Mom were a kind of life support, keeping all the old places close, as she and I summoned Sophie in each other. It was safe. It worked, until it didn't work anymore. I was growing increasingly sullen on the phone, and when I spoke, my voice trembled, to my horror. I sounded like a pouty four-year-old, self-absorbed and incoherent. And poor Mom—bewildered, exhausted—would ask, again, what was wrong. At my inevitable "I don't know," she would sigh and ask if it was okay if she put me on speakerphone; Dad had just come home.

⚬

Back when we lived in Atlanta, when we would drive up and visit Grandma and Grandpa in Indiana, Sophie and I had two favorite games, both of which involved recording our voices. The first was taping ourselves on a Fisher-Price recorder and then dying laughing when we played it back out loud. The other game required one person to sing along to a Walkman with earphones on, while the other rated her. This game was genius because it was equally enjoyable for both participants: it was really fun to sing, as though you were Bonnie Raitt, and hilarious to hear the other person sing as though they were good at it, when they sounded awful. At the end of the song, the one who had listened would give the other a score (our games were rarely without some kind of competition) and we would switch.

⚜

Mom's voice: warm, with a tinge of southern, concerned, always ready to laugh, to empathize, to analyze. Her voice was my connection to home, a combination of notes, a nearly internalized timbre. Before the friction arrived, the dissonance, our Skype calls would be one, two, three hours long. The delight of your own echo, a few notes higher, harmonizing.

⚜

I loved the singing group for many reasons. It was an unapologetically nostalgic, cheesy connection to America: half the songs we sang, selected from enormous binders on the whims of the participants, were American songs I had despised growing up, the kind of thing you hear when you're eating a burger at Wendy's: "Sittin' on the Dock of the Bay," "I Just Called to Say I Love You," and

"Bridge over Troubled Water." I adored these songs now, walked around Kreuzberg humming them, and got choked up when I sang them with the group.

It was also an intimate way to hang out with Germans without speaking German. To sing next to someone can be more communicative than speaking to them, letting your voices blend and rise together. I began loving the German songs we sang there, too: "*Abends will ich schlafen gehen*," "*Koffer in Berlin*," or the lovely Yiddish hit, "*Bay mir bist du sheyn*." It calmed me down, kept me in the present tense.

I had always been a little embarrassed of my voice growing up, compared to Mom's; she was so clearly talented. But here, my voice felt strong, sure, and steady. In a country where I was constantly whispering, unsure of the German declination in a sentence, or the proper article, I sang loud.

The singing group is where I eventually met Matthias, a shy documentary filmmaker who sang along with the enthusiasm of a thirteen-year-old at a Justin Bieber concert. I didn't really pay much attention to him until we sat next to each other one day. There was a gentleness to the way he held the sheet music to "Born to Be Wild," his hands shaking ever so slightly, and how he didn't wipe away my spit when it landed on the paper accidentally. How he toasted me with the inexpensive red wine the singing group drank together, as we looked each other in the eyes, true to German tradition. He had grown up in East Germany and was utterly unenamored of the US. I liked that. He had a dog he called Martin Luther in a ground-floor apartment in West Berlin, in a quiet corner of Schöneberg, and a year after we first kissed, on the U-Bahn ride home from the singing group, I moved in with him. He often worked late in his shared studio space downtown, and I had the dog and the apartment to myself, where I watched the linden tree in the courtyard turn yellow, petted Martin Luther, and practiced my lines.

⚬⚬

Matthias had a quiet air of loss about him, even though none of his friends or family had passed away, except his grandma on his mother's side. He was an unabashed Romantic who shot films about the lives of rural farmers in Romania and about disappearing languages and crumbling churches. We had our first fight about American farming: I somehow found myself defending large-scale industrial farming, something I was normally against. His naive insistence that it would be possible to go one hundred percent organic by 2030 and his insinuation that it was the American hunger for profit that prevented it had me channeling my grandfather, defending the use of insecticides and corn subsidies.

But most of the time we drew the line at gentle teasing and concentrated our wrath on shared enemies: the architectural nightmare of Potsdamer Platz, the hipsters taking over Neukölln, and the predictable rich-people babble of seventy-year-olds in Charlottenburg over *Kaffee und Kuchen*. Martin Luther, with his dark eyes and honeyed fur, kept us from being too negative, whining for a walk on beautiful fall days, coaxing us to Tiergarten and Schlachtensee, making us stare and be silent.

When Matthias asked me to marry him, my fourth year in Berlin, I realized how hollow my easy declarations of permanence in Berlin had been. A large part of me had never bargained on actually settling. Berlin had been somewhere to recover from the bruises of Shanghai, and the city's cosmopolitanism had soothed my craving for other wanderers like me. It was similar to how I pictured the different levels in Lavender's video games: I would earn enough points through my language skills and my voice-over gigs to pass the Berlin level and move onto the next one, who knows where. It was horrifying and delicious to truly imagine staying, to become an immigrant instead of an expatriate. On the one hand, I felt like I had finally arrived; on the other, I worried that telling myself I had found home in a foreign country was pure denial, a way of constantly reopening the wounds of homelessness.

On the nights it felt like the apartment wouldn't get warm enough, when Matthias was shooting a documentary in some forgotten Hungarian village, and when I couldn't get "The Sound of Silence" (which Alex, from our singing group, always insisted on singing) out of my head, I would get Martin Luther up onto the sofa with me and try to ascertain what Sophie would say about the whole situation.

Now that I wasn't talking to Mom as much, I really wished I had Sophie around; sometimes I felt like I missed her now more than I ever had before. Not to do wedding-prep stuff with me, or be my maid of honor; I didn't care about any of that. But to help me find home again. To know whether or not it was okay to settle, to leave our family, our country of four, to start a new family, with Matthias, in Germany. And of course I knew, somewhere in my bones, that she would have been happy for me, as the tired old cliché went. But I needed to hear her say it out loud.

A Taste of Blood

Madison, Wisconsin; Berlin, Germany; Moscow, Russia, June 2011

F or the past three days, Elise has walked around with the taste of blood in her mouth. Literally. On Tuesday, at the age of fifty-seven, she was summoned to the dentist for a thirteen-year-old's surgery: a wisdom tooth extraction. Her father had performed them on many of her friends, the richer ones, when she was a teenager. She'd envied their convalescence: the days in bed, the ice cream, the attention. She had begged him to take hers out, too, but he'd insisted that her teeth were growing in perfectly and there was no reason to fuss with nature.

And now those teeth, or the holes where they used to be, ache like hell. *See, Daddy?* she thinks. You could have saved me all this pain. Which is ridiculous, of course; it would have just come earlier, and at his hands. She feels a surge of missing for her mother, wishes Ada were still around to comfort her, the way she always pampered her children when they got the flu or a strong cold. Ada had never second-guessed their ailments, even when it was obvious they were trying to skip a geography test or avoid seeing an awkward date in the cafeteria. A familiar chill settles over Elise, as this cherished vision of her mother is corrected and clouded by the one time that Ada didn't believe in what was ailing her daughter. "You shouldn't tell such tales, Elise." Elise hates this reckoning, especially since Ada's death two years ago. *You're still dragging that around?* Ada murmurs in Elise's mind, her mellifluous southern drawl sharpening to a bark: *Well, get over it!*

Elise lifts a hand to her throbbing jaw. She imagines this is what men must endure, at least a couple of times in their lives: getting punched in the face. Has Chris ever been in such a fight? She couldn't say. Surely an elbow thrown in a basketball game would have done similar damage. Without the routine physical violence of being assailed by cramps and blood every month, she thinks, men have to take it out on each other.

Her own bleeding stopped four years ago. Elise had mourned and celebrated menopause as a rite of passage. Or at least that was how her friend Laura, who always wears turquoise and knows how to phrase things like that, had put it. Laura made menopause sound like you were Aphrodite in ancient Greece, lying in a pomegranate grove, relishing your own ripening (also Laura's phrasing), and not yourself, stuck in traffic on the Beltline during an NPR donor drive, frantically turning up the air-conditioning. For Elise, menopause simply felt like a dull recognition of age, the way that her current diet of soup and smoothies seems like a cruel foreshadowing.

God, she feels out of it. The dentist forbade her coffee for three days, and without her seven a.m. cup, nothing comes into focus. She's also been abstinent from yoga, a morning class she's been militant about attending three times a week for the past two years. Plus the fact that summer still hasn't come to Madison, after all the winter they endured, snows up through mid-April. On cool June days like this, overclouded, fallish, her body longs for Mississippi sweat.

❧

In addition to healing from her surgery, Elise is planning a wedding, and she sits at the dining room table now, bridal magazines strewn across the knotted pine surface. Not her own, though when she attended her lesbian friend Paulina's wedding last year, at the arboretum, it had looked like a lot more fun to throw a wedding after fifty, to just hang out and get drunk and talk to whomever you wanted to talk to, and to not have all kinds of crap in your hair. To wear sandals, not high heels. Or maybe that was just a perk of being lesbian.

Elise is planning Leah's wedding, or at least helping her plan it, although Leah hasn't been returning her phone calls or emails about caterers and flowers and music. Which is fine with Elise, as she has decided to interpret Leah's silence as carte blanche and is going for everything she would have had at her own wedding in Mississippi thirty-three years ago, if Charles Ebert hadn't been counting every penny. Hence flowers from the Kriegsteins' former homes—honeysuckle and tiger lilies to evoke Atlanta, bougainvillea and orchids, flown up from Florida, to suggest Singapore. A soloist and a string quartet *and* a classical guitarist at the reception. A live band *and* a DJ. Elise is taking care to inflect it with what Leah loves too, of course: a couple of W. H. Auden readings during the service, and a regional, all-organic buffet.

And even though she knows she shouldn't—but her teeth hurt and isn't she allowed a little bit of wiggle room on such a day?—she wonders what it would be like if she were planning Sophie's wedding. (*Not instead of yours,* she tells Leah, in her head. *Don't accuse me of that.*) Who would Sophie be marrying? Someone gallant, someone all-American, someone who said "ma'am" at the end of his sentences. Which would make you dismiss him, Elise reminds herself. But she had always pictured someone like that for Sophie: someone traditional, strong, someone who could stand up to Sophie's stubbornness and her glory.

Is it healthy to think of Sophie as often as she does? Since moving back to Madison with Chris after their second stint in Singapore, Elise, after years of teaching at American schools, has reinvented herself as an interior designer, one of the most sought after in Madison, according to the *Wisconsin Monthly*: "thanks to her natural artistic streak, her years abroad in Asia, and her southern eccentricities." The last bit had sounded like a backhanded compliment to Elise, which she gets a lot of up here. The smile, the smooth compliment, which hurts you in the gut only later, as you're driving home. Midwesterners are afraid of southerners, she knows. Afraid of southern whites, for being the presumably racist descendants of slave owners, and afraid of southern blacks, for being black.

What does that have to do with Sophie? Ah yes, Elise's mind snags on the connection: interior design. Her new career has often offered Elise a fresh insight into grief: its awkward untidiness, its stuttering expressions of lost love. The room at the back of the house, the one her clients inevitably show last: the son who committed suicide, his 1996 Nirvana posters peeling off the walls. Or the closet full of a dead wife's Neiman Marcus dresses; the unfinished baby room before a miscarriage, half-painted. Elise takes special pride and even, to some degree, pleasure in assisting her clients with these rooms, these secret aches. The magazine profile of Elise didn't mention it, but this is her truest talent: guessing at the people who live, or lived, in the rooms she's remaking, intuiting their desires, their shames, who they want to look like, who they want to forget, and who they are. Elise always tries to steer the design back to who they are.

She's also partial to the couples who've just moved to the city, the ones who will relocate again in another three years. She walks through the rooms with the wives, discussing where they can fit all the antiques from their former homes in Zimbabwe, Rio, and Bangkok. Sometime she surprises herself, however, by being short with these women, usually when they start talking about how thrilled they are about this latest move, about how much they love traveling, and, more than anything, how great it is for their husbands' careers. Liars, Elise thinks, and gives them a list of local therapists' phone numbers before she leaves.

Laura doesn't think that Elise thinks about Sophie too much. Last week, after yoga, she had reached out and grabbed Elise's hand while they were having bran muffins and Top of the Morning energy shakes at the local health food store.

"You're still her mother," Laura said. "Of course you think of her."

"But fifteen years later—"

"That's right, Elise," Laura says firmly, and slightly bossily. "Sophie is twenty-eight now. Not 'would be' twenty-eight. She is. And you still have to tend to her, inside."

Elise always wavers between being comforted by Laura's convictions and dismissing them as well-meaning bullshit. Laura hasn't ever lost anyone; she's just read a lot of self-help books.

Another wave of pain hits Elise in the pit of her mouth. She needs a matinee and some ice cream, she decides, even if it is forty-five degrees outside. Elise gathers her purse and keys and kisses her two yellow Labs on their heads; they thump their tails, as if they want to go for a walk. They don't. At sixteen and fourteen, they have quite outlived themselves, especially Robo, or, as they now simply call him, the Elder.

✢

That night, Elise opens an email reply from Leah, which reads, "Sounds great, thanks Mom!" Sent from her iPhone. Elise's email was full of questions; how is "sounds great" an answer to any of those? Elise reads the email out loud to Chris, who is sipping a generous glass of merlot and reading the paper. "Teenagers," he says, and they laugh. It's their little joke, that Leah is embarking on an adolescent rebellion now that she avoided at fifteen. Or maybe she was just too wrapped up with Sophie's death... Elise is making excuses for her again, she knows: Laura's warned her against it. "She's acting like a cunt, Elise. Don't fall for it." Laura loves to swear; it's all over the poetry she writes, which is why they won't print it in their church poetry anthology, even though they attend the most liberal church in Madison. Laura calls it censorship, every year.

Elise wishes, like she does about her wisdom teeth, that the pain of separation with Leah had come earlier, when it was supposed to come. She's already lost one daughter, and for the last few years, she's had to deal with a second one drifting off, too, at thirty. But at least they're having the wedding here, she thinks. Leah and Matthias could have eloped, or been ridiculously European and not gotten married at all. And Elise likes Matthias, who is kind, forthcoming, funny, charming. He has a clipped German accent that reminds Elise of her days in Hamburg, a time she remembers rosily, when she and Chris were deeply in love, in love with their love, and Elise's pregnancy.

She and Chris pore over potential wedding reception venues: the Mill, a renovated factory downtown; the Madison Museum of Contemporary Art; Highlands Golf Course, which Elise instinctually dismisses, knowing Leah; Sugarland Acres, a working farm, which Chris vetoes, pointing out the potential for a distracting cow manure odor. They settle, finally, on Quivey's Grove, a quaint historical estate in the countryside. The photos online boast large, shady elms and a sweet white picket fence, a tiny detail that obscurely sells Elise on the place. How strange, Elise thinks, to be choosing all this for Leah, the way she would lay out the girls' clothes for the next day in London. She hopes that this passivity on Leah's part does not extend to her relationship with Matthias. But Leah closed the door on such inquiries with her new *I need some distance* edict, last year.

You've got the goddamn Atlantic Ocean, Elise had wanted to scream. *That's not distance enough?* How dare Leah say she needed distance? If anyone, Elise was the one who needed distance, from all of the motherly overtime she'd put in: the late-night calls, the empathizing, the tolerating of Leah's weeping, a sound Elise had grown to find extremely irritating (shuddering sighs, snotty intakes of breath, self-indulgent crying, crying, crying); but that never meant Elise had ever considered distance something you could simply ask for, like a Christmas present.

This is the worst part of being a mother, having to live in the thrall of your child's tyrant. Women are so fickle, Elise thinks. So kind to men and so willing to sacrifice their relationships with one another. But Elise had never treated Ada that badly, even if she'd deserved it.

Chris looks at her inquisitively. "Enough," he says. "Let's get you to bed."

❧

The next morning, the sun is out, blinding and beautiful. Zack, Robo's much dumber son, has his chin on the bed, staring at her. His father is curled on the floor, his blond fur whitened in the sunspot. Elise grimaces as the pain comes back, swallows a pill by her bedside, and stares at the room, blinking, trying to bring herself to the day. She's canceled all her meetings with clients because of her wisdom teeth, which imbues the morning with a summer vacation feel. Elise had lived for summers in Vidalia as a child: days spent at the country club pool, burning your feet on the hot concrete, shrieking in the water, throwing glances at the boys on the lounge chairs opposite, heading home in the quiet, cooler dusk, urging Ivy to come on, we're almost there.

Elise's mind alights, briefly, on Ivy. Funny that after all those years of drama—Who's Ivy dating now? Where's the band touring? Is Ivy *on* anything? Or is Ivy's wide smile, her fast talking, her piercing gaze, just Ivy being Ivy?—her little sister's life has become relatively calm. Ivy has settled in Monticello, a small town not far from Vidalia. She'll call Elise every few weeks just to chat, not to ask for money or confess her sins, as in the old days. Now she and Elise exchange laughs about their dogs, or Vidalia, or Ada. But one month ago, Ivy had called sounding worked up. In the past, that tone had signaled a downward spiral, but this time it turned out that Ivy had good news.

"Some kids want to make a documentary about Choked by Kudzu," she said. "They're raising money on something called Kickstarter to get us back on a reunion tour. They might call you and ask some questions; I don't know."

"Is there anything you want me to keep quiet?"

Ivy laughed, her scraping, gravelly laugh, like a car pulling out of a driveway. "Just make me sound glamorous," she said.

Elise thought, for days, about what she would tell them. Would she mention Ivy's wild years? The biker boyfriends? She would have the cameras set up in the living room, she decided, and she would sit on Ada's (reupholstered) couch, one leg tucked demurely underneath her. She would wear her pale lavender cashmere sweater. She would be compassionate, concerned: the responsible older sister surrounded by Asian antiques. Probably the interview would get sidelined by that;

they would inevitably want to hear about Singapore and China. She would grant them a tour of the apartment, she decided, if they asked.

But they never called. Elise checked with her brother Dodge; they had called Grayson, Dodge told her, but not him, thank God.

"We got off lucky, huh?" he said, and Elise murmured a response.

For a few days, she thought about emailing the filmmaker—Ivy had told her his name, which Elise had immediately Googled—but she thought it would be too transparent, too attention seeking. This morning, Elise feels uncomfortably petulant about not getting the call: in preparing for the potential interview, Vidalia and Ivy have crowded back into her life, with no payoff; and Vidalia inevitably means Paps, too, sulking in the corner, shady now, opening his arms for a hug.

Elise forces herself out of bed. Chris is gone; Elise dimly heard him moving around at four this morning, packing for a six a.m. flight. He'll be traveling for a week: Moscow, Dubai, Riyadh. If anything, he travels even more now than before. Elise supposes she minds, in some place, but that place has grown so protected over the years, so tired of hurting and missing and trying, that his absence hardly registers now. There was a time, Elise reminds herself, in Philadelphia, when she had so eagerly anticipated his departures, when they had given her license for—for what? Elise can't remember anything but a vague thrill, a shivery wildness that she associates with the months before her second pregnancy, something she's only ever felt again in those married-couple crushes you have with other people's partners: an unspoken complicity across the room, starved glances at the dinner table, lingering, nonsensical conversations with fourth glasses of wine on windy balconies, too-tight hugs good night. And with Bernard, of course, Elise's only other lover. Laura often begs her to tell the story of Bernard again, the way Sophie used to insist that she read *Goodnight*

Moon night after night. Bernard has become a close friend now. He and Elise write each other long emails, lightly flirtatious. Bernard and Rebecca are still in Southeast Asia, living in Jakarta, a chronic expat fate Elise is relieved she escaped.

Elise makes herself a cappuccino in their expansive kitchen, taking quiet pride in all the design details, the way she would sometimes feel, watching her girls approach from afar, walking in step, chattering. Later, when it was just Leah, Elise had been too distraught, too worried, to dwell in that easy motherly pride. She'd wanted to run forward and hug her awkward, lonely, now only child, but knew she couldn't, that it would make Leah shrug away, and so the waiting, the forced, casual smile. There is some relief in the distance now. To not know every heartache, every real or imagined threat Leah perceives.

Be careful how much you invest. Which parent had said that? Was it Ada? A veiled warning against premarital sex? Or more likely Charles, lending his cautious advice about renovating the first house Chris and Elise had owned in Atlanta?

On days alone like this, before she leaves the apartment, Elise floats between homes and voices. Their apartment, the penthouse of a newly built set of luxury lofts, has walls of windows overlooking Lake Mendota. Despite the view of Madison outside, the apartment's objects—the Chinese peasant paintings, the London pine table, the pottery from Singapore, the life-size terracotta warrior from Wuhan—toss Elise back and forth, between cultures and continents. She doesn't mind. After years of trying to adjust to new places, acquire new best female friends, conquer new cities, Elise is content to not be anywhere when she's at home.

⚘

At noon, she drives to Heritage Congregational Church, for a meeting with Mi-Yun Kim, the pastor who will lead the wedding service, a bubbly young Korean American woman who routinely cracks up the wealthy, largely white congregation, who pride themselves on their progressive political views despite their elderly Republican parents.

"I would usually be having this meeting with the engaged couple," Pastor Kim begins. "But I understand that they're in Berlin."

"That's right," says Elise, feeling slightly guilty, as though she had engineered the whole thing such that she could steal the meeting from Leah. The same irrational guilt she feels at airport security: some part of her always expects them to find a concealed weapon in her carry-on.

"Perhaps I can set up a Skype call with them," Pastor Kim muses.

"You can try." Elise smiles. "But those two are hard to pin down."

"Right." Pastor Kim nods briskly. "As long as they show up to the altar! Ha!"

Elise laughs politely.

They run briefly through the program. "I was thinking, a light sermon, nothing too serious—a couple poetry readings, some music," Pastor Kim suggests.

"Precisely what I had in mind," Elise says. "I mean, what I've discussed with Leah."

"This must be difficult for you, having her so far away," Pastor Kim says.

"It is." Elise has no desire to get into this with the preacher now. "But I'm just happy that she's happy, and that she's found someone." She feels like a Hallmark card.

"Of course. Now, let's go over the organ music, so I can send an email to the organist later today."

☙

The afternoon flies by with a meeting with the florist, who is testy on the subject of wildflowers on the picnic tables outside ("They'll wilt; wouldn't your daughter prefer peonies?"), and a torturous tasting with a caterer, which Elise realizes she should have canceled, as she can eat only the soft things: the gazpacho starter, the mashed potatoes, the crème brûlée. She is too embarrassed to admit that her teeth hurt too badly to tear into the steak, so she lets them think that she's either vegetarian or a halfhearted anorexic. She remembers the years Leah swore off food, like some third-world activist launching a hunger strike, how she would move things around her plate, order two starters, while Chris and Elise had three courses, the grim pride on Leah's face as her cheekbones sharpened, her angles narrowed, insisting, all the while, that she was fine, just not too hungry. Trying to get to Sophie, Elise knew, to the prepubescent body that Leah had been so jealous of at twelve, when she acquired curves, and further still, to Sophie's skeletal status, now departed. Leah! Elise feels a throbbing in herself, has to check it, remember that Leah's okay now, healthy, about to be married, after all: Isn't that what a mother wants? For her child to have a happy ending?

☙

In Berlin, which lies in the Central European time zone, it's seven hours later.

"Is it white?"

"Maybe."

"Long?"

"I forget."

Leah and Matthias are sitting on a bench outside a bar, sipping Augustiner beer, their eyes trained on the soccer game, talking wedding dresses. Matthias has been trying to pry details from Leah since she bought her dress with Elise in December.

"Lacy?"

"Maybe."

"Veily?"

"That's for me to know and you to find out."

Leah loves tossing out these American English ten-year-old comebacks to Matthias, who never heard them when he was growing up in Leipzig: "Finders keepers, losers weepers." "It's a free country." When he was ten, Matthias and his friends had shoved down winter wool caps over the victim's eyes, screaming "Night in America!" before sprinting away, a bizarre game based on time zones, given that they lived in the shadow of the Berlin Wall, and the idea of travel to the West was a cruel joke.

Leah and Matthias turn their attention back to the game: Portugal vs. Norway. It's a qualifying match for next year's championship, when every bar, restaurant, and Späti (the ubiquitous, largely Turkish-owned convenience stores) shows the matches live, with flat-screen TVs jerry-rigged to the outside walls, the sidewalks crammed with benches.

Leah is grateful for the noise of the match, the easy distraction, the neat geometry of skilled passes and the graceful arch of crosses over the field. From her years of soccer in Singapore, she knows what to yell at the screen, which moves to admire, what kind of defense looks sloppy. Fifteen years ago, seeing a player fall on the field would have turned her breath shallow, would have treated her to a panic attack in the bathroom, biting her fist. That's all settled to a quiet hum now. The game is also a welcome distraction from a fight she and Matthias had earlier this morning, which they've been tiptoeing around ever since, alternately snarling at each other, licking their wounds, then nuzzling heads, nipping ears, then snarling again and retreating to separate corners of their apartment.

In seventh grade at Shanghai American School, sitting out yet another miserable slow song at a middle school dance (inevitably Bryan Adams's "Everything I Do"), watching Sophie dance with a freckled British boy, Leah had known, in the pit of her stomach, she would never get married: that was Sophie's path. Yet here she is now, on the cusp of marrying Matthias, that jerk, she thinks, though not without affection.

When Leah was twelve, they moved to China. When she was fifteen, her little sister died. When Matthias was eight, his father tied him to a pole outside for swearing (a loose knot, Matthias had emphasized to Leah, so that he could have escaped if he'd tried, but he'd remained there, whimpering stubbornly, for five hours). Leah hates being left alone, or any sudden, unexpected change in plans. Matthias hates boundaries and having to say sorry. Leah likes testing boundaries and hates being the first to say sorry. Matthias likes traditions and manners, which Leah often scorns. He is more excited about planning the wedding than Leah. He is the one who writes Elise back.

This daily role-playing, role shifting, with characters as predictable and boring as those in a passion play, without the redemption; this eternal back-and-forth, the squabbling, the jealousies, the resentments—it's not unlike a sibling relationship, Leah thinks sometimes. How bizarre to have a partner again, to have an inseparable. How infuriating, how brilliant. She punches Matthias hard, in the shoulder, and points across the street. "Punchbuggy black, no punchbacks," she says.

"I gave that to you, I totally saw that car an hour ago," Matthias says, unwittingly echoing Sophie, a light German accent inflecting his slang.

"Oh, come on!" Leah yells at the screen, as the Italians botch another shot on goal. She feels herself relaxing, letting down her guard, which she very much meant to keep up, as Matthias draws her in for a hug.

⁂

At halftime, it begins to pour, and the crowd hunches inside a tiny bar that smells of cigarettes and stale beer. Leah, standing next to the open door, shivers as a blast of rain smatters the back of her neck. Earlier in the day it was blazing, as sweaty as Atlanta in July. Now it sounds like Singapore outside—the percussion of a tropical torrent—but it's turning chilly. When Matthias and Leah leave the game, cycling back to their apartment along the canal, it feels and smells like fall.

Leah remembers the confusion of the heat in Singapore, how it never lifted. Those deceptively mild nights, perfumed with frangipani, when Robo would sleep in her bed, to ward off nightmares. Robo. Her mother had insisted on the name, uncharacteristically refusing any compromise. Before Sophie died, when the sisters had wanted to remember what the seasons felt like (for it was always summer in Singapore), they had cranked up the air-conditioning until it was freezing, and piled on sweaters, talked about things like apple cider and Thanksgiving. It worked until you looked outside, saw the thick, tropical vines swaying, that bright blue sky, the unrelenting sun.

In Shanghai, the weather had been indistinguishable from the pollution. Sometimes Leah takes a gulp of exhaust smoke on a busy road in Berlin, to remember China, the same way she inhales a passing stranger's cigarette smoke, to summon the feeling of a Saturday-night bar on a pale Tuesday afternoon.

If she's been alive for thirty years, two alone, in Hamburg and Philadelphia; thirteen with Sophie, in Philadelphia, London, Atlanta, Madison, Shanghai, and Singapore; and fifteen alone again, in Singapore, Ann Arbor, Shanghai, and Berlin, does she have a sister or not? And if Matthias has known her for only the last two years, in Berlin, what does he know of her? Do you have to know someone to marry them?

"Punchbuggy red," Matthias yells, from his bike, and decks her left arm.

You choose your friends and your boyfriends, your colleges, your curtains, your type of bread, your granola, your poison, your pants, your tattoo, your postcards at the museum shop. But not your losses. For a long time, Leah's loss chose for her. Or, rather, chose to make everything hard, assigning Sisyphean tasks like Be Skinny, Go after Distant Guys, Nothing If Not Wildly Successful. Now things feel more relaxed. Be with Matthias. Stay with Matthias. Let Mom handle the wedding. Don't stress out if you forget the German word for "yellow bell pepper." Just say it in English. Back at their apartment building, in the courtyard, Leah locks her bike in the dark, stumbles up the stairs beside Matthias. She brushes her teeth with him, making faces in the mirror, snuggles up next to him in bed.

It is ten months to the wedding. Leah anticipates it with the mild delight of an upcoming birthday party: she can't tell if her lack of excitement, comparing herself to several other female friends she knows who've gotten married, stems from denial or a suspicion of Big Life Events. She'd felt equally underwhelmed, she remembers, by college graduation.

But in ten months, walking down the aisle, Leah will be trembling. Sneaking glances at friends, holding her father's arm, taking hits of the honeysuckle in her bouquet. Seeing Matthias waiting for her, in his self-selected forest-green bow tie, Leah will smile, slowly. For once, Leah will not question her presence in that place, but simply feel at home, humbly grateful for her mother's subtle, loving arrangements.

But for now, in bed, she just feels restless.

"You still awake?" Matthias asks.

"Yeah."

"What should we have for the midnight snack?"

"Huh?"

"At the wedding?"

Leah rolls her eyes in the dark. Who cares? "How about White Castle?"

"What's that?"

"The most disgusting American fast food possible. Gray burgers."

Matthias lets out a critical sigh, one that Leah knows means *You're not taking this nearly as seriously as you should be.*

⌘

"I'm serious," Chris says. He's sitting in a sauna, naked, sweating with men from the Russian joint venture, at the CEO's dacha outside Moscow. They've just beaten each other with birch branches, and in this open atmosphere, Chris is hoping he can sell them on the benefits of extending the joint venture to Siberia. But the Russians look like they aren't into discussing anything at this point. Borgev, the CEO, who kept walloping Chris's back at dinner after making crude jokes, is leaning back with his eyes closed, looking embalmed. Andrej, his son, who is poised to step up as the CEO, the one Chris really needs to convince, lifts a finger to his lips. "We talk later," he says. "Now, relax. Sauna."

But it's hard for Chris to relax in a sauna, where his body urges him to get out: it's just counterintuitive to sit stewing in these temperatures. Saunas seem to Chris the perfect symbol of Russian and Northern European masochism: why choose to relax in an environment that is, by definition, deeply uncomfortable? It's too hot in the sauna, too cold when you jump in an icy lake, and too weird when your foreign business partners are swatting you with branches. Chris prefers the American form of chilling out: taking a John Grisham book and a dog down to the dock on the lake, sitting in the sun with a cold beer. Chris says a silent prayer of gratitude to his ancestors, for getting the hell out of Europe. Mechthild sends him a silent *Bitte schön* back.

Later that night, after several more rounds of vodka, the businessmen get confessional. Borgev begins. "And to think, five years ago, Dmitry would have been here with us," he says, heaving a huge sigh, like a wooden ship sinking.

Through his vodka-sharpened senses, Chris notices that Borgev's son, Andrej, looks distinctly uncomfortable.

"Borgev oldest son is killed by Russian thugs," says the man next to Chris, a fat, wheezing sales manager whose name Chris immediately forgot as soon as they were introduced. "He was going to be the CEO. Now Andrej must do it."

Chris thinks Andrej has the potential to become a skilled CEO. He's sharp, perceptive, and has a good handle on the market. But he doesn't have the bluster of his father, or of most Russian businessmen. Though he drank rounds of vodka with everyone, he got quieter, not louder. He would make a great business leader outside of Russia,

Chris thinks, but he won't last a day here. Chris wonders, briefly, if he should act on this insight soon, sell off Logan's shares in the joint venture before Borgev retires. But this call to action recedes just as quickly as it came, and Chris relaxes back into the circle of men. They are sitting around a candlelit table, with tiny vodka glasses in front of them, the table laden with Russian dishes: pickled tomatoes; cold herring; beet salad; thick, dark bread; slices of nearly translucent green melon.

"You have how many children, Chris?" Borgev asks, looking up blearily from his reverie.

"One," says Chris. "But two before. I also lost a child. A daughter."

"It is terrible," says Borgev. "And this daughter, the one still alive. She work in your company?"

"No," says Chris. "She is a newspaper reporter." Technically, this isn't true, but it's the career that Chris had always wished for Leah, and hopes might still happen, once she gets out of this silly voice-acting business.

This produces a wave of hilarity among the crowd. "A reporter!" Borgev shoves his son. "Like this one! He also want to be a journalist!" Andrej smiles, embarrassed. Borgev slaps his thigh. "In Russia! What a joke. I take him out of literature study and put him into business. Because I need someone I can trust."

This, of course, prompts a toast to trust, and more vodka.

"My younger daughter, Sophie, wanted to be an engineer," Chris says, surprising himself. He never permits himself to think about this, let alone mention it in front of wasted Russian colleagues. "I think she would have done very well in this business."

Borgev shakes his head. "What is it Tolstoy says? About death?"

Andrej shrugs, annoyed, a look that Chris has caught from Leah before.

Borgev takes it down a notch. "God gives, and God takes away."
He lifts his glass. The others follow suit.

By now, Chris's head is swimming.

"This daughter of yours, Chris. Is she married?"

"Engaged," says Chris.

"Too bad," Borgev says, already laughing at his own joke, before
he's said the punch line. "Otherwise I would offer her Andrej."

For a second, in his vodka-addled state, Chris considers it. Most
likely they would be a good pair. Andrej seems serious, well inten-
tioned, a reader. Who is this Matthias, anyway? Chris has met him a
few times: he is nice enough, smart, but Chris is still uneasy. Watching
Leah and Matthias, he remembers his engagement with Elise. They
wrote each other a letter every day while he was studying in Stuttgart
and she was teaching in Atlanta. Sometimes he thinks that was their
happiest period: the anticipation of being together, before it actually
happened. How does he warn Leah about the bitterness that comes,
the disappointments, the personal failures? Maybe she already knows.

Chris is dreading the wedding. He tries hard to hide it, but he
wishes it weren't happening at all. It means he has grown old, that
Leah is staying in Germany. It is another step away from their time
as a family, with Sophie. I've stayed the same, Chris thinks. Traveling, working, meeting with customers. But Leah and Elise are barely
recognizable as the daughter and the wife he knew. Elise, with her
expanding interior design business, her feminist friends, her guarded
nonchalance. He watched Leah closely in Berlin, the last time they
visited her. Her face and body changed when she spoke German; she
looked like a stranger to him. I've stayed the same, he thinks, stubbornly, and feels suddenly betrayed.

I should get some sleep, he thinks. What time is it in Madison?
Five in the morning.

"Wake up, Chris!" Borgev is yelling. "We take car to Moscow, go to fun bar downtown. Only forty minutes to city center. Still early!"

Andrej helps Chris up apologetically. "I can take you back to your hotel if you want," he says quietly, in the corridor. "We'll just tell my father that we'll meet him there; he'll forget all about it in an hour."

⚘

Andrej and Chris settle into the back of Andrej's black Lexus. Andrej murmurs something to the driver and they head down the gravel driveway back to the main road.

"You must miss your brother," Chris says, to break the silence.

"Yes," Andrej says, and then, after a pause, "Well, we were very different. He thrived in this life. He loved the energy, the money, even the danger." Andrej is quiet until they turn on the highway. "I think it's bullshit. It's ugly. I wanted to study abroad, get a journalism degree at NYU, come back here and make a difference. Oh well." He laughs, joylessly. "I shouldn't be telling you any of this."

"I'm glad you're telling me," Chris says. "You know, business was my ticket out of a life I didn't want, on my parents' farm. So for me it was a chance to escape. But I see how it is the opposite of that for you."

"Very much so," says Andrej heavily. "Well, we'll see. How long I last."

They have entered Moscow's suburbs now, tall Soviet apartment blocks sliding by. "How is your daughter now? After her sister's death?"

"It was hard for her," Chris says. "But I think she's doing okay now." He doesn't say that he is worried she will never recover, that none of them will. Who would they be if they did? He doesn't want that, either.

"The place they are going tonight, it is where Dmitry got shot. Whenever my father gets drunk, he goes there." Andrej shakes his head. "Sometime I think, he hopes they kill him there, too. Or he will kill them. It is good your family is better," he says. "Dmitry's death really fucked our family up."

Chris doesn't know what to say to this, so he simply says, "Your English is incredible."

"Hollywood," Andrej says. "The cheapest American education."

They do not speak for the rest of the ride, and Chris drifts off.

⚘

After he has been dropped off at the hotel, back in his slick suite, he feels irritatingly awake. He opens his laptop, glances swiftly through emails. On an impulse, he opens a picture he has saved on the desktop: one of the four of them, Chris, Elise, Matthias, and Leah, at the lake house last summer. He tries, in the smiles of Leah and Matthias, to judge whether they are happy, whether they will be enough for each other. Then he looks at himself and Elise, trying to remember what he felt that day. All he can see is that the sun is in everyone's eyes, they are squinting, laughing at Zack, who has wandered into the bottom of the picture. Then Chris pulls a photo from his briefcase, the one he always carries when he travels: the four of them, Sophie, Leah, Chris, and Elise, on the Great Wall of China. He looks at his two daughters smiling, holding each other tightly. Leah has told Chris and Elise, in the last two years, along with other sundry revelations, that she was rabidly jealous of Sophie, miserable in China; but she looks happy here. Everyone looks happy. They must have been happy. If they weren't happy back then, then when?

❖

Of the four of us, I'm the only one who can go back, whenever I want, to wherever we were. I can touch down in Singapore without landing at Changi Airport (although I sometimes stop by, to sample the hard candies they give out at passport control, which Leah and I always loved: the ones with the penguins on the plastic wrapping, a weird polar welcome from a tropical island). I wind through Little India, which we seldom visited when we lived there, but which I love now: the loud voices, the iced tea and the lime juice in small plastic bags, the patterns of saris, like looking up at the stars.

I wander over to the harbor, stare at the boats and the cranes. One good thing about dying young is that you don't lose your curiosity, the excitement that made me ask Dad, over and over when I was alive: How does that work? What makes that move? The same impulse that made me take apart Leah's Discman when I was ten, and she freaked out, but I put it back together, didn't I? People think the dead are all knowing, but it's not true, at least not for me, not yet: information is revealed in agonizingly slow stages, as far as I can tell. I sit in on physics classes at Singapore American School, at an empty desk in the back row, and make mental notes about quarks and black holes and Schrödinger's cat.

When we were little, Leah and I used to hold our breaths passing the cemetery, exhaling and giggling when we couldn't hold it in any longer. I avoid cemeteries now, too: they're comfort for the grown-up living, not for the young, and not for the dead. I do go back to the soccer field where I collapsed, sometimes, for sentimental reasons. It's not a space of horror for me, like it is for Leah. It's like going to visit an old house, or the place where you had your first kiss. If anything, I feel a quiet pride, and I guess that's what keeps me going there: there's less and less these days from my time alive that conjures any emotion in me. Grand Ada says that's a good sign; it means I'm ready for the next level, which makes me excited and a little nervous, the way I used to feel before any of our big moves as a kid.

"Next level?" I asked her once. "Like a video game?"

"How should I know?" she said, kind of condescendingly. "I never fooled around with that trash." Then she was gone. I can't wait until I can learn that disappearing trick. She says it's not so hard.

I go back to our old houses too, of course, especially the one at Cairnhill Road, where it rained in the kitchen, where Robo was a little puppy. Another benefit of leaving the quick behind: I can find out things I always wanted to know before, like where the heck the name Robo came from. I look in Mom's files (they're not files, of course, but that's the best way I can think to describe them to you) and sure enough, there's the story of Robo Cop, lost in the woods, cuddling up next to Mom on the mountain summit. It's satisfying to piece it all together.

And upsetting, to learn the bad stuff: about Paps, about Grand Ada, about Mom. The next time Grand Ada showed up, I yelled at her until I had no more "breath." She just kept mumbling, "I'm sorry, I'm sorry, I'm sorry," until we were both as empty of emotion as winter trees of leaves. And that was that—for Mom's sake, I tried to stay angry at Grand Ada, but after that confrontation, the fury was gone. The dead can't stay mad, contrary to what stupid ghost stories will try to tell you. To the dead, revenge is as laughable as sleep. Both irrelevant to us now.

I read Leah's files first, of course, desperate to know everything about my mysterious teenagey sister, and missing her like crazy. Seeing the files wasn't as good as being back with her, alive, but it was the closest I could get, and it shed light on a lot I didn't grasp back then.

Some of it I knew, of course, like how she was kissing Ana's brother, Lane, the summer before I died. Ana and I had a special club devoted to encouraging their budding relationship, FSLA, the Future Sisters-in-Law Association. But I hadn't gotten the chance to read Leah's and Lane's breakup faxes, which I did with bated breath. In some ways, it was beautiful to be able to be closer to Leah in this new way, flipping through the pages (still speaking in metaphor, you understand), pretending, sometimes, that she was whispering it to me in the dark, in the twin bed over.

I was shocked that she had been, or still was, so jealous of *me*. I mean, what with the weird mature hindsight you get as soon as you kick the bucket, I *got it*, I understood the whole sibling rivalry business and Leah being older, and shyer, and not having curly hair, or whatever, but I hadn't known what a big deal it was for her. Reading it I had a strong flash of human emotion, something I haven't had for years now, which you experience often in the few short years after you die, the same way the ones you leave behind have flashes of death in the first years of mourning. I felt sad at being resented, even as I blushed with a feeling of triumph.

But the funny thing is, I'd been jealous of her, too. I mean, I wasn't as hung up on our differences as she was, but even that preoccupation of hers was something, I admit, that I envied a little bit in her; she had a focus, a quietness, a way of overthinking that I never had. I mostly saw how adults admired it, because it made her seem smart and more like them. Plus, being older, she got to do everything first: go to school, read, get her period, have a real kiss (with Lane, which I watched with Ana, from behind some bushes, although apparently, according to Leah's files, we missed the real first one, which took place two days before). I had a just-for-fun kiss before I died, even before Leah's kiss, which I know would have driven her crazy had she known, a sweet tiny one from a freckled British boy, on my cheek after the sixth-grade school dance, as formal as a handshake. Jonas Crockett. Now an investment banker living in Surrey, last time I checked.

People alive these days are pretty psyched about Facebook, but they should try being dead. Status updates from anyone you feel like accessing, anytime. Mostly I just stay tuned to my family, and Ana, of course. I've heard that the less you access the living, the better chance you have of getting to the next level, but I'm not too worried about it. That's another nice thing about being gone; I used to be crazy about winning everything, whether it was a race down the sidewalk with Leah or a board game. I don't have that urgency anymore; I just know what I want, like Robo the Elder lying in a sun spot. I also check in on him now and then.

I have a feeling that Leah's wedding will be one of the last times that I duck back down to be with them. At first, I would go pretty often. I didn't miss a single family therapy session for the first six months. But it gets more and more tiring, and now I can feel myself losing the knack for the dive, kind of the same way, just at the end of my life, I felt myself moving into adolescence, losing that kid quickness. And then, just on the cusp of it—a few days away from my first period, it turns out; you can read your own files, too—bam, snatched away, who knows why. What with all the knowledge you get up here, that's nowhere in the data, the *why*. Maybe in the next level. I'm not even sure I want to know.

But I'm excited about Leah's wedding, maybe even more than she is, because I know what it means for her. And the great thing about being dead, I have to say, is the pure joy you can possess for other people, especially the people you could be kind of annoying to or resentful of when you were alive. I'm not sure where I'll stand, next to

Mom, probably, or maybe I'll move around during the ceremony, try not to make too much noise, or cast any accidental shadows. I hope they have steak. And dancing, to oldies. And that it's everything that Leah really hopes it will be, which she won't even admit to herself. I know my older sister.

And then it's time, probably, for a little vacation, flitting around to my new favorite places to watch: the North Pole, Chinese construction sites, Costa Rican rain forest. And then there're some briefings scheduled in September, which I'm looking forward to: it's a big deal to be allowed to participate. I think I get to do it even earlier than usual because Grand Ada coached me, and I've gotten to shadow her on some of her briefings.

After I passed, Grand Ada was the first dead person I met. You're allowed one person from your life before, a dead family member or a friend, to be your mentor, and Grand Ada chose me. She's pretty different from how I remember her when we were both alive. As a dead person, she's a lot more sassy; she makes jokes about how I'm her intern, and talks about which TV actors she would want to sleep with, if she were alive. I was relieved to see Grand Ada, because when you first die, you miss everyone in your family so much, just like they miss you. And even though all the rhetoric down there is about how great it is that the dead don't feel pain anymore, how they're in heaven (Yeah, right: I wish! Gummy bears for every meal and no Meditation Instruction ever!), what they don't know is that pain becomes something we look forward to, or even cling to, because it is, as weird as it sounds, a consolation. Here you see the pain ending; you know it's being lapped away even as you feel its pang, like the summer days growing shorter on earth. I wanted so badly to tell Leah this, during all those years of racking hurt for her, but there was no way, except to be a breeze in the trees, her favorite song: to inhabit her safest spaces. That's one thing Meditation Instruction is good for.

The four of us. Leah, Chris, and Elise still look for me, for a second, in restaurants, when they sit down at a table set for four; just as I, sometimes, when waking (again, speaking in metaphor), forget that I'm not in the bed next to Leah, being woken by Mom or Dad for school.

Who knows what the next level is? There are all kinds of rumors flying around. Some say that you totally forget your past, or that you were never a "you" to begin with. Others scoff at that and say that the next stage is gradually losing individual feelings, so that you start to vibrate with everything that's being felt everywhere. But the guy who said that is a big hippie, everyone agrees. I even heard someone say the next stage is being a house. A house? I don't know. It's a little frightening. But I draw courage from Leah, down there, composing an invitation list with Matthias, writing an email to Mom about which poems the pastor should read. I'm glad she's getting married before I move on. The dead still need the living sometimes, to remember what choice feels like, just as they still look to us, the dead, to enter their own inevitability.

Acknowledgments

Many thanks to—

My parents, Karen and Steve Sonnenberg, for enduring interminable living room readings when I was a kid, for patiently repeating my name until I looked up from books, and for their deep underground river of love and support.

My extended family, the Sonnenbergs and the Stevenses, for giving me a fierce sense of family ties and belonging, no matter where we were in the world.

My agent, Jenni Ferrari-Adler, for believing in *Home Leave*, offering invaluable writerly wisdom, and, along with the rest of the Union Literary team and its subagents, helping this book find its homes.

My editor, Helen Atsma, for her scintillating sense of story and character and for her encouragement and presence, even during a rapidly unfolding chapter of her life; and to everyone at Grand Central, for their fabulous work.

My German editor, Ulrike Ostermeyer, for her inspired suggestions and support, and to everyone at Arche Verlag in Germany and AST in Russia.

My closest friends and readers, especially Kayla Rosen, who saw this book through every stage, including the awkward pubescent one, when most would have avoided it in the cafeteria; my Berlin writing

Acknowledgments

group, Emily Lundin, Florian Duijsens, and Clare Wigfall; my CGS gals, Danielle Lazarin, Christina McCarroll, and Mika Perrine; my friends in academia, nonfiction, and design, who offered fresh perspectives, Nasia Anam, R. Jay Magill, and Karen Schramke; and my Minneapolis crew, Bonnie Marshall and R. D. Zimmerman.

My teachers, i.e., heroes: Beth Burney, Kim Gage, Bob Dodge, Ginny Donahue, Patricia Kuester, Gish Jen, Patricia Powell, Lan Samantha Chang, James Wood, Peter Ho Davies, Eileen Pollack, Nicholas Delbanco, Michael Byers, and Julie Orringer.

My director at HKU, Page Richards, for emphasizing the importance of maintaining a writing practice as a writing instructor, and for grasping my deep connection to Asia.

My lamplighters, Renate Becker and Elizabeth Bowen.

My *Montags Gesangverein*; for giving me a suitcase in Berlin.

My love, Erwin M. Schmidt, for his deep caring and clear-eyed faith.

And to my sister, Blair Sonnenberg, for teasing me, coaxing me, knowing me, and loving me, still.

About the Author

Brittani Sonnenberg was raised across three continents and has worked as a journalist in Germany, in China, and throughout Southeast Asia. A graduate of Harvard, she received her MFA in fiction from the University of Michigan. Her fiction has been published in *The O. Henry Prize Stories 2008* as well as *Ploughshares*, *Short Fiction*, and *Asymptote*. Her nonfiction has appeared in *Time*, the Associated Press, the *Minneapolis Star Tribune*, and NPR Berlin. She has taught creative writing at the University of Michigan, Carleton College, and the University of Hong Kong. She is currently based in Berlin. *Home Leave* is her first novel.

Reading Group Guide

Discussion Questions

1. The first chapter of HOME LEAVE is told from an unusual point of view. Why might the author have chosen to begin her story with the house itself? How did that decision set the tone for the rest of the book? What kind of connection do you have with your physical home? If your house could speak, what stories might it tell?

2. How would you compare Sophie and Leah? How do they compare themselves? Do they strike you as having a typical sibling relationship?

3. When we first meet Elise, she is struggling with feelings of shame, but by the end of the novel she has reclaimed her sexuality. Did you think Elise and Chris's marriage would endure all that it did? Would you have expected the woman who once played in a Christian rock band and worried that marrying Chris "would mean a life of debauchery and drunkenness and scant-to-no clothing" to have so dramatically altered her relationship with shame?

4. How do the Kriegsteins understand chance? Fate? How would you answer this question, posed in "The Good Years" chapter:

"If they had stayed in the States, would *it* have happened? Was Sophie's death a foregone conclusion in any geography, a heart failure built into her system that would have struck her down on any continent?"?

5. The author writes from many points of view. Which perspective did you most identify with? Have you ever imagined what stories a long-ago relative or someone recently deceased might tell about your own family?

6. In what ways is Elise a nontraditional mother figure? In what ways does she conform to traditional maternal roles? Do you find yourself identifying with her? When?

7. Each Kriegstein seems to change with every city the family lives in. Can you imagine your own life in a far-flung locale? How might your life look different? What might stay the same?

8. What does home mean to you? Is it where you grew up? Where you currently reside?

9. HOME LEAVE is full of turning points—both expected ones, like planned moves, and unexpected ones, like the first time someone touches Sophie's hair in Shanghai. Which ones resonated with you the most? What are some turning points you remember from your own life? Were they planned or surprising?

10. Would you have gone along with Sophie's plan to run away from Shanghai? Have you ever felt persuaded by a family member to do something you knew was risky, the way Leah was seemingly persuaded by Sophie?

11. Sophie, during a family therapy session, tells Leah, "Trust your own deaths." What do you think she means? What does that mean to you?

A Conversation with Brittani Sonnenberg

HOME LEAVE is a work of fiction, but you have also lived all over the world, and sadly lost your own sister at a young age. Why did you decide to use those elements of your personal story in a fictional setting, rather than in a memoir?

While I initially experimented with writing a memoir, and exploring some of the autobiographical material in HOME LEAVE through nonfiction, I was unsatisfied with the results. As I wrote, I didn't feel that urgent curiosity that is crucial for good writing. Instead, I felt as though I were merely reporting events. I put the memoir aside and turned my attention to short fiction. But I still found myself strongly drawn to the basic setup—an American expatriate family abroad, two sisters, a tragedy—and I decided to start from scratch. This time, I allowed myself the freedom of fiction: I drew on real-life events while creating wildly different scenarios, inventing characters, rewriting outcomes, etc. You might think, given the pain of losing my younger sister, Blair, I might have wanted to make that story end differently for the Kriegsteins, and keep Sophie alive. But I wanted to look closely at how a family that lacks a geographical home (and considers the family unit itself "home") deals with loss when one of its members suddenly dies.

Once I began working on the material as a novel, I started having a lot more fun. One of the chapters I most enjoyed writing was "The People's Square," in which Sophie and Leah attempt to run away from home (or "run back home," as Sophie puts it). Although my sister and I complained a lot about Shanghai to each other, we never put our grievances into action. It was exhilarating to push the emotional truth of that era—our longing for Atlanta and the familiar—into a new "truth," an imaginary series of events. If plot is simply the result of choices that characters make and the consequences that follow, it holds true that by introducing new choices, and thus new consequences, a new story emerges, and, with it, a new family.

You live in Berlin, Germany, but you're a US citizen and your extended family resides in the United States. Where is home for you? Has that answer changed for you over the years?

I suppose I would say that I have several homes. I'm going on my sixth year in Berlin, which is the longest I've lived anywhere (my family lived in Atlanta for five years), and I enjoy the sense of belonging that comes with staying put, even if I still feel foreign on a daily basis. Then again, feeling foreign also feels "homelike" to me! I tend to say I am from Atlanta when people ask, just because it's the easiest answer, but if my interlocutor has a patient air I might add that my family moved to Asia when I was twelve. Or, if I'm feeling provocative, I may simply answer that I don't have a home.

Aside from Atlanta and Berlin, I also feel a deep connection to Shanghai and Singapore. Our time in those two cities profoundly challenged and changed me, and I think any place where you experience significant growth also becomes a home. It resides in you, even when you have ceased residing in it. Like the Kriegsteins, my family also traveled to the US in the summer when we lived overseas, and we spent a great deal of time at my grandmother's mountain house in North Georgia. So the word "home" also strongly evokes memories from that region: piney mountain air, blackberry cobbler, the gentle peaks of the Smoky Mountains, vegetable roadside stands, hot, briny boiled peanuts, and the teasing banter of my cousins and Southern relatives.

The Kriegstein family moves from Europe to Asia, with stints in the United States in between. But also explored in the novel is the dramatic shift Chris undergoes as he moves from a rural world to an urban one. Why did this migratory story also interest you?

I think Americans possess a strong capacity for reinvention. But reinvention is often spurred both by profound confidence—I can be someone else, somewhere else—and profound insecurity—I don't belong here; I crave transformation. What interested me most in Chris's character is how the values he learns on the farm and on the basketball court as a kid (work hard, don't complain, stay humble) remain vital for him as his career accelerates and he becomes a successful, jet-setting CEO. Chris is able to manage his daunting travel schedule and work demands precisely because of this steadiness. He is eager to leave the farm but he never rejects its ethos, whereas Elise winds up shedding many of the Southern Baptist beliefs she grew up with in Mississippi.

You have lectured and written on the subject of Third Culture Kids. Can you explain what a Third Culture Kid is?

I think that David C. Pollack and Ruth van Reken, two sociologists who have written extensively on the subject, have come up with a good definition. According to them, "A third culture kid is a person who has spent a significant part of his or her developmental years outside the parents' culture. The TCK frequently builds relationships to all of the cultures, while not having full ownership in any. Although elements from each culture may be assimilated into the TCK's life experience, the sense of belonging is in relationship to others of similar background." (Pollack and van Reken, *Third Culture Kids: Growing up Among Worlds*, Nicholas Brealey Publishing, 2009.)

This definition helps explain why living overseas impacts children much differently than their parents. For Elise and Chris, "home," for the first eighteen years of their lives, was inarguably Chariton and Vidalia, respectively. For Sophie and Leah, "home" is a flexible construct. To some degree, the same is true of the girls' trans-national identities, even if they carry US passports. After eighteen years of living across three continents, Leah doesn't feel fully American, a fact made painfully obvious when she goes to college and finds herself surrounded by "real" Americans. Often, TCKs struggle with feelings of inauthenticity, of not having "full ownership in any one culture," as van Reken and Pollack put it. I, too, spent my college years grappling with what the novelist and TCK Joseph O'Neill has called "personal placenessness." Over time, however, I have discovered just how widespread this phenomenon of displacement is, and have deeply benefited from the community of others who are similarly bereft, and/or similarly searching. Due to globalism's advance, those who have a secure notion of home are increasingly in the minority, and the rest of us—TCKs, CCKs (cross-culture kids, for example second generation Chinese-Americans), immigrants, exiles, nomads—understand that we may never truly feel "at home" in any one place.

One theme of the novel is loss—and how a family moves on, or doesn't, following a tragic death. And grief and mourning is ex-

pressed differently around the world. In your travels, have you found that people from other cultures deal with death in a healthier manner than Americans generally do? Or vice versa? Or is grief simply grief, no matter the place?

I do think that, to a certain extent, "grief is simply grief" everywhere. When we listen to music, even if we don't understand the lyrics, we can usually guess whether the song is about budding love or searing heartbreak, because it speaks to shared human emotions. That said, I think grief is closer to the surface in some cultures than in others, where it is neatly tucked away. In Cambodia, for example, where I lived for six months in 2001, the grief from the deaths of millions of Cambodians during the Khmer Rouge regime was still palpable. When I told people there I had lost a sister, I often received weary, understanding nods—they had lost sisters and brothers themselves, though in much more horrific circumstances. In the US, despite the numerous shelves dedicated to grief and mourning in bookstores, death feels like a much more awkward subject to broach. I'm not sure whether some cultures' methods of dealing with death are healthier than others; I think each culture's various methods represent a long evolution of what Lionel Trilling called "manners and morals," and evince, more than anything, our stumbling bewilderment in the face of death and the loss of those we love. For years, I shunned therapy, perhaps because it seemed too "Western" to me; I've since found it to be tremendously life-giving.

How does your reading life influence your writing life? Did any books or writers in particular influence you as you wrote HOME LEAVE?

My reading life strongly influences my writing life. Often, the feeling I have when reading brilliant books is of receiving courage for my own writing. When I was in college, I struggled, as I mentioned above, with the sense of not belonging to any one culture. I was just beginning to write fiction, and this insecurity manifested itself in the fear that I would not be able to set a story anywhere convincingly, because I did not know any one place well enough. But reading Joseph Conrad and V.S. Naipaul, who each had their own struggles with displacement and "belatedness," as Naipaul puts it, helped me envision a way in which I might draw on all of my homes, rather than dismiss them as long layovers.

Ha Jin and Eudora Welty have also been strongly inspiring authors for me: I admire how they both manage to evoke foreign settings (China and the American South, respectively) for audiences largely unfamiliar with those regions. They succeed in doing so, I believe, for the same reasons: richly drawn characters and a great sense of humor. "After Cowboy Chicken Came to Town" by Ha Jin and "Why I live at the P.O." by Eudora Welty are two of my favorite stories, and ones I go back to again and again. Finally, as I was drafting HOME LEAVE, and experimenting with which novelistic form best suited my material, I also drew inspiration from authors such as David Mitchell and Jennifer Egan, whose formally adventurous fiction urged me to take the my own risks.